CW01662101

Wes

A HAMMOND BROTHERS NOVEL

CHRISTMAS AT WHISKEY MOUNTAIN LODGE IN CORAL CANYON™

BOOK TWO

LIZ ISAACSON

feel good fiction
ELANA JOHNSON

ISBN-13: 978-1638764168

Chapter One

Wesley Hammond refused to be a former CEO who walked out of his corner office, with two walls of floor-to-ceiling windows, carrying a brown box with his belongings in it. He'd already carted out the sad plants, the family pictures, the toiletries he kept in his desk drawers, his clothes, and all the menus of the downtown Denver establishments that delivered until midnight.

He'd done that by taking a few things every day over the course of the past few weeks, after the board had approved the transfer of power from Wes to Laura. She'd been in his office every day too, six days a week, and Wes found himself getting along well with her. Better than he ever had before.

Laura had the passion for HMC that Wes had started with, and he knew in his heart that this transition was good for him, and good for the company. It didn't make leaving for the last time any easier, though.

His heart beat down two paths, and he could hardly determine which one to go with. Excitement that tomorrow, he didn't have to get up, shower, shave, and put on a suit. He didn't have a schedule to stick to. He didn't have a call at six a.m. to accommodate the branch manager in London. He'd have to be in charge of his own schedule now, and he'd sorely miss Myra, who kept him looking knowledgeable, and Matthew, who always made sure Wes arrived in the appropriate place on time.

Or trepidation that he had no schedule to stick to. No phone calls to make. No one in charge of him, except for him.

"Are you ready?"

He turned at the voice he'd worked with for so long to find Myra standing in his office doorway. "Yes," he said, picking up his briefcase. "Is Matthew done?" His secretary had been on the phone with a regional manager out of Pittsburgh fifteen minutes ago, talking fast and trying to get something taken care of before the weekend started.

"He just hung up," Myra said. She entered the office fully now, walking toward him with a smile on her face. "What are you going to do tomorrow?"

Wes took a deep breath, smiled, and blew it out. "Well, tomorrow's Saturday, and I'd love to sleep in and then find somewhere to play golf."

Myra gestured to the windows behind him. "You've looked outside, right?"

Wes turned and looked, though he'd seen the snow falling earlier. It hadn't stopped all day, and it had a certain magic about it. "Yeah," he said. "No golf. Maybe I'll go skiing."

"I didn't know you skied."

"I don't." He faced her again. "Never had the time, but I will now."

Myra laughed lightly with him, and she turned to go back out the door. "I'm going to miss you, Wes. You're the best boss I've ever had."

"That's because I'm not your boss," he said.

"You always acted that way," she said, nodding. "And I appreciated that."

"Laura's good," Wes said. He'd told Myra this many times. "You can leave anytime too. It's only her that can't fire you for the first twelve months."

"No, Laura is great," Myra said. "I'm hoping things will just continue on as they are, and that if we work well together, that I can stay. I've loved working for a family company."

"Our benefits are excellent," Wes joked as they left the office. He didn't stop and look back. He'd never go inside again, loosening his tie after a stressful meeting and asking Matthew to screen all his calls.

"Even if I left now," Myra said. "I have an excellent retirement, because you allow employees to invest in the company too."

"What do you own?" Wes asked.

"I'm almost to two percent," she said.

"That's amazing," Wes said, truly surprised. "You cash those out, that's what? Two million?"

"Three and a half," she said. "At the employee rate."

"Good for you, Myra," he said, stopping at Matthew's desk while the man scurried around, putting files away. He never left for the day until his desk sat clean and pristine. He claimed that then, when he got in the next day, he knew right where everything was.

Wes looked at Myra, with her honey-colored hair and dark brown eyes. She'd been an excellent assistant—and a good friend. "How's Janey doing?" he asked.

A smile lit Myra's face at the mention of her daughter. "Great," she said. "She sent me a picture of the palm trees this morning, just to rub it in."

Wes chuckled, wishing he were in Florida, on the beach along the Gulf of Mexico. He'd even go back to school to do it, as Janey was. The fact was, Wes could go to the beach now. Any beach. Anywhere. Any time. He had plenty of money. The truth was, the cold had never bothered Wes, and sometimes he actually craved it. So he wouldn't go to the beach.

His mind moved automatically to Wyoming, and the woman he hadn't spoken to in five weeks now. His last conversation with Bree Richards hadn't ended well for him, and every time he tried to hear her voice again, he couldn't.

That particular aspect of Bree had fled his memory, and he hated that. He hated that she'd broken up with him too, though he could admit that they hadn't actually been dating. A better way to say it was that she'd cut off their conversation. He'd asked her if she was sure she didn't even want to talk to him anymore.

She'd said she'd met someone else—up there in Coral Canyon. Up where Wes didn't live. He couldn't tell her then that he'd been planning to come meet her in person come February seventh—which was tomorrow. He'd erased her voicemail, and she'd apologized a bunch of times.

Wes had too, because he was sorry things between them hadn't really been able to take off. He felt completely stalled, stuck on the ground, reaching for the stars that seemed so far above him that he'd never touch them.

He stifled the sigh threatening to come out of his mouth and looked at Matthew when he said, "Ready. And I'm buying tonight, so pick your poison." He grinned, and Wes had the sudden urge to grab the man in a hug.

So he did, ignoring the grunt of surprise that came from Matthew. Wes clapped him on the back a couple of times, stepped back, and gave Myra a quick hug too. "You guys have been amazing," he said, his emotion stuck way down deep in his stomach. That was one thing this job had taught him—how to contain emotions until he was alone and could deal with them.

"Thanks for putting up with my moods, and my wild changes, and well, my everything." He nodded, glad to have that out of the way. "And I want to go to Rothburg's, so you better bring the platinum card."

Matthew grinned and held it up. "Right here, Wes." He glanced at Myra. "And you've literally been the best boss—and friend—I've ever had."

"Same," Myra said.

Wes looked at them, the bond between them fourteen years in the making. "All right, then. I wish you guys could come with me."

"Where are you going?" Matthew asked, picking up his own briefcase. The three of them started toward the elevator.

"I'm going to take a little cross-country trip," Wes said,

deciding on the spot. "I think I'm going to fly to Maine, rent a truck, and visit every state in the country." And if he started back east, he wouldn't get to Wyoming any time soon.

He couldn't believe he even wanted to go to Wyoming. He wouldn't even recognize Bree if he saw her, as he'd never seen a picture of her. Colton had gone back to Coral Canyon several times over the past five weeks, as his girlfriend lived there. His brother was preparing to make the move permanent in the next couple of days, and Wes would've volunteered to help had Colton not hired a moving company.

"Sounds amazing," Myra said. "I can't wait to see your pictures."

"Yeah," Wes said, stepping onto the elevator. "Because I only post on social media when I travel." The three of them laughed, because that was true, and Wes knew it. He wished he knew what to do with his life now, and all he could do was trust that God would lead him where he was supposed to be, when he was supposed to be there.

Maybe something would come up in Vermont. Or Georgia. Or South Dakota. The possibilities were wide open, and Wes's excitement finally outweighed his fear of the unknown.

* * *

The months passed, and Wes decided he'd need to go back to New England when it wasn't wintertime. That had been a mistake. He'd hit Florida during baseball season's spring training, and that had been fun. He'd watched the cherry orchards bloom in Michigan, and he'd dug his toes into the white sand along those beaches bordering the Gulf of Mexico.

He experienced the spring thunderstorms in Texas, where the thunder could roll through the sky for a full minute before it clapped. Where the rain could douse a man in under ten seconds. Where he finally found all those cowboy roots he'd come from.

His great-great-grandfather had owned a ranch in Texas, and Wes had visited it and met the people who ran it now. The Stokes were great people—a big family like the Hammonds. Lots of boys, all of whom still worked the ranch where they lived.

He'd experienced summer arriving in the Rocky Mountains, and as he crossed the border from his home state of Colorado to Wyoming, his throat only hitched a little bit.

The past six months had taken him to thirty-nine states, and Wyoming was number forty. He only had ten to go, and plenty of time and money to get to them. He'd heard Alaska was beautiful in August, and his plans included hiking in the Tetons in Wyoming, visiting Yellowstone National Park in Montana, hitting something in the Idaho panhandle—maybe the quaint town of Coeur d'Alene—as he headed toward Seattle.

He then planned to get on a ship that would take him to Alaska, where he wanted to see as much wildlife as he could, hike any trails he was fit for, and simply be outside, where he felt closer to God than he did anywhere else.

The trip had been good for Wes's soul, that was for certain. He spoke to his parents often, as well as all of his brothers. The family party at New Year's had been good for them, bringing them closer as a family unit. Ames and Cy had started to stray, and if Wes were being honest, so had he.

He sent them pictures of his day and told them the random museums he'd visited. Cy had told everyone that he'd met a woman in Oceanside, and he wanted to bring her home to meet everyone. The plans for that were still being made, and Wes figured he could fly to Denver from almost any city in the world. If his quest to visit all fifty states got interrupted for a few days, he wouldn't die.

He hadn't had any revelations about what he should do once he'd visited the last ten states on his list. He didn't have to do anything, he'd told himself a thousand times. He could go out to the family farm and help his parents with it. Ames had been doing that more and more, and it was actually good for him to have that purpose in his life.

Wes simply wanted a purpose too.

He didn't set his GPS specifically for Coral Canyon, though he certainly knew the town's name. He drove into the beautiful mountain town just before the Fourth of July, and he admired their Main Street that had red, white, and blue flags, banners, and streamers on all available surfaces.

People seemed to be everywhere, and he decided to find somewhere to park and then something to eat. It wasn't nearly as hot here as it had been in Denver, and he sure did like the higher elevations. The magnificent Teton Mountain Range sat in the distance, towering up and piercing the cloudless blue sky.

A measure of joy and peace filtered through him, and Wes

had the distinct impression that he'd like to live in a town like this. He pushed the thought away because it sounded crazy. He couldn't live here, though his brain immediately started questioning him. *Why not?*

Colton lived in Coral Canyon, and Wes had always been close to his brother. He pulled out his phone and called Colton, always preferring to call over text. He supposed he was old-school that way.

"Hey," Colton said. "Are you in town?"

"Just finding somewhere to park," he said.

"Downtown?"

"Yep."

"It's crazy downtown right now," Colton said. "You should've come here. We can take the ATV's over."

"You ride an ATV around town?"

"Everyone does," Colton said, and Wes reminded himself he wasn't in the big city anymore. He hadn't been for a while. He did love a big city, but he'd also fallen in love with all the remote towns that existed along the highways in this country, and he loved the ones where the roads had no lines on them, no sidewalks bordering them, and kids riding bicycles down the middle of them.

He'd grown up in Ivory Peaks, which was exactly like that, and Wes suddenly wanted a town like that where he could settle and stay. Maybe meet a woman and have a family. He was nearing fifty, though, and in order to have a family, he'd need to find a woman several years younger than him.

People do it, he told himself. He had to, because he didn't want his legacy to be the fourteen years he'd spent running

HMC, or the fourteen before that going to school, learning the ropes of the manufacturing business, and investigating politics.

Thankfully, his cross-country trip had put the idea of him running for governor to rest, and his father hadn't brought it up again.

"We'll meet you at Stagg's," Colton said. "It's a great place, and you can't miss it. Has tons of big antlers on the outside."

"Fifteen minutes?" Wes asked.

"Fifteen minutes," Colton said. "Just me and Annie."

"Great. See you then." Wes hung up as he spotted a parking lot up ahead with a troop of Boy Scouts standing at the entrance. "And it's just me," he muttered to himself. Always just him.

He pulled up to the boys in uniform and handed them a ten-dollar bill so he could park. With his wallet in his back pocket and his phone in his hand, he got out, taking a nice, deep breath of the mountain air he loved so much.

Oh, yes, Wes needed to find a town like this to live in. He loved the busyness of it, knowing that all of these people would soon retreat back to their lives, homes, and jobs, and then Coral Canyon would go back to being the small town with big charm.

He smiled at the hanging flower pots outside of the bakery, and the window display in the pet palace. If he'd owned a dog, he'd definitely have gone inside to see what clothes or toys he could get for his barker.

Colton was right; Wes couldn't miss Stagg's. And not just because of the antlers, but because it was very popular, and several people milled around outside on the sidewalk. He stepped through them to the hostess station, and asked, "How long for a party of three?"

The woman standing there scanned her list. "Twenty minutes."

"My name's Wes," he said.

"Three?"

"Yes, ma'am."

She looked up at him, and Wes grinned at her as he tipped his cowboy hat in her direction. A warm smile spread across her face too, and Wes's spirits lifted. Perhaps if he found somewhere permanent to stay, he *could* meet a woman and make a real life for himself.

He turned away from the hostess station and found a patch of empty cement to wait for Colton and Annie. He listened to the others around him talking, barely paying attention to what they were saying.

Wes had been trying to focus on how he felt, and he absolutely felt comfortable here in Coral Canyon.

Maybe this is your final destination, he thought. He automatically resisted the idea, but it wouldn't go far.

Then he heard a voice that flipped a switch inside him, and he instinctively turned toward it. "All I'm saying is I'm not doing that dating app again," the woman said.

Wes searched for her in the people waiting beside him, his heart banging against his ribcage now. *Bang, bang, bang.* His pulse moved into his ears, and he couldn't hear whoever Bree was with. He couldn't see her either.

Somehow, Bree's voice cut through the other noise, the

hammering of his heartbeat, all of it. "And I'm not calling *him*," she said. "So don't even suggest it."

He found her sitting at one of the tables-for-two on the other side of a black railing. She shook her hair, dark curls falling over her shoulders and down her back. She looked at the woman across from her, who held up both hands as if surrendering. Wes had to get a better look, and he wasn't sure who he touched or pressed through to get closer. He just knew that he now stood a couple of feet behind Bree's friend, his view of her clear and focused.

She was absolutely gorgeous, and Wes felt like someone had stunned him. He gripped the railing with one hand as her friend said, "So, what are you going to do, Bree? Stop trying?"

"Yes," Bree said, the word almost a shout. "I'm going to stop trying. I don't need a man in my life. All they do is break my heart."

Wes wanted to shout that he wouldn't. That he hadn't. That *she'd* been the one to cool things between them, before they'd even had a chance to see if they'd get hot.

She looked at her friend with dark, soulful eyes, and Wes knew he could get lost in them. She wore makeup, but not too much, and when she reached up and tucked her hair behind her ear, he caught sight of dark purple fingernails.

He'd once told her that he'd dated a woman with bright red nails, and that he'd hated them. *What color would you choose?* she'd asked.

Purple, he'd said. *A nice, dark, deep purple.*

Just like what she had on her fingers.

It means nothing, he told himself. She hadn't remembered

that conversation. Even if she did, she'd just told her friend she wasn't going to call him. At least he hoped he was the *him* she'd referenced.

His phone rang, startling him away from the railing. The last thing he wanted was for Bree to see him. But she did look over to him, as he literally stood maybe eight feet from her. Her eyes swept over him, past him, maybe not even seeing him.

He ducked his head anyway, never more grateful for a cowboy hat than he was in that moment. Colton's name sat on the screen, and Wes swiped on the call, his heart beating at him to get out of there. Now.

"Hey," he said. "Stagg's is super busy." He walked away from Bree, part of him begging him to stay. Telling him to go back and pull up a chair and say, *Hey Bree. You might not remember me, but I haven't stopped thinking about you in six months. I'm Wes Hammond.*

Stick out his hand. See if she'd shake it.

"Can we go somewhere else?" Wes asked, desperate now. If Colton didn't agree, Wes would simply march back to his truck and find something else to eat in the next town he came to.

And I'm not calling him.

"Sure," Colton said. "Oh, I see you. We'll make a plan."

"Great." Wes hung up, still striding away from Stagg's—and the most beautiful woman he'd ever laid eyes on.

Chapter Two

Breeann Richards sighed as she opened her desk drawer and put her purse inside.

"Rough day?" Willie asked from the next desk over.

"When the Fourth is over," Bree said. "Life will be normal again." She collapsed into her desk chair, knowing that her exhaustion came from more than just working two jobs. It came from the additional debt she'd incurred over the five months she and Alex had dated. The man said he drove a tour bus, but he never seemed to have any money to do anything. And he wanted to do expensive things, like go river rafting and go out to eat at expensive restaurants.

Because of him, Bree had another gash on her heart, thousands of dollars in credit card debt, and this second job working for a temp agency, helping other people find jobs.

"At least the restaurants won't be so crowded," Willie agreed. She went back to her computer, and Bree should too. Her phone rang, though, and a small blip in her heartbeat told her she hadn't gotten over Wes yet. Sure, she'd just told Elise she wasn't going to call him—and she wasn't.

Didn't mean she couldn't fantasize about making that call and hearing that voice.

But this call had Graham's name on it, and Bree swiped it open. "Hey, Graham," she said.

"Heya, Bree," he said. "We've decided to go ahead and hire a butler."

Bree couldn't help smiling. "I think it's so odd to call them that," she said. "But all right."

"It's better than bellhop," Graham said. "And besides, he'll have to help with more than just taking bags to rooms."

"What else?" Bree said, jiggling her mouse to get the computer to wake. "I'm assuming you called me, so I can make a job listing for you?"

"That's right," Graham said. "We want him to have experience with horses."

"You're only looking for males?" Bree asked.

"No, anyone," Graham said. "But they have to be able to carry heavy baggage up and down stairs."

"I'll put sixty pounds," Bree said, typing information into an intake form for new listings. "Horse care required. What else?"

"Cooking is a plus. Customer service," Graham said. "Current driver's license, with no accidents in the past three years. He'll be a valet too."

"Valet," Bree said.

"Patsy would love someone who can be part of the admin team," Graham said. "So a business background maybe."

Bree's eyebrows went up as she keyed in the info. "How much are you paying this person?" She wondered if she could lift sixty pounds, as she had all of these other qualifications.

"It's a full-time position," Graham said. "Though we don't have room at the lodge for them, so they'll have to come up the canyon every day. I don't know. Beau said seventy-five."

"Thousand?" Bree couldn't keep the surprise out of her voice.

"Yeah," Graham said. "If we can get someone who does all these miscellaneous things, but really has a business mind...the lodge needs that. Patsy does a great job of running things day-to-day. You all do." Graham exhaled heavily. "We think we just might need someone with more of a, I don't know, some type of background that can help the lodge stay current. Maybe even expand. Thrive."

"Yeah," Bree said. "I know what you mean." Whiskey Mountain Lodge was a stunning mountain villa, with views of the Tetons that were unmatched. All the rooms were fully booked almost all the time, especially in the summer. They did fine. But they weren't growing. Even Bree felt stagnant in her position there, and she wouldn't mind some help with the horses, and some new blood to offer new ideas for events.

"Okay," she said. "Let me read this back to you." She did, outlining the requirements for the job, the salary, and then she asked, "When do you want it to close?"

"Can we leave that open?" Graham said. "Open until filled."

"Sure," Bree said. "I'll get this processed, and it'll be on the website by tomorrow morning."

"Great," Graham said. "I'll tell Andrew, and he'll get the word out."

"Perfect." The call ended, and Bree finished up with her end of posting the listing. It would take a few hours for the system to generate the listing, and she clicked the final approval box and got the process going.

She met with a couple of people as they came in to look at the job board. She took two more listings, noticing a man hanging around outside the workforce office. That wasn't entirely uncommon, as sometimes people had to work up the courage to come in and admit they needed help finding a job.

Coral Canyon was booming right now, though, and there were more jobs than people to take them. She was still considering applying for the butler position at the lodge herself.

By the time the office closed, and Willie and Bree could go home, the loitering cowboy had left. Thank goodness. Bree didn't need any more experience with handsome cowboys. No, siree. She was done with them, thank you very much.

Still, in the back of her mind, and in the tiniest corner of her heart, she still wanted one—a good one. There had to be a good man out there somewhere, didn't there? One who didn't lie about his name, and one who didn't lie about his job, and one who wouldn't bleed her dry financially and emotionally. Right?

She closed her eyes and asked the Lord, *right?*

He didn't answer, of course, and Bree was starting to wonder if He ever would. She banished that poisonous thought though, because all she had to do was go outside and look at the mountains to know God existed.

And if He existed, He wouldn't abandon His children here on earth. Bree simply had a harder time communicating with him than other people did. *Seemingly everyone*, she thought, but she put that out of her mind too.

Pastor Clemens had said the Lord spoke to different people in different ways, and Bree couldn't carry the burden of comparing herself to anyone else when it came to the Lord too. Heaven knew she was already doing it in every other aspect of her life.

Willie exited the building first, and Bree turned to lock the door behind them. They had the next two days off, and Bree couldn't wait for her four-day weekend. When she turned, Willie gave her a hug, and they walked toward their cars.

Willie's phone rang, and she said, "It's Connor," with a laugh in her voice. "See you Monday, Bree."

"Yeah, bye." Bree didn't wait around to hear Willie chirp hello to the man who wanted to be her boyfriend. She pressed against the rising jealousy in her stomach, telling herself that she didn't need another low-life cowboy loser in her life. She didn't.

"Ma'am," someone said, and Bree looked up. Adrenaline spiked in her body, sending her pulse flying though her feet froze.

The cowboy who'd been loitering near the windows had taken up camp near her car. He actually sat on the tailgate of his truck, his long legs dangling toward the ground. He certainly looked the part of a Wyoming cowboy, but he hadn't sounded like one. He carried more of a Texas twang in that *ma'am*, and Bree couldn't help taking in his strong jaw, that long, sloped nose, and his dark gray eyes.

Her pulse picked up for an entirely different reason now, and she tried to put the brakes on it. Unsuccessfully. She'd broken up with Alex five weeks ago.

"Did you need a job?" she asked. "I saw you outside earlier."

He shook his head, changing it to a nod only a moment later.

"Is that a yes or a no?" she asked.

He nodded, and she wondered why he wasn't speaking.

"We have a website," she said, reaching into her purse and pulling out a card with all the information he'd need on it. She thought he could definitely lift sixty pounds—probably a hundred—right up over his head. But if he couldn't talk, he couldn't get the job at Whiskey Mountain Lodge.

Customer service was a requirement. She stepped toward him and handed him the card, her fingers coming dangerously close to his. "If you look there, you can see all the openings. We have a ton of stuff right now."

He looked at the card and then her, and Bree had a severe sense of déjà vu. Did she know him? Where had she seen his face before?

She knew a lot of people around Coral Canyon, as she'd moved here years ago. She'd left home the day after getting her high school diploma, and she hadn't been back in nineteen years now.

A pang of missing hit her, and she supposed she should at least call her parents that weekend. See how patriotic things were in Mountain Dale. But Bree knew there'd be red, white, and blue everywhere, same as here, though the two towns existed in two totally different states.

"If you need additional help," Bree said. "There's always a couple of people here to go over things with you." She put a kind smile on her face, though her energy for the day was nearly gone. "My name's Bree, and I work every day. Well, we're closed tomorrow and Friday for the holiday, but first thing Monday morning. I only work until noon, usually. Today was just weird."

She commanded herself to stop talking, wondering why she was still babbling on in the first place. She didn't want to admit that she felt something magnetic pouring from the handsome cowboy on the tailgate, and he was holding her in place.

Adjusting her purse, she stepped toward her car. "Okay, bye." She wanted to kick herself in the teeth. He didn't need to know her work schedule, or that she had another job up the canyon that she worked—usually—from one until whenever everything was done.

At least she wouldn't have to come down to the workforce office for the next four days. She'd just opened her door when the cowboy said, "Thank you, Bree."

She froze again, her heart pittering, and then pattering, and then pouncing. It seemed to take a very long time for her eyes to lift from where she'd been searching for her keys in her purse to the man who'd just spoken.

She knew that voice.

She knew this man.

How?

While she stared at him, he cleared his throat and jumped down from the tailgate. He kept his cowboy hat dipped down, keeping that gorgeous face from her sight, and walked toward the driver's door.

"Wait," she said—more of a blurt really. "Do I know you?" She went halfway around the front of her car, keeping some distance between them. He hadn't parked immediately next to her either, and two spaces separated them.

"No," he said, pulling open his door. "Thanks." He lifted the card and got in his truck. The engine started and he pulled away before Bree could even move.

Confusion riddled her mind, and her eyebrows pulled down. She did know him—or at least that voice. She'd heard that voice say her name before.

A wild, terrible thought entered her mind, and she spun to watch the black truck disappear around the corner.

It couldn't be.... Why wouldn't Wes just say who he was?

Her throat had never been drier, and yet, Bree couldn't move. When she finally thawed, she couldn't get her phone out of her purse fast enough. She still had Wes's number. She'd just call him and ask him if he was in town and had happened to talk to someone about a job today.

"But you gave your name," she said. "So if it was him, he'd know it was you." She looked down the road again, half-expecting the truck to come back. Bring Wes back to her. Could that really happen? Could she and Wes have a second chance at...whatever they'd started the first time?

She got behind the wheel of her car and started the engine

so the air conditioning would start to blow. Then she dialed Wes, clenching her teeth while she squeezed her eyes shut, a constant prayer streaming through her mind.

Three rings. Then four. Five.

His voicemail kicked on, and it was so impersonal and a recording, so she couldn't really identify if he was the same man who'd literally said six words to her. Frustrated, and not wanting to leave a message, she hung up.

He'd see she called. Then he'd either call her back or ignore her. "Please let him call me back," she said as she pulled out of the parking lot and went the same direction as the black truck had. She thought of no one and nothing else for the long drive back to her cabin up the canyon from town.

Time for her second job to begin.

* * *

Wes did not call back. The patriotic parade on the Fourth of July found Bree waving a miniature American flag with one child in her lap and two more on the blanket beside her. Rose and Liam always needed help, and Bree loved their triplets.

She worked around the lodge on Friday, prepping everything for the next couple of weeks so she wouldn't have to work so late into the evening. Saturday, she did the same, putting on a children's craft class, taking a group horseback riding, and coordinating a fishing expedition for the guests at the lodge that holiday weekend.

She found some solace and comfort at church on Sunday,

but her question of *who was that cowboy?* had yet to be answered by anyone, man or divine being.

Monday, she woke early and made sure Patsy had everything she needed for that morning's mountain yoga class, and then she drove down the canyon to the office. She scanned the parking lot, her heartbeat ricocheting around inside her chest.

The black truck wasn't there. The gorgeous cowboy didn't come in. Bree wasn't sure why she felt so defeated and disappointed. She should've known someone like her wouldn't be able to attract the gaze of a man like that. Still, she'd been dreaming of Wes, and she'd almost texted Colton to ask him to send her that picture he'd shown her once, months and months ago.

But she didn't want him to know she'd never truly let go of his brother. She'd told him at least a dozen times that she'd made the right decision when she'd called Wes and ended their phone calls. Even after she'd broken up with Alex—and Colton had been the first to know—Bree had denied him concerning Wes.

"All right," he'd said. "But he's not dating anyone right now...."

Bree just needed a break. She drove back to her cabin and hurried to eat lunch before heading over to the lodge to make sure the afternoon check-ins went well. She liked to have brochures and schedules of their upcoming weekly activities on the counter, and she always worked check-in to help with the traffic and to answer any questions about events.

Bree loved working at Whiskey Mountain Lodge, and she truly felt like part of the Whittaker family. She loved Elise,

Patsy, and Sophia, and she wasn't surprised to enter the office and find she was the last to arrive.

"Afternoon," she said to the others, reaching up to secure her ponytail a little tighter. She'd grown her hair out in the last six months, and she liked how feminine the longer locks made her look.

"There you are," Patsy said. "We have the Kings coming today, and I need to be here for them. But Graham hired a new —butler, I guess?—and he started this morning. Could you help him this afternoon?"

"He hired someone already?" Bree asked, stowing her phone in the back pocket of her shorts.

"Yes," Patsy said. "He's pretty great too. Smart, articulate, strong." She smiled and picked up a piece of paper. "He did great this morning with check-out, and I think he earned fifty bucks in tips."

Bree's eyebrows went up. On top of the seventy-five-thousand-dollar salary, the guy probably didn't need the fifty bucks in cash. Or maybe he did. Bree had learned a long time ago that she didn't know the intimate details of anyone's life. Not really. She could never know what really went on behind closed doors, and she'd learned that at a very early age.

Patsy handed her the paper. "It's Colton's brother."

Bree's heart positively stopped, and her eyes dropped to the paper while her mind raced. Colton had four brothers; it could be any of them.

But *Wesley Hammond* sat at the top of the paper, and Bree's fingers lost their capability to hold a single sheet of paper. It fluttered to the ground.

Then Patsy said, "Ah, here he is. Wes, come in. I have some VIP clients this afternoon, so Bree is going to be your trainer for check-in." Patsy was smiling for all she was worth, and Bree knew why.

She knew a little bit about Wes Hammond, and he could charm the socks off of anyone. Patsy touched Bree's arm, and that thawed her enough to turn around.

She came face-to-face with the man she'd given the job card to last week. The devilishly handsome cowboy sitting on the tailgate.

He still wore that delicious hat, his in a shade of charcoal instead of the white one Colton wore all the time. Those dark eyes drank her right up, and Bree could scarcely breathe. He wore a T-shirt with an outline of Wyoming on it, with a pair of jeans and cowboy boots. He was tall and tan and lean and luscious in every way.

"Bree," he said, and oh, how wonderful it was to hear her name in that deep, rich-as-gold voice. "I'm Wes. Nice to meet you." He put out his hand, and Bree simply stared at him, her heartbeat crashing like cymbals in her ears.

Chapter Three

Foolishness ran through Wes, as he continued to look at Bree, his hand stuck out in front of him. She simply gaped back at him, unmoving.

He cleared his throat and threw a look at Patsy. Pulling his hand back, he looked back at Bree. "Okay." He didn't know what else to say or do. "I'll just see you at the desk." He turned to go back to the check-in desk, wondering what in the world he was doing here.

He should just go home. Or better yet, continue with his plan to visit every state in the Union. He could do that; the weather was beautiful today. He wasn't stuck in Coral Canyon the way Colton had been.

He could leave.

He *should* leave.

In fact, he should've left last week, before the Fourth of July. Before this insane job interview. Before he'd come face-to-face with the beautiful Bree Richards and been rejected—*again*.

"So stupid," he muttered to himself. He was used to having a lot of eyes on him, but the ones boring into his back weren't from people admiring the way his suit coat pulled across his shoulders or marveling at how he'd managed to secure a lucrative deal.

He turned to go out into the living room, as the check-in desk was really just a podium in the circle drive in front of the lodge.

"Oh," someone said, and Wes balked as a warm body collided with his. The scent of chocolate rose into the air, and warmth seeped through Wes's brand new T-shirt. "I'm so sorry."

A woman stood there, an upturned plate of cookies in her hand. One still clung to his shirt, and it fell to the ground as the sticky chocolate released. "It's my fault," he said, bending at the same time as the woman.

He bumped into her again, this time knocking her a bit backward. Heat flared in his face, because he knew Bree could still see him. The woman laughed, but Wes really wanted to sink into the floor and disappear.

"Sorry," he said, picking up the errant cookies. He didn't know what to do with them, though, and their warmth and gooeyness told him they'd recently come out of the oven.

"It's fine," the woman said. "Who are you? I'm not sure we've met."

"Wes," he said.

"The butler," someone behind him said, and Wes jerked

his attention to Bree. "And apparently, he's still learning to buttle." She grinned at him and then the woman. "Hand me the cookies, Laney."

Laney did as Bree said, and Wes pressed into the wall behind him, trying to get out of the way. He should've helped Laney to her feet, but Bree did it. He should've apologized again, but Laney just took the paper plate and continued down the hall to the office where Wes had "met" Bree. He should've ducked his head and used that ridiculous cowboy hat he'd had Colton help him buy to hide his face as he got the heck out of this lodge.

Instead, he stared at Bree, desperate for her to say something.

"Hey," she said, her smile made of nerves.

"Hey."

"You're here."

"Yes." Wes's brain seriously couldn't come up with more than one word at a time, and he wondered where all his confidence had gone. Where the easiness that had always been between him and Bree had decided to hide.

"*Why* are you here?" she asked, gesturing to the expansive living room in front of him. "Doing this?"

His heart beat too fast, and his defenses went straight to the ceiling. "You may or may not remember that I don't have a job anymore," he said coolly. "This sounded like a decent gig, and Colton's been trying to get me to Coral Canyon for months." None of that was a lie, though Colton had stopped suggesting Wes move to Coral Canyon permanently about March.

Bree glanced over her shoulder, and Wes followed her gaze. No one stood in the hall watching them. She put her hand on his elbow and urged him to move into the living room. "You were the CEO, Wes. This is a butler position."

"So what?" he asked.

"You lived in a high-rise penthouse."

"And now I live out of my truck." He narrowed his eyes at her. What was she trying to say? That he didn't belong here? He already knew that. Maybe his heart had been hoping for something different. In his fantasies, Bree shrieked when she saw him, ran toward him, and he got to scoop her up into a big hug as they both laughed.

Then he'd set her on her feet and envelop her in his arms, lean down and....

He cleared his throat, wishing the insane and ridiculous imaginations would disappear too. Because the woman currently looking back at him didn't have a shriek or a smile anywhere in sight.

She removed her hand from his elbow, and Wes kept walking toward the door. He didn't have to explain anything to her. He really didn't.

"Wes," she said as his long legs put distance between them.

"What?" he barked over his shoulder. "It's almost time for check-in." He dang near ripped the front door off the hinges as he opened it and stepped outside. He loved how the sun heated the air in the summer, but the mountains helped it keep a cool note in the atmosphere. He loved the scent of pine trees, and the sweeping hillsides full of greenery. At night, he loved listening to the crickets sing songs to each other, and he hadn't heard that in a while—until he'd arrived in Wyoming.

"Do you know how to do check-in?" she asked.

"No." He arrived at the podium and looked down at the tablet there. "You're supposed to show me."

"It's super easy," she said, and she began detailing where he should tap and what he should do. She talked the way she always had, and her voice did the same thing to Wes now that it had six months ago. He could barely grasp what she was saying, because her voice mesmerized him.

"Did you get that?" she asked, and Wes blinked. No, he had not gotten that. But checking in seemed easy enough. Tap on the name. Give them the right key. Welcome them with a smile. Take their bags to the right room. Done. Easy.

"Yes," he said.

With the explanations done, the two of them stood at the podium with nothing to do. The storm in Wes's soul urged him to simply quit and walk away. He didn't need this job, and he couldn't stand the idea of working here at the lodge with Bree so close and also so astronomically far away.

"Listen," she finally said. "I need to apologize."

Wes turned his attention toward her, the empty parking lot not all that interesting. "For what?"

Bree shifted her feet, an expression crossing her gorgeous features that Wes could only identify as regret. "For last winter. For breaking up with you—I mean, I'm not sure *breaking up* is the right term. For ending our conversations." She drew in a long breath, looked out over the parking lot, and sighed out all the air. "I miss talking to you."

"You do?"

Their eyes met again, and Wes couldn't help the way his hopes lifted. He tried to tether them to the ground, but they kept rising and rising.

"Yeah," she said, a small smile touching those lips. "I just...."

"You met someone else," he said, his throat raw. The words he shouldn't say surged against the back of his throat. But no way was he going to tell her he'd thought about her every day for the past six months. No way he could vocalize that he'd dreamed about seeing her here, or that he'd imagined kissing her.

No way, he told himself even as his eyes dropped to her mouth. His gaze rebounded quickly, because they weren't anywhere near the kissing stage of their relationship, despite his imagination.

"Yeah." Bree folded her arms. "And he was a real...loser, and I already know you're not a loser."

"How do you know that?" he asked. "A butler is a real step down from CEO, wouldn't you say?"

Her smile fully formed on her face, and she shook her head, her dark locks swishing around her shoulders. "I know what you get paid, Mister. And it's a step up from me."

"How do you know what I get paid?"

"I put the listing on the job board." She leaned closer to him, her eyes searching his. "I'm assuming you looked at the job board? I mean, I gave you that card."

"Yes, well." Wes looked away. "I was going to tell you who I was last week. I was."

"Is that right?" She leaned one hip into the podium, giving her a great curvy shape that made Wes's throat a little too dry. "Why didn't you then?"

"Oh, you know," he said, trying to find something in the landscape besides the lovely Bree to focus on. "I was struck dumb by your beauty."

She burst out laughing, and Wes sure did like the sound of that. He hadn't heard it for far too long, and he ducked his head as he smiled.

"You're good," she said. "I'll give you that." A car pulled into the parking lot and right up to the podium in the circle drive. "Let's see how good you are with check-in. I mean, you already knocked the owner's wife to the ground and left a mess of chocolate in the hallway."

Horror moved through Wes, and he stared at Bree for a few seconds. Long enough that a man had to say, "Hey, so we're here...." before Wes could pull his attention from her face. She was teasing him, if the smile lodged on those lips was any indication.

"Yes," he said. "Welcome to Whiskey Mountain Lodge. Name please." He spoke a little too loud. A little too animated. Beside him, Bree giggled under her breath as the man gave his name.

Wes tapped and checked them in, handed over their key, and started to get their bags out of the back of the rental car while the man, his wife, and his three kids entered the lodge. Buttling wasn't all that hard, and when all thirteen rooms had their guests, Wes still felt like he had the energy to do more.

He'd never felt like that at HMC. That place had sucked

him dry, demanding long hours and then isolation in a huge office. Wes didn't mind the time alone so much as he did the feeling of not being able to stand long enough to make it home. And the thought of having to get up the next morning and do it all over again.

He hadn't realized how exhausted and overwhelmed he'd been as the company's CEO until he wasn't in charge anymore.

"All right," Bree said, picking up the tablet. "That podium goes up against the lodge, and I'll let you use those pretty muscles to get it there." She grinned at him. "And then, what do you think about telling me about all the places you've been while we eat dinner?"

Surprise darted through Wes. "Dinner?" he asked, easily picking up the podium and putting it where she'd said. "Us? Together?"

"Don't tell me you don't eat dinner," she teased. "I already know you don't eat breakfast. Or rather, that you only sip coffee for breakfast."

So she honestly hadn't forgotten their conversations. Wes found himself smiling too. "I eat dinner."

"Great," she said. "So we'll go see what Sophia made, and we'll sit with the guests."

"Are we allowed to do that?"

"Sure," Bree said as if she truly had the authority for him to eat at the lodge. Patsy hadn't mentioned that, but he went inside with Bree anyway. This place had the feel of pure luxury, and Wes had liked it immediately upon stepping inside. The furniture was tastefully done, clean, and comfortable.

He bypassed the huge staircase that went up to the majority of the rooms here at the lodge, and followed Bree through the living room to the kitchen and dining room at the back of the house.

He'd have knocked down the walls separating the two spaces a long time ago, but he could admit the lodge had charm in both areas. Both were huge, easily accommodating two dozen people, so the extra walls certainly didn't make the space appear smaller.

"Oh, this is bad," Bree said, stalling in the entrance to the dining room.

"What?" Wes peered over her head, trying to find the source of badness.

"Sophia made meatloaf." She turned her head toward Wes and lowered her voice. "It's not super great. Abort. Abort."

Wes chuckled and backed into the hallway. Bree followed him, took his hand, and said, "Hurry, before she sees us." She darted down the hallway, stopping just before another doorway. She peered around the corner, her hand in his so magical.

His skin tingled, and a shot of sparks moved up his arm and into his shoulder. "Let's go," she hissed, and she ran past the doorway and turned right down another hallway. Wes followed, and he had the very real feeling that he'd follow this woman anywhere. He wasn't sure how he'd fallen for her from just the sound of her voice, over the course of a couple of weeks of conversations.

But he had.

You started *falling for her*, he told himself. He hadn't gone all the way. Yet.

She burst out the back door, the sunlight and cool air such welcome friends. Bree laughed as she released his hand, and Wes pushed down his cowboy hat and grinned too.

"That was close," she said. "I need to make sure I check the menu before committing to entering the kitchen." She threw him a flirty look as she started down the sidewalk, walking backward for a few steps. "Come on."

"Where are we going?" he asked, already hurrying to catch up to her. He told himself not to be so obvious, but he was sure he'd already shown her all of his cards. Following her to the employment office. Stalking the sidewalk outside until she left for the day. Sitting on the tailgate and talking to her. Taking this job at the very lodge where he knew she worked.

Yep, it all added up to desperate. He probably could've written his feelings for her in the sky and been less obvious. He reminded himself that he was forty-seven-years-old, not fourteen. Not even seventeen. He didn't have to let his hormones rule his world.

"My place," she said. "I make some great ham and egg sliders, and they'll be ready in twenty minutes."

Her place.

Wes's night suddenly got a whole lot more interesting, but he managed to tame his voice into mild interest when he said, "All right, but my standards for sliders are pretty high, just to let you know."

Chapter Four

Bree mixed together the butter, mustard, and brown sugar, ready to be done cooking, though she'd only been in the kitchen for fifteen minutes. To be honest, she normally threw something in the slow cooker before she left for work and then opened a bag of rolls. Or she slid a frozen pizza into the oven and collapsed on the couch while it heated.

She slathered the melted mixture over the top of the sliders while Wes watched, seemingly intrigued. "Fifteen minutes," she said, sliding the pan into the oven. She turned and met Wes's eye, the man's good looks sending adrenaline straight through her. "Tell me about your adventures around the US."

He cocked his head slightly. "How did you know I was having an adventure around the US?"

"Colton," she said.

Wes rolled his eyes, and Bree grinned at him. "So?" she asked. "Favorite state you've been to?"

"Oh, I can't answer that," he said seriously.

"Why not?" Bree sure did like the vibe between them. It was fun and flirty, just like their phone conversations had been.

"I haven't been to all of them yet," he said.

"Seriously?"

"How can I have a favorite if I haven't experienced them all?"

"So you're telling me that you can't pick a favorite of anything unless you've experienced all of them previously." She folded her arms. "So you have no favorite ice cream. Or no favorite color. Or no favorite hike."

She knew he had a favorite hike, as he'd told her about the trail up into the mountains above Ivory Peaks, probably a couple of times.

The smile Wes put on his face made Bree's muscles start to melt. She leaned into the counter behind her for extra support, reminding herself that this man was dangerous to her health. She might like talking to him, but they came from two different universes.

He was rich and refined, and she hadn't finished college. Heck, she hadn't even *started* college. Did a few vocational classes in floral arrangement count as college? No, no they did not.

There was no way a woman like her could hold the attention of a man like him. She strengthened the walls around her heart, because he was already starting to creep in. And she didn't need to deal with another case of falling too fast for the wrong guy. She'd done that plenty of times now, thank you very much.

"I suppose I have a favorite flavor of ice cream," he said. "Do you happen to have any cookies and cream?"

"No, sir," she drawled. "We try not to keep ice cream in the cabin." It was too dangerous, because both she and Elise loved it.

"You're kidding."

Bree shook her head.

"We have to remedy this," he said. "Ice cream is one of my favorite foods."

She couldn't contain the smile for another second, and it spread across her face. "As I've said before, Mister Hammond, ice cream is not a food."

"What is it then?"

"It's a treat," she said.

"I'm pretty sure it's part of the dairy *food* group," he said, his eyes sparkling like moonlight off dark water. Bree felt a magnetic pull toward him, and it took every ounce of willpower she had to keep herself against the counter instead of moving closer to him.

"Bree," Elise called, and she turned her attention toward the front of the house, though she couldn't see the door from the kitchen. "Bree, I have the greatest news." Elise came tearing into the kitchen, and she stopped suddenly when she saw Wes sitting at the kitchen counter. He looked at her, and then back at Bree.

"You remember Wes," Bree said, relieved Elise had come

home. Bree had no idea what she would've done, but she was pretty sure it involved kissing.

Kissing. Ridiculous.

She couldn't believe she was even *thinking* about a relationship with Wes. Though, if she allowed herself to really examine the past six months, she hadn't *stopped* thinking about Wes.

"Of course," Elise said, smoothing down the front of her slacks. She wore a nervous look in her eye, where before she'd only broadcasted excitement.

"What's the news?" Bree asked, turning to open a drawer to get out the oven mitts. All these sliders needed was time to melt the cheese and heat the glaze on top of the sweet rolls.

Elise clasped her hands together and glanced between Wes and Bree. "It's kind of silly."

"I'm sure it's not," Bree said, though Elise did tend to get excited about little things. But the little things were important to her, and Bree thought more people should get excited about small things to keep the joy in their lives.

A smile crossed Elise's face. "I just got my tax EIN from the accountant. Two Green Thumbs is officially a legal business in the state of Wyoming."

"Elise, that's amazing news." She stepped over to her friend and hugged her. "Congratulations."

The timer went off on the oven, and Bree moved over to take the sliders out.

"Are those the breakfast sliders?" Elise asked. "This is the best day ever." She set about getting out plates and silverware, because Bree tended to put too many scrambled eggs on the rolls, and Elise had plenty of experience with the breakfast sliders.

"Are you going to advertise next?" Bree asked, wondering if Wes would say anything else tonight.

"I don't know," Elise said. "I mean, I have work up here."

"Two Green Thumbs," Wes said. "Do you do gardening?"

"Lawn care, too," Elise said. "Landscaping. Anything outside, really."

"You should advertise for customers," Bree said. "You want to do this, Elise."

"Yeah, I know."

"I'll hire you," Wes said.

Both Bree and Elise stopped working to get ready to serve the sliders.

"You will?" Elise asked at the same time Bree said, "You don't even live here." They both stared at him, and Bree's heart started doing flips for some reason.

"I do live here," he said, meeting her eye again.

"You do?" she asked, her voice pitching up. "Where?"

"I got a place...somewhere," he said. "I don't remember the name of the street."

"You don't remember the name of the street." She didn't mean to say it with so much sarcasm. "I think you're lying, Mister Hammond."

He removed his cowboy hat and pushed his hand through his thick, dark hair. Bree figured he knew exactly what he was doing, and that such a move would make her resolve weaken.

"Well, Colton's yard needs some work, anyway," he said.

Bree gave him a smug smile. "Colton lives on Talent Street."

Wes snapped his fingers. "That's it." He just grinned at her. "I know how to get there, and that's all I need, I guess."

"Oh, no," Elise said. "You need a couple of these sliders." She waited while Bree cut around each roll and then scooped a glorious, cheesy and scrambled egg slider. She put two on each plate Elise had gotten out, and Bree slid a plate and a fork over to Wes.

"I'll admit I've never seen anything like this before," he said.

"It's delicious," Elise said, lifting hers and taking a bite. Bree waited until Wes picked up one of his sliders and took a bite, and she knew the moment he fell in love with it. She could see the surprise in his eyes, as well as the way they started to roll back in his head.

A moan came from his throat, and he chewed and swallowed. "This really is amazing." He finished his first slider in only a few bites, and Bree finally picked hers up. "So, you work here and at the employment office?" he asked.

Bree almost choked on her scrambled eggs. She managed to swallow without coughing, and she nodded. "That's right. At least for right now."

"Why's that?"

Elise looked at Bree then, plenty of her familiar anxiety in her light eyes. She knew why, as did the other ladies at Whiskey Mountain Lodge. Colton knew too. And for some reason, Bree didn't want Wes to know.

Oh, and she knew the reason. He'd think she was pathetic, and Bree already thought that about herself. She didn't need the sexy, handsome cowboy billionaire to know it too.

Thankfully, his phone rang, and Wes let it distract him. "It's Colton."

"You better take it," Elise said, and Wes stood up to do just that.

"Thanks," Bree said under her breath as the man left the kitchen and answered the call from his brother.

"Oh, my goodness," Elise said, fanning herself with one hand. "Bree, that man is *gorgeous*." She giggled, and Bree couldn't help smiling too. "You're going to go out with him, right?"

"What?" Bree asked, already shaking her head. "No. No way, Elise."

"Why not?"

"Why not? How about let's start with the fact that his jeans cost more than I earn—from both jobs—in a month? Or that he's from a completely different league than I am." She shook her head. "No, I'm not going to go out with him. Besides, he hasn't even asked."

"Okay, but just think for a second," Elise said, retrieving some errant scrambled eggs from the pan. "He's supposedly on a trip around the country to visit every state. Yet, he's stopped here. I think that says something."

"I disagree," Bree said.

"Second," Elise said as if Bree hadn't spoken at all. "He got a job here. Here, Bree. A job. He doesn't need a job."

"No, he doesn't." She heard what Elise was saying, she just didn't want to acknowledge it.

"I'm just saying—he's already asked." Elise gave her a pointed look and put the last bite of her slider in her mouth.

Bree turned away from her friend and roommate and started washing the few dirty dishes she'd created to make the sliders. She'd washed the bowl she'd cracked eggs into when Elise said, "I'm going to go shower."

"Okay," she said. She hadn't heard Wes leave, but she couldn't hear him talking either. Her nerves wouldn't settle, and she worked her way through the sink and finally loaded the dishwasher.

"Hey," Wes said, coming back into the kitchen. He radiated power from his broad shoulders, and he'd definitely command any room he entered. "I have to get going. Thanks for dinner." He slid his arm around her effortlessly, and Bree's heartbeat crashed against itself inside her chest. He bent down before she could even move, pressed his lips to her temple, and stepped back. "See you tomorrow?"

"Yeah," she said dumbly.

"Great." He grinned at her, turned, and left.

Bree had no idea how long she stood in the kitchen, but her left foot had started to fall asleep before she moved. Pinpricks and tingles spread through her foot, and she wanted to make it to the privacy of her room before Elise found her staring off into outer space over a quick, five-second exchange.

A touch. A kiss.

Bree closed the door behind her and pressed her back into the wood. A sigh slipped between her lips, and she closed her eyes, already reliving the weight and warmth of Wes's hand along her waist, the pressure of that mouth against her temple....

Maybe, she thought.

"No," she told herself. "Remember who you are. Remember who he is. A lion does not fall in love with a mouse."

Chapter Five

Wes woke just before the sun and got dressed in his running clothes. Colton liked to put in a few miles before breakfast, and Wes said he'd join him. Never mind that he hadn't gone running in the past six months, other than that one time in Louisiana when that Rottweiler had chased him.

Because he was closer to fifty than Colton, Wes took several minutes to stretch before he left the guest bedroom he'd been given. Colton lived in a very large and very nice house in a newer part of town, and when he and Annie got married, she'd move in here with him.

The wedding wasn't for another couple of months though, and Wes would be back in Coral Canyon for that. He'd planned to loop back through after he'd visited the West coast. He still had plans to see all the states, but he could spare some time.

How long, he didn't know. What he did know was that he

wanted to spend more time with Bree, though she had seemed a tiny bit standoffish last night.

"Ready?" Colton asked when Wes made his appearance in the kitchen. He took a sip of coffee, and Wes shook his head.

"You drink coffee before you run?"

"I can't seem to do anything without a little coffee in me," Colton said, grinning.

"You're younger than me," Wes said, leaning into the counter so he could stretch his hamstring again. "And I haven't run in a long time. How fast do you go?"

"Not fast." Colton set his coffee cup down, a wicked grin curving his lips. "Let's go."

Wes followed his brother out into the garage, and it was clear that Colton was going to run fast. He'd been training since he'd moved here, and Wes spied a bicycle on the wall. He pulled it down and swung his leg over the bar.

"Cheater," Colton said when Wes caught up to him.

"Dude, I can barely keep up on a bike." Wes would get plenty of work out of cycling, because Colton ran *fast*.

"Tell me what you're thinking about Bree," Colton said, and how he could talk and run at the same time was amazing to Wes.

"I don't know," Wes said, because he didn't. "I just...when I saw her sitting there at that restaurant, I knew I wanted to stay. So I'm staying for now."

"Are you serious about her?"

"Of course," Wes said, looking at Colton.

"She's had some rough waters in the dating pool." Colton wouldn't say more than that, and Wes didn't really want him to. He wanted to get to know Bree on his own terms, and to do that, he needed to talk to her on his own. Share things the way they used to do.

He'd done that through phone calls, and the seedling of an idea rooted into his head. He'd call her as soon as it was a decent hour, and maybe he'd find a way to work in asking her out.

* * *

Later that day, after Wes had worked the check-outs in the morning, he drove down the canyon, following the electronic voice directing him to Springside Energy. Andrew Whittaker had called as Wes was stepping out of the shower, and he wanted to meet at the family energy company to go over business strategy.

Graham had flat-out told Wes during his job interview that he and his brothers were interested in increasing the productivity of the lodge, and that they'd love to hear his ideas. He'd been ecstatic to learn that Wes had been a CEO of a family company too, and he'd obviously passed the information on to his brother.

Andrew ran the public relations and marketing at Springside Energy, though Wes knew all the Whittakers had plenty of money. He could almost smell it on them, though they didn't put on airs or treat anyone poorly.

Wes had plenty of money too, and there was simply a way Graham had carried himself that testified to Wes about his means. Graham reminded Wes so much of himself, except Graham had managed to find a wife and start a family.

Wes felt his age keenly as he pulled up to an immaculate building with a couple of fountains out front. A sprawling sign read Springside Energy, and Wes could see the wealth pouring from the building itself.

His skin itched as he walked toward the doors, and he wasn't sure why. He didn't want to return to downtown Denver and HMC. He didn't want the corner office on the top floor. Yes, it had been hard to walk out that last time. But it had absolutely been the right thing to do.

Wes kept in touch with his old assistant and his former secretary, and they both seemed very happy at HMC. His cousin, Laura, had taken over, and both Matthew and Myra didn't have a negative thing to say about her.

He pushed through the front entrance and into the blessed air conditioning. A woman looked up from the reception desk, a smile blooming across her face. Wes noted her beauty, but there was no bubbling, boiling chemistry the way there was with Bree.

His heartbeat accelerated, and all he'd done was think about the woman. *Get yourself together*, he told himself. He wasn't sure what it was about her that called to him so strongly, only that she possessed it. In the past, he'd never had to work very hard to get a woman to like him or go out with him, but Bree seemed to have some resistance keeping her from a real relationship with him.

He'd always been the one holding the women at arm's

length, and he'd never been this excited about a relationship before.

A potential *relationship*, he reminded himself as the woman asked him who he was there to see.

"Andrew," he said, wondering if last names were needed. "Whittaker."

The woman didn't so much as flinch. She reached smoothly for the phone and pressed the number one. "Andrew," she said. "You have a visitor." She lifted her eyebrows, and Wes knew secretary speak.

"Wesley Hammond," he said.

She repeated the name and hung up a moment later. "He'll be down in a few seconds."

"Wow, seconds," Wes said, smiling. "Your elevators must be much faster than the ones I'm used to."

She smiled and shook her head. "He seemed very excited to see you."

"Oh, well." Wes smiled at her and moved to the side. "I'll just wait over here."

But he didn't have to wait long. True to his word, Andrew appeared before a full minute had passed, and Wes supposed that was only seconds.

"Wes," Andrew said, striding toward him. He wore an expensive suit in dark blue, a white shirt and tie, and a cowboy hat. Wes was still getting used to the abundance of cowboy hats in Wyoming.

"You must be Andrew." Wes shook his hand, both men smiling.

"Thanks for coming," Andrew said. "Let's go up to my

office." He led the way back to the ultra-fast elevators, which did move quite quickly, and down the hall to an office with a wall of windows, just like Wes's old one.

He paused in the doorway and scanned the space, finding Andrew's office completely different than the one that had housed Wes for fourteen years. Evidence of Andrew's family lingered everywhere in pictures on his desk, toddler artwork magnetized to the front of his desk, dirty fingerprints on the windows in front of him, and even a brightly colored plastic cup on the small table next to the door.

"Sorry about the mess," he said, striding past all of it. "My wife has been sick, and I've had the kids in the office with me."

"How many kids do you have?" Wes asked, finally entering the office.

"Three," Andrew said. "My one-year-old just started walking, and I can't keep up with him." He chuckled, and Wes smiled too. He couldn't even imagine having a one-year-old, and yet, something paternal yawned within him that he'd never felt before.

"Another son who's almost three, and a daughter who just turned six."

"Oh, so when your wife is down, it's all hands on deck."

"Plus some," Andrew said. "Come sit down. I can't promise that chair isn't covered in bananas, but I think Lois wiped it down before she sat there this morning." Andrew gave him a bright, beaming smile, and Wes sure did like him immediately.

He prided himself on being a good judge of character, and this man had a spirit about him that couldn't be denied. So

Wes sat, and he folded his hands in his lap. "So, what can I do for you, Andrew?"

* * *

That afternoon, Wes carried bags from the circle drive to the rooms upstairs and down. He didn't see Bree in the lodge, and he had a feeling he should give her some breathing space. With the job done, he tipped his hat to Patsy and headed out to his truck.

On the way down the canyon, he dialed Bree. Their relationship had started on the phone, and maybe Wes just needed to get back to those roots. He'd surprised her at the lodge yesterday, and while she'd been friendly and made him dinner, there'd definitely been an invisible wall between them.

"Hey," she said easily, and Wes's grin could've lit a whole city.

"Hey," he said.

"Where are you right now?"

"Driving home," he said. "Well, driving back to Colton's."

"So you're not at the lodge?"

"Nope."

"I must've just missed you," she said. "I just came in to see how your second day was."

"It was just fine," he said. "I mean, it's finding a name on a list and carrying a bag to a room."

"Yeah, seems a little basic for you," she said. Her voice definitely held a hint of coolness.

Wes didn't know what to say. He didn't need the job at the

lodge. Bree knew that. Wes knew that. He wasn't even sure what his end goal was.

Yes, you do, he told himself. He just didn't want to admit it out loud.

"Tell me about your day," he said. He'd soothed himself after distressing meetings by listening to Bree's voice. He'd relaxed at night while she told him about the hiking trails in the Teton Mountains. All at once, Wes knew what he wanted to ask Bree.

"Oh, it was a day," she said. "I did have to break up a near fight at the employment office today."

"You're kidding."

"I am not." She laughed, and Wes wanted to turn around and go back to the lodge. Maybe they could find a private spot to talk, and he could somehow figure out how to hold her hand while she told this story.

But she continued talking, and he continued driving while she told him about two men who wanted the same job. In the end, they'd both applied, and a disaster had been diverted.

"I don't remember you working at the employment office last Christmas," he said.

Bree didn't respond, and Wes could feel the tension even though they were miles apart.

He gave her a few seconds, and when she still didn't speak, he said, "It's summertime, and I think you told me about a hike I simply had to do in the summer. What was the name of that?"

"Diamondhead," she said, her voice hardly her own.

"Would you go with me?" he asked, drawing a breath and holding it.

"I can't, Wes."

"Why not?"

"I don't have time."

Wes thought of the employment office and the lodge. She worked at both, and he knew she hadn't last year. He wanted to know her financial situation, because he could solve it.

His father's advice entered his mind though Wes had it memorized. *You can't save everyone*, his dad used to say. Probably would still say if he knew what Wes was thinking. *Don't spend your money with your heart, boys. Use your heads.*

"Okay," Wes said, trying to make his voice as light as possible. "I'll look it up."

"Tell me about your day," she said, and Wes suddenly didn't want to.

But he said, "I met with Andrew Whittaker today. He wanted to talk business strategy and how he and his brothers can improve the lodge."

"Oh? Is that right?"

"Yeah."

"What did you tell him?"

"I told him I have no idea how to run a lodge." Wes had enjoyed the conversation though. "He wants me to meet with Patsy and see what's happening at the lodge and see if the two of us can come up with some improvements."

"Are you going to do that?'

"Probably," he said. "I haven't talked to her about it yet."

"Mm."

The silence that settled between them radiated awkwardness, and Wes didn't like it. They'd never had this kind of silence before, and a slip of sadness moved through Wes.

"Wes?"

"Yeah?"

"I can go on that hike with you this weekend if we go Saturday morning and we're back by ten."

A grin chased away all the melancholy in his soul, and he let the happiness out through a chuckle. "All right then. What time do we have to meet to be back by your deadline?"

Chapter Six

Bree woke on Saturday with nerves parading through her body. Her shoulders ached too, from a particularly hard horseback ride she'd led yesterday afternoon. She was glad she'd gone though, because she enjoyed nothing quite so much as exploring nature from atop a horse.

She loved hearing the moms and dads talk to their kids about the things she pointed out, and the cries of excitement when they saw wildlife. Wyoming and the Grand Tetons in the summertime were simply breathtaking, and Bree loved her job at Whiskey Mountain Lodge.

She wished it was the only job she had, but she'd gotten over dwelling on things she couldn't change. With the extra money she made at the employment office, she estimated she could quit at the end of the year and go back to working full-time at the lodge only. And if she didn't get herself into another disastrous relationship, maybe her heart will have healed by then too.

"So what are you doing with Wes?" she asked herself as she measured coffee grounds, set the maker to brew, and turned her attention to packing a sandwich. They wouldn't be gone over lunch, but she'd need to eat breakfast, and she didn't care if that meal came with the traditional breakfast foods or not.

"Why are you up so early?" Elise asked as she came into the kitchen. "I mean, yay, I don't have to make the coffee." She grinned at Bree as she got down a couple of mugs. She was already fully dressed, her light blonde hair pulled up into its customary ponytail, and perky.

Bree wasn't a morning person, that was for sure. She did manage to smile at her cabinmate and say, "I'm going hiking with Wes."

"Ooh, Wes," Elise teased. "He is gorgeous, isn't he?" She added a giggle to her question, though Bree knew she was serious.

"He is." She sighed like his handsomeness really put her out.

"Oh, okay. What's wrong?" Elise poured two cups of coffee and nudged one closer to where Bree stood peanut buttering bread—something she'd been doing for the past five minutes. Snapping to attention, she finally put the knife down and reached for the strawberry jam Celia made.

"Nothing's wrong," Bree said, but she couldn't quite erase the misery from her voice.

"I know you, Bree," Elise said. "And something's wrong. I thought you'd be thrilled to see Wes up close and in person."

"Yeah, I thought so too," Bree said, finally abandoning the sandwich to look at Elise. "It's just...I have a really bad track record with men. What if I'm missing something with him? What if he's not what he seems?"

After all, Jay hadn't been. Jay hadn't even been the man's real name. And Alex hadn't been the guy he'd portrayed himself to be on the dating app either. They'd both taken something from her, and it was more than a piece of her heart and some of her pride.

She'd lost her confidence completely. Not only that, she didn't trust herself anymore, not when it came to choosing the right man to spend time with.

"He's Colton's brother, and Colton says he's a good guy," Elise said. "I think you might be overthinking this."

Overthinking something was Bree's superpower, and she didn't know how to turn it off. "I just think...I don't know what to think." That was the problem, but Elise clearly didn't get it.

And how could she? Bree hadn't told anyone about the root of her problems, because she couldn't go down into that deep, dark hole and confront them.

"Bree." Elise stepped to her side and put her hand on Bree's forearm. They looked at one another, and so much compassion streamed from Elise. Bree loved the other woman, and she tried to smile at her. It shook on her mouth, and Elise pulled her into a hug. "You're smart," Elise whispered. "And strong. And don't think you don't know what to think. You know how to feel, and maybe just see how today goes on the hike."

She pulled away but kept her hands on Bree's shoulders. "Okay?"

Bree nodded, her throat too tight to speak. Elise smiled and backed up, turning to open the fridge a moment later. As she poured cream into her coffee, Bree's emotions loosened, and she could breathe normally again.

"What about you?" she asked Elise. "Are you going to go out with one of Colton's brothers?"

Elise pealed out a string of laughter. "Are you kidding?" She shook her head, still giggling. "Not a chance."

"He said he'd, and I quote, 'hook you up.'" Bree grinned at Elise, glad the conversation had turned lighter.

"I know what he said," Elise said, lifting her mug to her lips. "And I told him in no uncertain terms that I wasn't interested." She sipped, her light green eyes dancing with merriment.

"You don't date very often," Bree said. "Why is that?"

Elise shrugged with a sigh. "I mean, I don't know. Brandt really stomped on my heart, you know? And Wyoming doesn't seem to have a man that doesn't own fifteen cowboy hats. So." She shrugged. "I don't want to move, so I either need to figure out how to like and trust cowboys again, or I need to be happy on my own."

"You don't like cowboys? How did I not know this?" Bree picked up a spoon and started stirring sugar into her own coffee.

"Brandt was a bull rider," Elise said. "He was born with spurs on—or so he liked to say." Her features turned hard for a moment, which was so uncharacteristic of her. "And he broke my heart, so no, I don't really like cowboys."

"I'm sorry, Elise," Bree said. She'd heard about Brandt

before, of course. She just hadn't realized how deeply his exiting spurs had scarred Elise.

She waved her hand. "It's fine. It's been a couple of years, and I just need to figure out how to get back on the horse."

"I've done it," Bree said. "But I keep picking the wrong horse, so that's why I'm thinking it's safer to just stay in the cabin from now on."

"But not this morning," Elise said. "You love hiking, and you've always liked Wes. Just try to have an open mind." She took another drink of her coffee and set her mug in the sink. "I have to run, because I'm doing that herbal class this morning." She grabbed her visor and a jacket from the back of one of the kitchen chairs. "Call me when you get back from your date."

With that, Elise strode out of the cabin before Bree could tell her the hike wasn't a date.

The more she thought about it as she filled a hiking backpack with her breakfast and the pouch with water, Bree thought perhaps this hike with Wes *was* a date. Her heart rebelled at that idea, though her mind seemed completely okay with it.

She'd made arrangements with Wes to meet at the trailhead to Diamondhead. Did meeting for a hike count as a date? She'd met plenty of men at restaurants, the rodeo, the movie theater, and classified those outings as dates.

So this probably was too.

When she pulled into the trailhead a half an hour later, Wes's enormous black truck waited in the lot. A few other cars did too, but in an hour or so, this lot would be full and cars would be parked down the road.

Wes got out of his truck, already wearing a smile to go with his khaki shorts and bright blue T-shirt. It had a horse on the front, with the words KENTUCKY, and for some reason, that made Bree smile.

Wes certainly seemed like the real deal. He didn't mince words, and he didn't put off an air of importance, though she knew he had more money than a lot of people. Probably more than Graham and his brothers, and that was saying something as they were all billionaires.

In that moment, she realized Wes was a billionaire too.

He had to be.

And she worked two jobs to pay off debt she'd incurred from her last, idiotic boyfriend.

Shame moved through Bree, and everything inside her laced tight. When Wes reached her, his backpack slung sexily over one shoulder, she could barely lean into him.

"Something's wrong," he said instead of hello.

Bree couldn't really contradict him, because something was wrong. He was here with her. Didn't he know what a loser she was? How had she hidden it from him?

"Wes," she said, unsure of what else to say.

He looked closely at her, his dark eyes probing yet kind. "What's wrong, Bree?"

She shook her head, because the way he said her name with such care made all the tight parts of her loosen. No one had used such tenderness when saying her name, and she didn't know what to make of it.

"I just...." She looked up at him, needing him to know who she really was. Then he could make a more informed decision about whether he really wanted to waste his time with her. "I don't know what you're doing here," she said. "You, you know, being you, and me, well, being me."

Confusion filled his expression. "You being you? What does that mean?"

"It means we're not from the same worlds, Wes. You're rich and powerful and able to travel the whole country for months at a time. And I'm...I work two jobs, because I incurred some debt in the past six months I can't pay off with just one salary." The dam broke behind her tongue, and Bree just kept on going.

"You're amazing and wonderful, and I don't know. I'm not. We don't belong together, and I just think you're making a mistake, and you should know I'm not on the same level as you."

She took a deep breath and forced herself to stop talking. But at least the truth was out now. It hovered between them, and Wes even fell back a step.

He blinked a couple of times and glanced around, though no one else had pulled into the parking lot yet. "You think we don't belong together?"

"I think you'll eventually realize what a loser I am," Bree said. "So yes. I think you'd be happier with someone more of your caliber."

"What makes you think you're not my caliber?"

She gestured to the truck, the fancy backpack he wore. "It's obvious, Wes."

"Because I have money and you don't." He wasn't asking.

"That's one of the reasons," she said, getting dangerously close to things she didn't want to talk about.

"I don't care if you don't have money," he said, his dark eyes flashing with a warning. "And if you're unhappy working the two jobs, I'd pay your debts off too."

"No way," she said, taking a step forward. Her own resistance to that sparked through her. "Absolutely no way. I can manage it."

"All right," he said coolly. "But money is not important to me."

"That's because you have it," Bree said.

Wes blinked at her again, and she was sure he wasn't used to people talking to him like this. She wasn't sure why *she* was talking to him like this. She liked him. He was gorgeous, and strong, and why was she trying to sabotage their relationship before it had even really started?

"I can accept that," he said. "And try to be sensitive to your lack of funds." He flashed a brief smile. "But hiking is free, and I think you're one-hundred percent wrong when you say we don't belong together." He slipped his free arm through the backpack strap and tightened both of them. "*You're* smart, and talented, and wonderful, and I know exactly what I'm getting when I look at you."

Bree let his words wash over her, and they did scrub out some of the tainted parts of herself that Alex had left behind.

"I don't make mistakes, Bree," Wes said, grinning now. "Except for the one where I haven't really done much physical exercise while I've been driving around the country. So just try not to show me up on this hike, okay?"

She allowed herself to smile too, because Wes was just so darn charming. "You don't make mistakes." She scoffed. "Everyone makes mistakes, Wes. Even CEOs." They started toward the trailhead, their booted feet crunching against the gravel.

"Well, I'm not a CEO anymore," he said. "So I guess you might be right." He reached for her hand, interlocking his fingers between hers. "Oops. Is this a mistake?" He squeezed, and Bree's whole world got brighter.

Her skin tingled, and electricity shot up her arm and into her shoulder. She hadn't had such a powerful physical reaction to a man's touch in a long time—not even with Alex or Jay—and she squeezed Wes's hand back.

"If it is, I kind of like it," she said.

"I really like it," Wes said, his voice almost too quiet to hear. "Now, tell me about the hike. The trees we see. Everything."

Bree smiled, this time the action sinking all the way into her soul. Holding hands with Wes calmed a lot of her fears and getting her thoughts out of her head had helped too. She was able to enjoy the feel of his skin against hers, and tell him about the lake they encountered, the swans and pelicans that visited it, and the views of the Tetons they could see once they reached the top of the loop.

"I love listening to you talk," Wes said once they started down the second half of the loop. "Can I call you tonight after you finish at the lodge?"

"What will we talk about?" Bree asked, because she'd never had a man tell her he liked listening to the sound of her voice.

"I don't care," Wes said. "I just want to hear your voice again tonight." He gave her another grin, and Bree felt her world shift again. Maybe he could be something good in her life. Maybe Elise was right, and all Bree needed to do was have an open mind.

"I guess if you called," Bree said, flirting with Wes now. "I'd answer."

"Perfect," he said. "Now tell me what's going on with those trees. They're all dead." He glanced at her, and she followed his gaze to the right, where yes, the mountainside of trees had died.

"This part of the mountain got infected with brown rot," she said. "It's a type of tree fungus that kills whole forests...."

Chapter Seven

Wes really could listen to Bree talk all day. He got her back to the trailhead by ten, though, and he managed to sneak a hug from her before she climbed behind the wheel of her car and drove away.

He'd gone back to Colton's, where he'd showered and then taken his coffee to the back porch. He didn't have email to check. No social media he cared about. He didn't read much fiction, and he didn't have a device to do it on anyway.

He just sat and watched the leaves blow in the breeze while he let his mind move wherever it wanted to go.

He'd go up to the lodge later that afternoon to work the check-in shift, and he wondered if he'd see Bree. Maybe they could talk in person instead of over the phone.

"Slow down," he told himself. He knew he was in deep with Bree already, and their conversation from that morning had shown him why she had some walls between them. He hadn't had to remove bricks from a wall to get to a woman before, but he could figure it out. He took another sip of his coffee, his thoughts leading him toward a prayer.

Help me to know what to do and say with Bree Richards, he prayed. He didn't want to add more unrest to her soul, because he sensed she already carried around more than enough.

"Bless her," he whispered, adding his voice to the breeze. "Help her to see her own worth."

He could see it, and he knew God could see it. Why was it so hard to see one's own value? He wasn't sure, but he'd struggled to find the good inside himself in the past, and he felt like that was where Bree currently was.

"Help me to get where she currently is," he added. "And show her how wonderful she is."

Satisfied with his prayer, he leaned back in his chair, his eyes drifting closed. They'd met at the trailhead at six o'clock, and while Wes used to get up that early to go to work at HMC, he hadn't been using an alarm for months now. He yawned, and a few minutes later, started to drift into a nap.

Bree followed him there, and Wes sure did like that.

* * *

"Yes, ma'am," he said later that day. "I won't drop this. It'll go right on the bed." He smiled at the woman who seemed made of sharp angles and prickly thorns. Apparently her bag contained some valuables, and she'd lectured him for a solid sixty seconds on how to carry it and where to put it to protect them. As if he couldn't carry a bag and set it down properly.

He preceded her up the steps and down along the railing to the hallway. She was staying in room eleven, which sat down the hall on the left. He unlocked the door for her and entered the room, holding the door as she squeezed in past him. Her eagle eyes missed nothing, and Wes cringed as the spring-loaded door crashed closed behind him.

The woman—a Mrs. Buckley—actually yelped, and Wes offered her an apologetic smile. "That door is a bit loud," he said.

She pursed her lips and patted her perfectly set hair. Mrs. Buckley actually reminded him of his mother in her younger years. Always made up just right. Always proper and prim. Always with eyes that saw everything and ears that heard everything.

He set the bag on the bed gingerly and turned back to her. "Anything else, ma'am?"

"What time is dinner?" she asked, though Patsy had gone over everything downstairs just a few minutes ago.

"Six-thirty to eight," he said. "Tonight's menu is prime rib with baked potatoes." He could memorize information too, and he added his best customer service smile to the sentence.

"That's right." She set her purse on the desk in the room, and Wes started for the door. He didn't need a tip to make ends meet, and he didn't need to make anything awkward for anyone.

"Let us know if you need anything," he said as he opened the door. This time, he didn't let it slam closed, and relief poured through him when he'd escaped Mrs. Buckley.

"Can I ask you something?" someone asked, and Wes turned down the hall toward the voice.

"Sure."

"My one son wants to do the cooking class tomorrow afternoon," she said. "And the other wants to go to the movie. They're at the same time. Can they split up?"

"I think so," Wes said. He'd just checked this woman in forty minutes ago, and he remembered she had a thirteen-year-old and a six-year-old with her. "The cooking is for ages twelve and up, and a parent isn't required to be there. The movie is for all ages. So as long as it's your older son going to the cooking class, it should be fine."

She nodded, a smile forming on her face. "Great, thanks. We're excited to be here."

"We're excited to have you here," Wes said, wondering when he'd become part of the "we" at the lodge. But he had, and he liked it. He'd liked traveling the country too, and he still had those ten states to visit. But Wes had always liked belonging to something or someone, and until he'd quit as CEO at the family company, that something had been HMC. His family too, and he still belonged there. But his parents were getting older, and Wes didn't want the pressure from his father to run for governor, or the constant needling from his mother about when he might get married.

Wes returned to the podium outside to find Patsy had left. Everyone must be checked in, and Wes turned back to the double-wide front doors of the lodge. He hadn't mentioned anything to her about what Andrew had said yet, and he wondered if he should.

From what he could tell, the lodge was booked every night for the foreseeable future. He wasn't sure what could possibly be improved, as the events and classes here were unlike anything he'd seen before. The guests seemed content and happy—maybe not Mrs. Buckley, but she was an exception. Why she was staying at a lodge up the canyon instead of one of the nicer hotels in town, Wes didn't know. It wasn't his business to ask the guests why they'd chosen Whiskey Mountain Lodge for their home away from home.

But maybe they should, he thought. Maybe that was how the Whittakers could take the lodge to the next level. Find out why people came here and do more of it.

While he was still staring at the door, trying to decide what to do, it opened. Bree poked her head out, and Wes's day got a lot better in that one moment.

"You're still out here," she said.

"Yes, ma'am." He reached up and touched the brim of his cowboy hat. He had to wear it as part of his official butler uniform, and he didn't hate it. He'd only been in Wyoming for a little over a week, and he felt like a real cowboy in the hat, the boots, and the jeans.

"What are you doing tonight?"

"I have no plans." And it felt great. "Actually, I got a phone call a while ago, and I need to call the guy back."

Bree stepped out of the lodge completely and pulled the door closed behind her. "Who are you calling back?"

Wes's self-consciousness took over, and he reminded himself once again that he was forty-seven years old. He'd never had time to do everything he wanted to do, and now that he wasn't running HMC, he was taking life by the horns.

"It's Gentry Buchanan?" he said, unsure why he'd phrased it like a question. "I saw a flier at the coffee shop about guitar lessons, and I've always wanted to learn to play." He lifted one shoulder in a shrug, like it was no big deal that he needed to make this phone call.

Bree's eyebrows went up, and she leaned against the podium. "Guitar lessons, huh?"

"It's part of my post-CEO life plan," Wes said, itching to move closer to her but holding his ground right where he was, several feet away.

A smile crossed her face, and he wondered if she knew how stunning she was when she softened like that. Had anyone ever told her? Could *he* tell her?

He bit back the words, because he already felt on unstable footing with Bree. She'd placed him on a pedestal because of his money, and he needed to jump off that thing. So maybe a compliment would help.

"You sure are beautiful when you smile," he said, the words only getting stuck behind his tongue at the very beginning.

Her eyes flew back to his, shock and disbelief in them. "Really?"

"Really," he said simply. Surely she knew how he felt about her. It was obvious to him, and how often he called her, and how he'd invited her to go hiking with him, and basically how he'd put his whole see-the-whole-United-States trip on hold.

For *her*. So he could spend more time with *her*. So he could get to know *her*.

Maybe he needed to be more transparent.

"Bree," he said. "You must know why I stayed in town."

She ducked her head again, her dark hair falling out from behind her ear. He wanted to reach out and tuck it back, but he refrained.

"I put my trip on hold," he said. "I'm living with my brother for now. I stalked you at your office." He added a light laugh there, because he didn't like thinking of himself as desperate or a criminal. "I like you."

There. He'd said it. As if she hadn't known from six months ago, when he'd called after she'd left him a break-up message on his voice mail.

Bree looked out over the parking lot, an exhale passing her lips. "I know, Wes. What I can't figure out is *why*." Her gaze flitted past his, but he still saw plenty inside it.

"Why wouldn't I?" he asked. "You're gorgeous, for one. You're smart. You have a sexy voice. You're hardworking. You're resourceful. You can cook. You like horses and dogs, and they like you. Why shouldn't I like you too?"

"Oh, okay," she said with a giggle. "So if horses and dogs like a person, you like them? Is that it?"

"Sure," he said, dropping his eyes and studying the top of the podium near where she stood. "And you know, I'm thinking I need to hire someone to help remind me how to ride a horse." He took a step closer to her, his heart suddenly pounding out of control as he thought about holding her hand. "You know anyone who rides *really* well who can help me?"

"Yeah, sure," she said. "Beau Whittaker."

"Yeah, no," Wes said, flirting shamelessly now. He reached out and touched her fingers lightly with his. She didn't pull away, and he slid his fingers right between hers and held on. "I was thinking of this woman who leads groups from the lodge. I had someone just today say they're so glad they were able to book their week here, just for the horseback riding this woman does."

"That's not true," Bree said.

Wes finally lifted his eyes to her face, and she was looking back at him too. "One-hundred percent true, ma'am. You think I'd lie to you about that?" He placed his free hand over his pulse, which was still acting erratic. "I am not a liar. Cowboy's honor."

Bree's face lit up, and she smiled as she shook her head. "You're barely a cowboy, Wes."

"I'm wounded," he teased. "I'm a total cowboy. I'd just forgotten it."

"Yeah, because of all the shiny shoes and suit coats in your closet."

"Ah, another life," he said. "One I don't have to live anymore." He sobered, glad Bree's hand was still in his. He wanted to start every day in her presence and end it that way too. "Seriously, Bree. Don't you have time for one tiny riding student?"

She searched his face, and Wes kept his smile in place. After a few seconds, she finally released all the tension in her shoulders and neck. He'd won, and he knew it. But he didn't increase or decrease the smile.

"First," she said. "You're not tiny. You're huge. And second—"

"Huge?" he asked. "Is that a fat joke?" He had put on a little weight while driving around the country, sampling America's finest cuisine in the states he'd visited. But not that much.

She tipped her head back and laughed, and Wes chuckled too, more thrilled than he wanted to admit.

"No," she said. "You're not even close to fat. I meant tall."

"Tall is different than *huge*," Wes said, clearly teasing her still. "Maybe you should take a class on vocabulary."

"Yeah, I'll fit that in around my two jobs, my friends, and now my one *tiny* riding student." She rolled her eyes and shook her head, but Wes enjoyed the taste of victory as it moved through his soul.

"What was the second point you were going to make?" he asked.

"If you really want lessons, they'll have to be on Sunday." She lifted her chin slightly, and all Wes could think about was kissing her. Since they weren't anywhere near that step in their relationship, he simply let the fantasy run through his mind.

"I think I can handle a Sabbath riding lesson," he said. "Colton says church is in the morning."

"Yeah." Darkness coated Bree's expression for a moment, and she looked away from him.

Wes had been reading people for years, and he sensed something brewing inside her. "Do you go to church, Bree?"

he asked quietly, inching another step closer to her. Only the corner of the podium separated their bodies, and he ran his thumb in slow circles along the back of her hand.

"I do sometimes," she said. "But I don't really like it."

"Ah, the truth comes out." Wes knew religion generally wasn't something to joke about. "Want to tell me about that?"

"Maybe another day," she said, coming around the corner of the podium and joining him without any obstacles between them. She leaned into his side, and Wes reached up with his free hand and tucked her hair behind her ear. Their eyes met again, and he let his fingers linger along the side of her face, then cradle her jaw.

"You're stunning," he whispered. "I want to know everything about you. Good, and bad, and ugly, and all of it."

"I know," she whispered. "And that's what scares me the most."

"You have something to hide?"

She nodded, her eyes wide and afraid. "You don't?"

Wes searched himself, because he wasn't perfect. He definitely had things he regretted, and things he wished he'd done differently. Mistakes he'd made. Apologies he'd had to give. "A few things," he finally said. "But I trust you, Bree."

She looked away from him again, displeasure covering her face as she stared out at the parking lot. "I wish I trusted myself."

Wes released her hand and instead, put his arm around her waist, providing someone for her to lean on. He had no idea how to respond, because there was obviously a much larger story behind a statement like that.

Bree just sighed and leaned into his body, and Wes kneaded her closer, and they breathed together.

"You'll tell me when you're ready," he said. "And that's good enough for me, Bree."

"Is it?"

"Honestly, it is."

"Okay," she said. "Then we can start riding lessons tomorrow."

Happiness burst through Wes, and he smiled, thinking it would be easy and natural to press a kiss to her temple and ask her to dinner.

So he did both.

"No," she said, stepping away from him. "I can't go to dinner with you tonight. I came out here to ask you if you wanted to go to the movies with us tonight. We get dinner there."

Genuine pleasure moved through him. "Define *us*."

"Me and Elise. Colton and Annie. Patsy, Sophia, and you, if you want to come."

"So five women and Colton." Wes knew his brother was likable, and he'd always had women in his life.

"That's right." Bree grinned. "We've done it loads of times."

"How has Colton survived that?" Wes wondered, laughing in the next moment.

"Hey, he likes it," Bree said. "We're fun."

"Oh, I'm sure you are, sweetheart." And Wes had nothing else to do that night. "So you eat dinner at the theater?" That didn't sound appetizing at all, but maybe the theater food here was different than Colorado.

"Don't sound like you only eat caviar and filet mignon," she teased, pushing one palm fruitlessly against his chest. "It's good. They have pizza and flatbreads and salads and stuff."

"Ooh, flatbreads," he said in a British accent, catching her hand as she dropped it from his chest.

Time stilled for a moment, and they both wore smiles as they gazed at one another.

"All right," he said, breaking the spell. "What time and where am I showing up for this dinner-at-the-theater thing?"

Chapter Eight

Bree wore too much makeup to the movies, and she knew it. Her lips felt caked with gloss, but Elise insisted that she looked amazing and that Wes wouldn't be able to keep his hands to himself.

Bree hadn't been able to tell Elise that she'd already held Wes's hand. Twice. That morning on their hike, and that afternoon at the podium. He'd told her how beautiful she was, and Bree was still trying to figure out how to believe him. After all, all of her boyfriends in the past few years had told her how pretty she was. How easy to talk to. How charming—Jay's chosen word. And how smart—Alex's constant compliment.

Wes had used all of those too, and maybe that was why Bree didn't believe him instantly. She wished she could shake the doubts out of her head, but that simply didn't work. They filtered through her mind while she made her hair fall in gentle waves and while she covered up her sunspots with a foundation that smoothed out the texture in her skin.

Perhaps that was why she'd put too much on. She couldn't stop thinking about Wes and if what he'd said was true. If she could trust him, the way he said he trusted her. If she really belonged with a man like him. How long it would take him to get bored with her.

"At least you know his real name," she murmured to herself.

"It's time to go," Elise called down the hall. "Come on, Bree. Everyone's waiting."

She gave her hair one last pat and turned away from the mirror. "Coming." She left the bathroom and dodged into her bedroom to grab her purse. She hurried out of the cabin, where Elise waited down on the sidewalk. "Sorry. I'm coming."

"You're the one who orders the fried chicken," Elise says. "That takes ten minutes." She grinned at Bree and scanned down to her feet, where Bree wore a pair of black ankle boots that lifted her height a couple of inches. "You look so cute."

Elise looked down at herself. "Maybe you should help me with my wardrobe."

"Really?" Bree linked her arm through Elise's. "I'd love to, Elise. And then, we can see if the Whittaker brothers or Colton can casually introduce you to a few new men."

"They only know cowboys," Elise said. "But I was thinking maybe, if I could get a cute picture taken or something, I could sign up for that dating app everyone in town uses. You know, we don't get down to town much. Well, you do." Elise kept talking about Bree's new job, how she wanted to have a girl's day where they got their nails done, went shopping for a new outfit, and that Colton's birthday was coming up, and they had to get a cake decided upon.

"Don't you think Annie should take care of the cake?" Bree asked. She knew Colton's friendship with herself and Elise had been a sore spot for Annie in the past, and she didn't want to hurt her friend.

"She asked me," Elise said. "Yesterday, maybe? She wants us to make it, because Colton loves our chocolate cake."

"Then we have a cake decided upon," Bree said, echoing Elise.

"Not the *design*," she said as they finally reached the parking lot at the lodge. Patsy beeped the horn, as there were a lot of cars in the lot in the summertime.

They piled in with the other ladies who lived and worked up here at the lodge, and Bree was glad for the extra people, so she didn't have to talk so much. She was used to letting Sophia dominate the conversation, and she did on the drive down the canyon to the movie theater, because apparently, there was a guest in the lodge who'd checked in today who was "fussy."

Since Sophia worked in the kitchen and dealt directly with a lot of guests, she usually had some amazing stories. Patsy had dealt with Mrs. Buckley too, and the two of them traded stories all the way down the canyon.

At the theater, she couldn't pick out Colton's or Wes's truck, as it seemed like every man in Coral Canyon drove a big truck. The two men met them, along with Annie, inside the front doors of the movie theater, and Colton hugged Bree first, then Elise. He then took Annie's hand in his and said, "I can't wait to see if Carole can figure out how to keep her diner open."

"Oh, come on," Elise said, stepping with him and Annie. "We said you could choose the movie."

"And I did," Colton said, though he'd clearly chosen this romantic comedy for the company he kept. "And I'm *so* excited about it."

"Stop it," Annie said, laughing.

Patsy and Sophia had moved on to talk about the garbage disposal in their cabin, which needed to be fixed, and Sophia said she'd text Graham as soon as they sat down with their food. Bree watched them all start into the theater and head for the line to order dinner, and slowly, her attention moved to the last man standing there.

Wes.

Excitement zipped through Bree's bloodstream, even though she really wanted to hold him at arm's length. At the same time, she wasn't sure why he couldn't just get a little closer. The constant tug of war inside her exhausted her, but she managed to smile at him. "Ready for this?"

"I don't think I'm as excited as Colton," Wes said. "But I suppose if I get to sit next to you and eat something fried at the same time, I can count that as a win."

He was funnier in real life than he'd been on the phone, and Bree laughed with him for the second or third time that day. He didn't reach for her hand, something she appreciated. She wasn't exactly trying to hide her relationship with him from anyone, but she didn't need to broadcast it from the rooftops either.

They got in line behind Sophia and Patsy, and Wes hadn't had a moment to say anything before his phone rang. Mom sat on the screen, and he said, "It's my mother." He fumbled the phone to answer it, saying, "Mom, can you hold on for a quick second?" He pulled his wallet out of his back pocket and handed it to Bree, who almost dropped it. "Yes, just one second, I swear."

He pulled the phone away from his mouth and said, "I want the pepperoni and sausage pizza, with extra cheese if they'll let me have it. And a Diet Coke. Use any card in there, okay?"

"I don't—"

He gave her a grin and stepped out of line with, "All right, Mom, I'm back. See? That was only one second."

Bree held his wallet like it was a poisonous spider. She didn't need him to pay for her dinner. If he did, that made this a date.

Why shouldn't it be a date? she asked herself, and that sent her mind spinning too.

She watched him smile and laugh as he talked to his mother on the phone, and she honestly didn't know what that would be like either. She hadn't spoken to either of her parents in months now, and she could barely remember what their voices sounded like. Even when they did talk, there was no laughing. No good-natured humor about how long her mother would need to hold until Bree could talk to her. Nothing good about their conversations at all.

The worst part was, Bree knew all of that was her fault. She'd been the one to ruin everything in their family, and she'd left Vermont two decades ago and never been back. Twenty years was such a long road, and she had no idea how to bridge the gap between her and her parents. So she'd stopped trying —a long time ago, if she were being honest with herself.

"Next," a teenager called, and Bree snapped out of her awful memories. She didn't like spending time in the past, and certainly not with her too-small family at the forefront of those memories.

"I'll take the fried chicken," she told the girl. "Tots. And a pepperoni and sausage pizza with extra cheese. Two drinks."

The girl named some astronomical amount, and Bree was suddenly grateful she wasn't paying. If she'd come here with Alex, she would've been, and worry would've accompanied her for the rest of the night. As it was, Wes's card cleared quickly, and she took her buzzer and the two cups over to the soda machine to get the drinks.

She then joined her other friends as they all waited for their food. Wes came over and rejoined them a few minutes later, and said, "Mom wants you to call her," to Colton. "She and Dad are trying to make plans for the wedding."

"Did you just talk to her?" he asked.

"Yep." Wes smiled around at everyone. "Okay, let me see if I can get the names right." He went around the circle, and of course, he aced matching all the women to the right names.

Still, Patsy grinned like he'd just single-handedly achieved world peace, and she congratulated him on a well-done first week at the lodge. Everyone seemed completely taken in by Wes's charm, and Bree felt like she was standing on the wrong side of a pane of glass. Looking in. Pressing her hands against the hard surface, desperate to be accepted into the group too.

She wasn't sure why. Wes had said beautiful things that afternoon, and if anyone was in his inner circle, it was her. Why did she feel like such an outsider then?

"Yeah, go," Wes said. "We'll be in when our food is done."

Bree blinked, realizing they were the only two left again. "Sorry," she said. "I ordered the fried chicken, and it takes a while."

"It's fine," he said. "Can you imagine what the previews for this movie will be?" He shuddered, and Bree smiled at him.

"Why don't you have a girlfriend?" she asked, and all the playfulness slid right off Wes's face. It was nice to know he could be serious sometimes too.

"I worked too much in Denver to maintain a relationship," he said simply. "And then I've been on the road, so that wasn't really conducive to meeting a life partner."

"You never dated in Denver?"

"Uh, yeah, sure, I dated," he said, glancing toward the food pickup counter. No fried chicken had arrived yet. "I've actually been engaged twice."

Bree almost spit out the soda she'd just taken into her mouth. She managed to swallow it with only a slight cough. "Oh, wow. Twice?"

Wes nodded and took his own drink. "Yeah, neither of them got very far. I think I loved them on some level, but not the truly, deep level I needed to actually say I-do." He smiled as he lifted that one shoulder into that sexy half-shrug. "My mother is very disappointed in me, if you must know."

"Because you're not married?"

"Yes," he said. "She asks me about it all the time. Just now, in fact."

"She did not."

"I swear to you, she did." He put one hand over his heart as if making a pledge. "Absolutely, she did. She never lets a conversation happen without asking me if I'm seeing quote—someone special."

"Wow," Bree said. She wondered what her mother would ask her if they talked. Probably about work, and the lodge, and Wyoming. That was all they ever talked about. As if the weather in the Tetons was something that could take up hours of conversation and leave one satisfied.

"I have disappointed her," Wes said. "I do regret it. But Gray's been married, and he has a son. Cy too, minus the son. Colt'll be married soon. Our company's future is secure. I guess I'm...just really looking for that one woman who'll sweep me off my feet and make me wish I'd met her two decades ago." He gave her a small smile, but Bree had no idea what to say.

She'd known there was more to Wes than a fancy suit and a big bank account. She'd known that from talking to him last winter. But she didn't know that he could be deep in one moment, and romantic in another, and absolutely charming in a third. He was so good at all of those, and she couldn't help feeling like she was getting played.

"Oh, food's ready," he said as the buzzer went off on the table. He picked it up and stepped over to the pickup counter.

When he turned around, he had everything on a tray, and a few questions in his eyes. "Ready?"

"Yes," she said, stepping to his side and plucking one of her tater tots out of the cardboard tray. "I'm ready."

They walked toward the entrance to the theater, where she showed their tickets and they were told to go to theater twelve for their feature.

"How old are you?" she asked as they walked.

"Forty-seven," he said.

"Do you think we're too far apart in age?" she asked. "I'm only thirty-six."

"Only if you want to use that as a reason you don't want to be with me," he said, nudging her to the right as theater twelve came closer. "Because I don't care." He gave her a smile that wasn't entirely playful and headed into the dark theater first. The previews had already started, and Bree gave all of her attention to navigating to their seats in the near-darkness. Wes passed out their food and put up his footrest. Bree did that too and got all settled in.

Just as she took her first bite of the deliciously hot fried chicken, the movie began. As she ate and watched, she realized she didn't want a reason to not be with Wes.

So when she finished eating and noticed he was done too, she lifted the armrest between them, snuggled into his side, and relaxed as he put his arm around her shoulders. A sigh came out of his mouth, and then his lips lowered to her ear, "I guess the age thing doesn't matter to you either."

She shook her head, because it didn't. Gladness poured

through her that she didn't have that to worry about, and she settled in to enjoy the movie with her new boyfriend.

* * *

"Oh, come on," Wes said later, as the six of them finished ice cream cones at the shop next door to the theater. "It was obvious Rick was not going to buy the diner from the first ten minutes." He laughed loudly as Elise and Sophia protested. "Back me up, Colton," he said, looking at his brother and then Bree.

She said nothing, because he'd dug himself into this hole. Colton shook his head and said, "Bro, you've got to learn how to watch movies with women."

Bree grinned at him, and Colton's eyes sparkled with something she didn't like. She licked her ice cream as he got busy on his phone, and sure enough, hers buzzed in her pocket a moment later.

She rolled her eyes at him, the conversation between the two of them silent but loud at the same time. Wes was still trying to defend himself against Elise and Sophia, and Patsy threw in a comment every now and then too.

Colton nudged her with his foot, and she just glared at him. The message should've been clear. No, she wasn't going to talk about Wes right now. Not right in front of him, and certainly not with his brother. Even if she and Colton were good friends. Bree had a line she wouldn't cross when it came to her relationships.

"All right," Colton finally said. "We're causing a scene.

Let's go." He stood up, and since he was the pack leader, everyone soon joined him.

They took their laughter and loud talking outside, and Wes finally let the women go ahead of him. "Thanks for inviting me," he said. "That was fun."

"It was," Bree said. "I'm glad you came."

"She's *so* glad you came, Wes," Colton said, and Bree elbowed him in the ribs. He grunted and then laughed, and Bree wondered why he couldn't just act his age for a couple of hours.

"I'm going to put something gross in your birthday cake," she told him. "Pickle juice instead of milk."

He sobered quickly and stepped in front of her. "You wouldn't."

"Try me," she said.

"Okay," he said, holding up both hands. "I'm sorry. Honest." He glanced at Wes, who'd also suddenly turned a bit more stoic. "Bree makes a killer chocolate cake."

"Yeah?" Wes asked. "Where'd you learn to bake?"

Bree clenched her jaw, because she didn't want to say. "My grandmother," she managed to say, but the two words really hurt her throat coming out.

"Oh, where's your family from?" Wes asked, and pieces of Bree's sky started to fall.

"She doesn't talk about her family," Colton said quickly, coming to her rescue.

But that only made Wes ask, "She doesn't?" He looked at her. "You don't? Why not?"

"Can I talk to you?" Colton asked, grabbing Wes and practically dragging him away from Bree and Annie. Every muscle in Bree's body felt like someone had laced it with string and then pulled that string tight, tighter, tightest.

She looked at Annie, who wore an anxious look on her face too. But it wasn't like she knew about Bree's family either. She'd literally never talked about them, to anyone.

"Emily's calling," she said. "Excuse me." She too stepped away, turning her back to take the phone call from her daughter.

Bree felt like an island standing on the sidewalk. People she knew—friends—surrounded her, but she was absolutely all alone.

She'd felt like that since the day Bronson had died. An island all alone in a vast sea of people who could never understand her.

Chapter Nine

Wes got out of Colton's truck and reached back inside for the box of cupcakes they'd stopped to get. His younger brother had a serious sweet tooth, and Wes couldn't say he minded. Colton had been talking about The Chocodile here in Coral Canyon for months, and Wes would finally get to try one of their confections to see if they were as amazing as his brother said they were.

The night hadn't gone exactly the way Wes had hoped. Ninety percent of it had, he supposed. He'd flirted with Bree, and she'd flirted right back. They'd had a couple of meaningful conversations before the movie began, and she'd cuddled right into him for the bulk of the romantic comedy. Those kinds of movies so weren't his thing, but if he got to inhale the sweet scent of Bree's perfume, and trace patterns on her upper arm... he could deal with the ridiculous movie on the screen in front of him.

Colton had pulled him away real fast, though, when Wes

had brought up her family. "Look," his brother had said. "She doesn't talk about them. From what I can gather, something bad happened, and she never goes to visit. Never talks to them. So just let this go."

Wes didn't want to let it go, though. He couldn't imagine having a real, lasting relationship with Bree if he never got to know about her family. His curiosity had him oscillating between calling her and asking again, or driving up there and showing up on her doorstep to ask.

But something told him his brother was right. If he did that, he'd lose Bree for good. At the same time, she'd surely tell him eventually, right?

Bless her, he prayed silently as he followed Colton up the steps to the front porch of the luxury farmhouse his brother had bought.

"I'm gonna call Mom," Colton said. "Put those in the kitchen, and don't eat them all."

"How could I possibly eat them all?" Wes asked. "We got eight, and I just finished an ice cream cone."

"I'm just saying." Colton continued through the house and out the back door, where he lifted his phone to his ear and faced the woods behind his house.

Wes put the cupcakes on the counter but didn't open the box. He was stuffed from eating the whole pizza at the theater, even if it was a personal size, meant for one person. With that, the soda, and the ice cream, he thought he'd be eating cupcakes for breakfast.

Colton seemed to have a bottomless stomach, but the older Wes got, the less he could eat and be comfortable. And if there was one thing he'd learned in his forty-seven years, it was that life was too short to be uncomfortable by choice.

So he went upstairs to the guest bedroom where he was staying and changed out of his jeans and cowboy boots. When he'd first gotten the boots, he'd felt absolutely ridiculous. But he'd learned to wear clothes to play a part, and the boots made the guests at the lodge feel like they were getting the true Wyoming country experience. One man had even said that out loud to him.

Look, son, a real cowboy.

The son had not been impressed.

And Wes wasn't a real cowboy—at least not yet. But maybe if he learned to play the guitar and brushed up on his horseback riding skills, he would be. Bree sure did seem to like cowboys....

Frustrated that Bree was once again in the forefront of his mind, Wes put on his pajamas and went back downstairs at the same time Colton came in from the back porch. "Is she freaking out?" he asked. "The wedding is still six weeks away, right? And Annie's doing it all."

"Most of it," Colton said. "She's not freaking out. She's just wondering where we should cater the luncheon. I told her I'd take care of it." He put his phone on the kitchen counter and reached for the cupcakes. "I'm going to have the s'mores one. It's fabulous if you warm it up for seven seconds."

"So specific," Wes said, grinning at his brother.

"Oh, I've tested this," Colton said, turning to the microwave.

"Like you've tested Bree to see if she'll talk about her family."

Colt turned back to him and folded his arms. "She won't."

"But what if we had a real thing going?"

"We have a real thing going." Colton frowned. "She's a good friend. A close friend. She hasn't said a word to me about them."

"Yeah, but I don't want to be her friend." Wes didn't need to be shy with Colton. They were way beyond that at this point in their lives.

"Does she know that?"

"Heck, she better," Wes said. "I've embarrassed myself to no end, telling her all kinds of things and asking her out, and calling her all the time."

"What kind of things?" Colton grinned and that glint in his eye made Wes roll his eyes.

"I'm not telling you everything just because you gave me a bed to sleep in for a while."

"Yeah, well, if you're going to be here for longer than six weeks, you need to find your own place." Colton turned back to the microwave and took out his slightly warmed cupcake. "I've never been married before, and Annie's moving in here with me."

"Are her daughters moving in too?"

"No, they decided to keep the house where they grew up. She owns it, and Emily's getting married too. So Eden will live there alone until...well, she'll live there for now."

"I'll start looking for my own place." Wes sat at the bar and exhaled.

"So you're going to be in town for a while." Colton got a fork out and offered one to Wes, who shook his head.

"Yeah," Wes said. "I *really* like Bree, and I want to see if we could I don't know, have something."

"Something more than what you had with Claire and Lauren," Colton said.

"I proposed to both of them," Wes said. "I can do that much." He worried he might not be able to ever do the next step though. Would he ever find someone he wanted to take all the way to the altar? He hadn't been lying when he'd told Bree earlier that evening that he wanted a woman he couldn't wait to spend the rest of his life with.

He thought it was her, but he reminded himself that the relationship was still new—and that she really did have to trust him with *everything*, including her family—before they could even talk about something as serious as marriage.

"Well, Bree's awesome," Colton said, pointing his fork at Wes. "And if you hurt her, I *will* kill you in your sleep. She's been through enough already."

Wes blinked at Colt, a bit of betrayal leaking through him. "Isn't blood supposed to be thicker than water?"

"Not with her," Colton said. "She deserves the very best."

"Ouch," Wes said. "You don't think that's me?"

"Of course I think it's you," Colt said. "That's why I set you two up. I'm just saying, don't hurt her."

"What if she hurts me?" Wes watched his brother, sure Colt would come to his rescue then.

"Well, I guess that's a possibility," he mused, as if he'd

never really thought about it. "Somehow, though, I think you'll survive."

"Are you kidding me?"

"Oh, come on," Colt said with a laugh. "You'll get in your truck, and you'll go visit the other ten states you haven't been to yet. You'll be fine."

Wes frowned, but he didn't argue further. He didn't think he'd be fine if things with Bree didn't work out. She was the first woman who'd interested him even a little bit in the past couple of years, and he'd started to fall for her before he'd ever met her face-to-face.

Colton moaned over his cupcakes, and Wes glared at him. His younger brother didn't care though, and just laughed at Wes's displeasure. "I'm going to call Gray," Wes said. "Maybe he won't betray me if things go south with Bree."

"Oh, come on," Colton said as Wes walked away. "I've got your back, bro."

"Sure," Wes said, taking the stairs two at a time as he went up to his bedroom. He tapped and swiped to get the call connected to Gray. He wanted to see how his brother was doing at HMC, and how his nephew was faring this summer working on the ranch with their father, and yes, Wes needed a little support in this new relationship he'd embarked on, and he could tell he wasn't going to get it from Colton.

* * *

The next morning, Wes dressed in his black slacks and white shirt, knotting a tie around his neck. He hadn't been to church in several weeks, since he left the Bible belt and started north again. He'd liked going to church in the South, as they did more of a rock concert than a sermon.

Colton had promised him that Pastor Clemens gave a nice message every week, and that the choir was good. He said sometimes the older ladies of the church would have a potluck after the service, especially in the summer.

Wes couldn't smell any evidence that he'd get fed after the meeting when he walked in behind his brother. Colton seemed to have forgotten he'd come with Wes that morning, as he went down toward the front of the chapel and sat with Annie and her two daughters.

They'd saved just one seat for him, and Wes stayed near the doors, the lobby behind him, and the sunshine and the call of the wild beyond that. He could leave. He knew how to get a ride somewhere, and surely Coral Canyon had some kind of rideshare service.

He usually liked church, but something crawled under his skin that morning.

"Looking for somewhere to sit?"

He turned toward the female voice, though it wasn't Bree's. Elise stood there, and she seemed to be made of only light. White hair. Seafoam green eyes. She wore a white blouse with tiny sky blue horses on it, with a khaki skirt. If she had wings, she could fly up and away she was so *light.*

"Yeah," he said, thinking of Gray's words from last night. *Maybe I'll come up there. Get Mom off my back about finding another wife. Heck, you and Colton have done it.*

Wes reminded him that his relationship with Bree was

barely a week old, if that. He'd only started holding her hand yesterday. So maybe it was a day old. And when he'd talked to Gray, less than that.

"I'm sure they'll be room on our bench," Elise said. "If you can stand sitting by a bunch of women." She gave him a smile, and he automatically returned it. She gestured for him to follow her, and he did.

She didn't go down nearly as far as Colton, thank goodness, and she detoured to a side bench instead of a row in the middle. Also good, in Wes's opinion.

"Look who I found," she said, stepping over someone. That woman rose, and Wes came face-to-face with Bree.

"Oh, hey, you," he said. This day just got about ten times better, and he wondered how he'd missed her. Of course, he hadn't been looking for her from the back of the chapel.

"I was going to text you." She gave him a smile and sat back down. He settled beside her, hoping it was appropriate to hold hands in church, because he was fixing to do just that.

"Yeah?"

"Yeah, to see if you were coming this morning, and to make sure you still want to do the lesson. It'll be hot by the time we get out of here and eat lunch."

He leaned closer to her, the soft, powdery scent of her skin almost overpowering his manners. "Are we eating lunch together?"

She turned her head toward him, and if she'd just tilt her head back a little...he could kiss her. "You're welcome at the lodge," she whispered.

"Am I?"

"Well, I'm not cooking." She smiled at him. "If you want to eat together, we can go out, or we can go to the lodge. Celia cooks on the weekend, and she's made this sausage tortellini bake that has your name written all over it."

Wes chuckled quietly, easily slipping his hand into hers. "My name, huh? You think you have my taste buds all figured out?"

"That's right, cowboy," she said, settling their hands in her lap, where she covered his with both of hers. He felt like she was claiming him, and he didn't mind that one little bit.

He managed to sit still through the sermon, but he didn't hear a single word the pastor said. Colton apparently was going to the lodge for lunch too, so Wes rode with him. When they walked in, a wall of noise almost knocked them back outside.

"Holy cow," Wes said.

"It's always like this," Colton said. "Especially on the weekends. And during the holidays when the Whittakers are here." He led Wes through the house and into the kitchen, which was a huge room at the back that had two entrances. A giant table took up most of the space on the right, with a long counter dividing that part of the kitchen—which could technically be called a dining room, though it wasn't formal—and the area where the stoves, ovens, and cupboards were.

Wes looked around, completely overwhelmed with the number of people milling about. No way this many people were staying at the lodge. He knew—he'd carried their bags for them yesterday.

He saw Andrew Whittaker, and Graham, and he realized

when he saw another face that had the same shape as theirs that the Whittaker family had come for lunch too.

"How's it going?" Graham asked, shouldering his way through the crowd to stand in front of Wes. "Andrew said you guys had a great chat last week."

"Yeah," Wes said, shaking his hand. "Really great. It's going great." *Too many greats*, he told himself, still trying to find Bree.

"I think the four of us should sit down this week," Graham said over the din. "Me, you, Andrew, and Patsy."

"Sure," Wes said, though he still didn't know what he could do to help the lodge. He knew that was part of why Graham had hired him though, so he'd sit down with them if that's what they wanted.

"Perfect." Graham looked over his shoulder. "That sounds like one of mine, excuse me."

How he'd heard anything, Wes wasn't sure. And he'd thought getting together with his family brought on a headache. This was something else entirely.

A cool hand slipped into his, grounding him, and he glanced down at Bree. "This is insane," he said. Well, it was more of a yell, to be honest.

"I know." She grinned around at the complete chaos.

"You like this," he said.

She nodded, still smiling for all she was worth. Wes did like the happiness pouring from her face, and he tried to see what she saw, through her eyes. The press of bodies, the mass of cowboy hats, the wails of children, still appeared to be complete madness to him.

"All right, all right," someone said over the speaker system in the lodge. Patsy. "It's time for lunch, and we need everyone to quiet down." By the time she finished speaking, only her voice filled the air.

"We're glad to have everyone with us at Whiskey Mountain Lodge today," she continued. "Our friends, family, and guests that are like friends and family. We have our weekend chef in the lodge, and she's prepared three pasta dishes that I'll let her talk about. Celia?"

A pause, a crackle, and then Celia said, "For the little ones who don't like much spice, I made plain old spaghetti and meatballs. All beef meatballs, from our beef cows right here at Whiskey Mountain Lodge. Laney Whittaker raises those."

A slight cheer went up, and Wes saw a woman wave her hand as if she didn't deserve the praise. But Wes had worked a cattle ranch before, and it wasn't an easy job. Not by a long shot.

"If you like something with a little more kick, I've made a sweet and spicy chicken sausage tortellini bake, and our last pasta dish is a bacon mac-and-cheese. Side salads, of course, and garlic bread, along with our always-available soda bar."

"This is amazing," Wes said. "Totally different than during the week."

"Don't let Sophia hear you say that," Bree said, glancing around. "She has a bit of a jealousy issue with Celia."

"Is every weekend like this?" he asked.

"Usually just Sunday," she said. "Celia makes a big deal out of Saturday dinner and Sunday lunch."

"I know where I'm eating on the weekends," he said.

"All right," Patsy said over the speakers. "Here at the lodge, we start our weekend meals with a prayer. Today, I've asked one of our guests, Eileen Buckley, to say it for us. Mrs. Buckley."

A screech went through the speakers, which caused a groan to go up along with the movement of everyone taking off their hats. Wes swiped his from his head and ran his fingers through his hair, which he hadn't paid much attention to that morning.

Bree glanced at him, and he squeezed her hand as he placed his hat over his heart.

"Dear Lord," Mrs. Buckley started. "We are indeed grateful this day for so many blessings, including this lodge, all the people gathered here, and the food that's been prepared."

Wes thought she could say amen right there, and the prayer would be enough for the Lord. But she didn't. She went on and on, and Wes wasn't the only one growing restless.

"When is she gonna stop, Mom?" a child asked, and Wes smiled, his laughter starting to build beneath his tongue. He wasn't sure who chuckled first, but once they did, he couldn't hold his back.

Bree's grip on his fingers increased, but he couldn't help it. Still, Mrs. Buckley prayed on.

"Shh," someone said, and then Colton whispered, "Someone mute the speaker, and we'll all shout amen."

Wes was going to laugh right out loud, and he thought God might smite him to the ground if he did that during a prayer. He had no idea where the speaker system was, but it obviously wasn't in the same room as everyone else.

"Just a second," someone whispered, and Wes took a step back. He was seriously going to lose it. His shoulders shook with his silent laughter, and Bree said, "Stop it," but she was almost laughing too.

"Amen," Mrs. Buckley said, and there were enough other people who practically shouted it that Wes's laughter got lost among the noise.

"You're terrible," Bree said, shooting a look at him and then Colton, who was also laughing.

"That was six minutes," Colton said, tapping his phone, where a timer showed that the prayer was actually six minutes and thirteen seconds. "*Six minutes*, Bree. Who needs to pray that long?"

"You do, Mister," she said. "To repent for laughing at a little old lady."

Colton laughed again, but Wes just kept his smile on his face. When Bree looked at him, he said, "You tell 'im, sister."

"You're no better," she said, swatting at his chest. She wore delight in her eyes though, and Wes knew she wasn't really upset.

"Oh, I'm better than him," Wes said, grinning at her. "Come on, Bree. Tell me I'm better than him. I didn't say we should mute the speaker system."

"Oh, all right," she said. "You're *slightly* better than him." She stepped around him, though there wasn't anywhere for them to go. "Now, come on. If you want food around here, you don't dawdle."

Chapter Ten

Bree dumped her bag on the floor by her desk, about to drop the box of doughnuts or her coffee, and she didn't want to ruin either one.

"Bless you," Willie said, jumping up to help her balance the box of sweets before it tipped onto the floor. With that out of her hands, Bree was able to set her coffee on the desk.

She sighed and pushed her hair out of her face, already sweating, and it was barely eight a.m. "I brought doughnuts."

"And I will be forever grateful." Willie already had the box open, and she lifted one perfectly glazed treat out. "I love these doughnuts. They melt in your mouth. You can eat a dozen of them and not even know it."

"Definitely the best shop to come to town," Bree said, reaching for a doughnut too. Haloes proclaimed that their doughnuts came straight from heaven, and Bree had found their claim to be absolutely true.

One bite of the still-warm doughnut sent a wave of delight

through her, and she couldn't help moaning. The sugary glaze was just right, the dough light and fluffy, with crispy edges. Bree devoured the whole thing, deciding she could walk alongside her horse that afternoon as she did the riding tour. Then she'd ask Wes to take her on a hike, and hey, maybe he could bring dinner with him.

In fact, before she chickened out on the idea, she shoved the last bite of her doughnut in her mouth and pulled out her phone to text him. *Hike and dinner tonight? There are some pretty falls about a mile up a fairly steep hill not far from here. Not super crowded.*

She had no idea what time he got up, but she figured the former CEO didn't sleep until noon. So she wasn't that surprised when his response came immediately. *I'm in. What time?*

I'm done at the lodge at six, she told him. *Maybe you could hang around after you finish check-in and we can drive down the canyon together.*

I'm off today, he said. *I can get dinner though, and maybe you can come pick me up at Colt's?*

That works too.

"Who are you texting?" Willie asked, appearing at Bree's side. She tilted the phone so her friend could see it. "Who's Wes? You're going out with him?"

"It's a hike," Bree clarified.

"And dinner," Willie said. "And you're picking him up."

Bree giggled, because she did like Wes, and the more time she spent with him, the more she felt like she did belong with him. He was nothing but kind, and articulate, and the afternoon they'd spent together yesterday, chatting and saddling and riding had been some of the best hours of Bree's life.

"And you're smiling like a fool," Willie teased. "Bree." She singsonged the name.

Bree couldn't stop the foolish smiling, because Wes had just asked what she wanted for dinner.

You choose what you want to pack in. I like almost all food.

Instead of another text, her phone rang. "Ooh, he's calling," Willie said.

Bree swiped on the phone icon and said, "Hey," as she leaned back in her chair.

"Define 'all food,'" he said. "In fact, you said 'almost all food,' and I don't want to show up with something you can't stand."

Bree looked up at the ceiling, doing almost anything to postpone the moment she'd have to get to work. "The only place you could go that would make me wonder if we should keep seeing each other is Sushi Palace."

Wes burst out laughing, and even Bree started giggling. "So no sushi," he said.

"Absolutely no sushi."

"Everything else is fair game."

"And if you want bonus points, you'll get me the extra-crispy chicken sandwich at ChixPix."

"Oh, boy," he said, his voice making Bree wish she didn't have to work that morning. "I'll see what I can do about the ChixPix."

Bree giggled, sitting up as the front door opened. She sobered instantly as her boss strode inside the building. "I have to go," she said. "Thanks for calling, Mister Hammond." She hung up while Wes said, "I'll text you later," as quickly as he could.

She put her phone down, because it made no sense for a client or someone looking for a job to call her cell, and stood up. "Good morning, Marc," she said. "I brought doughnuts today."

"Oh, great." He smiled at her and took one from the box. "I've got Chris from the city coming in this morning. Will you show him back when he gets here? Apparently, they're doing a huge hiring fair, and they want us to get the word out."

"Absolutely," Bree said.

"Morning, Willie," Marc said, giving the other woman in the office a wide smile.

Willie giggled—actually giggled—and tucked her hair as Marc walked by. Bree had seen them interact before, and it had never been like this. She kept her eyes on Willie as she watched their boss walk the rest of the way into his office. He left the door open, and Willie sighed as she turned back to Bree.

When she caught Bree watching her, she cleared her throat and reached for another doughnut.

"What is going on there?" Bree hissed at her, swiping the doughnut box out of Willie's reach.

"Oh, don't you deny me another doughnut," Willie said, her bright green eyes flashing with fire. She was all bark and no bite, though, and Bree grinned at her.

She kept the box close to her chest as she asked, "Are you... did the two of you...what's going on with you and Marc?"

Willie glanced over her shoulder and then back to Bree. "Give me the doughnuts, and I'll tell you."

Bree immediately handed over the box. Then she grabbed her chair and dragged it over to Willie's desk, which was fairly close by anyway. "Start talking."

"He asked me out on the Fourth," Willie said, almost under her breath. "And we went out that weekend."

"And?"

"And he's cute, and fun, and we had a good time."

"What did you do?"

"We went to the boutique and walked around. Went to the rodeo. Dinner. You know, typical stuff that everyone and their dog went to that weekend."

Everyone except for Bree, though she did love a good rodeo. She hadn't had a date, and she could save her twenty bucks the rodeo ticket would've cost. Right now, she was saving as much as she could, and the only reason she'd brought in doughnuts was because she'd earned a free dozen by buying them for the lodge.

"And?" Bree asked again. "What about Connor?"

"We've been talking," Willie said. "And Connor has sort of faded away."

"Have you gone out again with Marc?"

"He went out of town this weekend," Willie said. "Our schedules haven't matched up, that's all."

Bree squealed, keeping it quiet enough that it wouldn't sound in Marc's office. "So you can show Chris into his office later."

"No, let's just keep things normal here," Willie said.

"Please, Bree? I just want it to be normal here, and if we just act like everything is normal, then it's fine."

"When are you going to see him again?"

"Hopefully on Wednesday night," Willie said, glancing over her shoulder. "Now get on over to your desk and get to work before he sees us gossiping over doughnuts."

"All right," Bree said, plucking another doughnut from the box before she rolled her chair back over to her desk. She needed to check her messages and get listings up that had been left over the weekend. She'd then print out the new jobs for the day and pin them to the board for anyone who came in physically looking for work.

The hours in the employment office passed quickly, because Bree had a lot to do and not much time to do it. When Chris arrived, she jumped to her feet and smoothed down her skirt. With a smile, she said, "Morning, Chris. Let me see if Marc is ready for you." She stepped back to his office and poked her head in. "He's here, sir."

"Great." Marc got up and came toward the door.

Bree backed out of the way and said, "Come on back, Chris," just as Marc reached her. She left the two men alone to talk business, but she knew she'd be putting jobs in like crazy tomorrow. Maybe even tonight, as sometimes Marc asked her to work online at home if they got a huge influx of jobs while she wasn't there.

Just as she was preparing to leave for the day, someone came through the front door. The sun shone in the front wall of windows too, and she couldn't see who it was.

"I got it," Willie said, standing up. "You go."

"Tell Marc I can work tonight," she said as she bent to get her purse out of her bottom desk drawer. She could have her hike and dinner, and stay up late to get the listings put in. As long as she had them done by midnight, they'd post in the morning.

"You have to work tonight?"

Bree straightened at the sound of Wes's voice. "Oh, hey." She smiled at him and looked at Willie. "This is my friend, Willie. Wills, this is, uh, my boyfriend, Wes Hammond."

"Oh, I'm the boyfriend." Wes grinned at Bree and then Willie. "Nice to meet you, ma'am."

"Oh, the boyfriend," Willie said, shaking Wes's hand.

"Okay, I'm leaving," Bree said, heat filling her face. "I have another job to get to."

"I'll walk out with you," Wes said, and that was when Bree noticed he carried a bag from ChixPix. "I got your lunch."

"He's a *good* boyfriend," Willie said, but Bree ignored her. Unfortunately, the sun shone brightly overhead outside, and it was mid-July, so the heat in Bree's face didn't dissipate once she left the building.

"Sorry about that," Wes said.

"It's okay," Bree said. "Nothing to apologize for." She took the bag of food from him. "Thank you for bringing me this. I guess we'll be having something different for dinner?"

"It's not sushi, don't worry."

"Sounds like you have a plan."

"Oh, I have a plan," he said. Before Bree even knew what was happening, he swept one arm around her waist and said, "See you tonight. You'll be by around six-thirty?"

"Yes," she said, surprised at his touch.

He kissed her cheek and stepped back, the smile on his face priceless. "See you then." And with that, he walked away. Bree stood in the parking lot near her car and watched him go, wondering why she felt like someone had poured magic into her veins.

Wes Hammond is made of the stuff, that's why, she told herself. Then she got herself in her car and aimed it in the right direction to go to her second job. She couldn't afford to spend too long thinking about Wes, or she'd find herself falling head over heels in love with him, and Bree simply needed more time to know if she could trust how she was feeling when it came to men.

* * *

Bree showed up at Colton's house wearing a pair of light cotton shorts and a tank top. She'd packed her backpack with a first aid kit, a full pouch of water, and a few snacks, as usual. Wes waited on the front porch with his own backpack, wearing light blue cotton shorts and a T-shirt with a giant baseball bat on the front of it along with the words *Louisville Slugger*.

"Hey, beautiful," he said, rising from the chair there. He shouldered his backpack and came down the steps on light feet. His hiking shoes looked brand new, and he hadn't switched out his cowboy hat for a baseball cap or a shade hat.

She liked the pet names he called her, and he'd used sweetheart and beautiful before.

"Hey." She accepted a hug from him, and they loaded into his truck. She directed him to the hike, which was about a twenty-minute drive from Colton's house, on a turnoff on the highway that led up to Dog Valley.

"Tiger Creek," he read on the sign.

"The falls are called Cub Falls."

"Cute." Wes reached for her hand, and she gave it to him, because once the trail steepened, they wouldn't be able to hold hands. "Good day?" he asked.

"Good enough," she said with a sigh. "Easy afternoon with just the one horseback thing, but I have to work tonight after I get home for my office job."

Wes slowed and stopped. "We don't have to go hiking."

"Uh, I ate four doughnuts this morning," Bree said with a smile. "We definitely *do* need to go hiking."

Wes chuckled and ducked his head. "All right."

"It's less than a mile up," she said. "It'll take us about half an hour. Then we'll eat, and it's much shorter to come down."

"I'm not in the greatest shape," he said, looking up the trail.

"You'll be fine," she said. "How many doughnuts did you eat this morning?"

"Oh, I didn't have doughnuts," he said. "I ate two cupcakes with my morning coffee."

Bree laughed, because she knew how much Colton liked cupcakes, and that had Colton written all over it. "Let me guess. The Chocodile."

"They have one called the shredded wheat cupcake," Wes said. "It was almost like eating a bowl of cereal."

Bree pealed out another lungful of laughter, because Wes's addiction to breakfast sweets made her happy. Being with Wes made her happy. Should she doubt that? What if what she was feeling wasn't real?

Why wouldn't it be real? she asked herself. And she had no answer. That was the biggest problem.

As the trail narrowed, and Bree moved in front of Wes to hike, she did something she should've been doing all along: she prayed for help, for guidance, and to know exactly what to do about Wes so that neither of them would get hurt.

Chapter Eleven

Wes rode the high from Monday night's hike for almost a week. Bree sure had been surprised at the table-for-two at the falls, where Wes had then served two fully plated meals from his backpack. Chicken cordon bleu rolls, with mashed potatoes, and roasted asparagus.

Bree had looked at him with stars in her eyes, and while he'd wanted to stay at the falls for a lot longer, she still had work to do that night, so they only stayed for forty-five minutes before making the hike back to his truck.

He'd wanted to kiss her in Colton's driveway, but Colton and Annie had been sitting on the front steps when he'd pulled into the driveway, and that fantasy still only lived inside Wes's head.

"Maybe today," he muttered to himself as he pulled into the parking lot at Whiskey Mountain Lodge. He was working the check-in that afternoon, though it was Sunday. He'd already held hands with Bree on the bench at church, able to listen a little more fully this week. Pastor Clemens had talked about serving one another through good times and bad times, and Wes had started thinking that he needed to do more in the service department.

He wasn't working much anymore, and he had plenty of money. Surely there was something around town that he could do to put his time and money to good use. Something he could do to bless someone else's life. He'd stopped to talk to the pastor and his wife on the way out, and they'd agreed to meet on Wednesday evening, after one of the church-sponsored classes.

He and Bree were set to enjoy lunch with the crew at the lodge again this week, then another riding lesson, and then Wes would do the check-ins before heading back to Colton's.

He hadn't mentioned to anyone but his brother that he'd called a real estate agent that week too, and he was hoping to be looking at houses this week as well. His stomach clenched at the thought of it, though he had plenty of money to invest in property in Coral Canyon. In this growing community, the house would have great resale value, and Wes wasn't worried about that. He still had the penthouse in Denver, too, though he'd done a sublet to a couple from Paris who'd taken a fifteen-month position in the city.

He had no plans for returning to Colorado, or where he'd live when he did. His parents lived outside the city, and he could stay in Ivory Peaks. Help with the farm, the way Gray and his son, Hunter, did.

Hunter lived with Wes's parents right now, and he was apparently tolerating the isolation of the farm. Gray worked in the city during the week, and only went out to the farm on weekends, and he'd told Wes last week that things were "going really well."

Wes still worried about him, because Gray tended to take on too much and wouldn't acknowledge it until he broke. Completely broke. So Wes would call him again tonight, after his buttling shift at the lodge.

Lunch was just as loud and just as crazy as last week, but Wes didn't hate it this week. He laughed with the Whittaker brothers and promised they'd meet this week for sure. He wondered how long that would go on until they would finally meet to talk about the lodge. But honestly, Wes thought they were doing a bang-up job at Whiskey Mountain. They were booked months in advance, and the reviews that came in were four and five stars. He wouldn't even know what to say to them.

"You ready for this?" Bree asked as they left the patio, where misters kept it cool despite the July heat, and headed for the stables.

"I didn't do too bad last week," Wes said. "So I think I'm totally ready for this." He took Bree's hand in his. "I wanted to ask you about something."

Everything changed in less than a breath. Less than a step. Tension poured from her, and she drew in a deep breath. Wes didn't like that, because it sent up a big red flag that indicated she had secrets. Secrets she didn't want to tell him.

Wes took a few moments to think through what he wanted to say. "It's nothing serious," he said. The stable neared, and Wes felt like the ground would vanish beneath his feet on the next step. The next step.

When there was still solid ground under his feet, he took a deep breath. "You asked me why I didn't have a girlfriend, and I was wondering what happened with Alex."

Bree stepped through the open door and into the stable, turning back to smile at him. "You want my dating history."

"Yeah," he said with a smile. "I mean, I told you I'd been engaged twice. Have any diamonds sat on your finger in the past?"

"Not even one," she said, holding up her left hand. "Never been married. Never been engaged."

Wes didn't need to punish himself, but as he reached for the saddle he'd used last week, he decided he needed to know. "I would like to know about Alex. I mean, we were talking when you met him, and you chose him over me."

Bree didn't answer right away, and Wes kept his head down as he took his tack outside and started saddling the big, beautiful, dark brown horse he'd ridden last week. His name was Chocolate Brownie. "CB for short," Bree had told him last week.

He'd managed to get on the horse last week, and this week was even easier.

"Good job," Bree finally said. "You got 'im saddled and ready." She beamed at him. "Let's see how he does under those trees that spooked him last week."

"You just want to see me jump off again," he teased.

"Not true." She smiled back at him. "But I do want you to

keep him calm. Remember how to get him to move? To go left or right?"

"Yes, ma'am." He clicked his tongue at CB, and added, "Let's go, CB." The horse didn't move, other than his long tail flicking at the imaginary flies around him.

"He's not a dog," Bree said. "It's just *go*. Go, CB."

The horse started walking forward, and Bree told her steed to "Go, Cookie," and her horse moved too. Her black-and-white horse was named Cookie Crumble, but Wes had learned that almost all the horses went by abbreviations of their full names. And they were all named after sweets, something Colton would've really liked.

The cowboy hat Wes now loved kept the sun off his face, but relief still covered him when CB moved under the cover of shade cast by the trees along the edge of the property.

"I chose Alex over you, because he was here and you weren't," Bree said. "That was all, really."

Wes looked over to her. "It was the long distance?"

"Yeah," she said. "And he was cute, and he asked me out to dinner, and I couldn't go to dinner with you." She shrugged. "I was stupid, I'll admit it."

"You're not stupid," he said.

"Yeah, well." Bree exhaled, a sound that was much too heavy for Wes's liking. "Remember how I said I don't really trust myself?"

"Yes," he said quietly. "I remember."

"It comes from my last few boyfriends," she said. "Alex was a freeloader. He said he had a job, but I think that was a lie. I paid for everything we did, and now I'm thousands of dollars in debt."

The horses clip-clopped along, the only thing disturbing the peaceful forest around them.

"In five months," she said. "It's amazing how much I spent in five months. That's why I have the job at the employment office."

"I can pay those," Wes said, thinking maybe this could be the way he could serve someone.

"Absolutely not," Bree said.

"It wouldn't even impact me," he said. "And Pastor Clemens said we needed to look for ways to serve each other. I've already set up a meeting with him and his wife for Wednesday to see what I can do." He looked at her, the idea of paying her debts growing and getting real teeth. "Why not you, Bree? Why can't I serve you?"

She shook her head. "I feel stupid enough about it already."

"Then go ask the pastor for help."

She wore a look of anguish on her face. "No, I can do this. I only have to work at the employment office until the end of the year, and I'll be out from under the debt. I can do this."

"Of course you can," Wes said. "You're strong and capable. But it's okay to ask for help too."

"I know." But she sighed again, and Wes wasn't sure she knew it was okay to ask for help. At least not help from him. "Anyway, my boyfriend before that was named Jay. At least that's what he told me. It was not his real name, and to this day, I don't know his real name."

"What in the world?" Wes asked.

"Yeah, exactly," Bree said. "And the worst part was that I dated him for six months. *Six months*, and I didn't know the guy's real name."

Wes just watched her, but she wouldn't look at him.

"The guy before that told me that I was a nice woman, but I needed to wear my hair longer, or else I look too manly."

"So he's a loser," Wes said, not bothering to keep the disgust out of his voice.

"He *was* a loser," Bree said. "And that's the problem, Wes. That's why I don't trust myself. I've never really had a good boyfriend. Ever. I always pick the losers." She glanced at him. "No offense."

"Do you think I'm a loser?"

"No," she said miserably. "But that doesn't mean I believe everything I've been feeling when I'm with you."

Wes wanted to ask what those feelings were, but he was still processing what she'd said about her previous boyfriends. "Okay, first off, you called your past boyfriends 'guys.' That's your first problem. I'm not a *guy*. I'm a *man*."

Bree just looked at him, and Wes really wanted her to know the difference. "I have plenty of money. Wesley is my real name, and I absolutely love your hair. Even if you shaved your head, I'd love it. I didn't start to fall for you based on what you looked like, Bree. I started to fall for you the first time I heard your voice. I started to fall for you when I realized how kind you were. I started to fall for you with every text and every call, and that happened long before I even knew what you looked like."

He drew in a deep breath, because he'd just laid a lot on the line too. "I'm too old to play games, to be honest. What you see with me, what you hear me say, is what it is. The end."

"I know," Bree said. "And that scares me too."

"You want to play the games?"

"No," she said. "I'm scared that one day, you're going to wake up and realize what I have with my last three boyfriends. That *I'm* the loser here, and you could do so much better."

"I have my eyes open," Wes said. "And I really don't think that's going to happen." He didn't want a woman he had to reassure over and over again, though, he knew that. Lauren had been on that end of the needy spectrum, and constantly telling her how amazing she was and assuring her that he was where he'd said he'd be had been utterly exhausting.

He looked through the foliage, the steadiness of CB beneath him comforting. Bree didn't say anything else, not even more instructions for riding the horse.

She eventually said, "We better get back so you're not late for your job."

"Okay," Wes said, and they made it back to the stables. He brushed down his horse, feeling a real connection moving through him. He cleaned and hung his equipment, and finally, he took Bree into his arms.

"Tell me we're okay," he said, his mouth right at her ear. Any ideas of kissing her today, though, had fled during the horseback ride.

"Yes, Wes," she said. "We're okay."

He pulled back and looked down at her. "Really?"

She smiled up at him and nodded. "Really."

"I sure do like you," he said very, very seriously.

"I sure do like you too," she said, and those were the best words Wes had ever heard. She tipped up on her toes, and Wes leaned down, his heartbeat crashing against his ribcage now.

"Wesley Hammond to the check-in podium, please," came over the loudspeaker. "Wesley Hammond to the check-in podium."

Bree started giggling, then laughing. "You better go," she said. "You're being paged."

"Can we pick this up later?" he asked, pulling her closer. "Right here. This moment. Later?"

"Yeah," Bree said, still laughing as the loudspeaker crackled to life again. "Now, hurry up. I'll wait five minutes and then head to my cabin."

"Ooh, sneaking around," Wes said as Patsy paged him for a second time in only ten seconds. He released Bree and backed up a couple of steps before turning around.

Then he hurried to his post, because the last thing he needed was to be paged for a third time. But he seriously couldn't wait to see Bree again...and get his kiss.

Chapter Twelve

Gray Hammond glanced at his sleeping son as he crossed the Wyoming state line. They still had quite the drive in front of them, but Hunter had said they should do it in one day. Gray hadn't minded, because there was nothing he liked more than a good road trip.

Truth be told, what he liked best about road trips were the sodas and candy he brought along. In fact, he reached for a Red Vine only to discover the box was empty. Frowning, he glanced at the seat between him and Hunter, where they piled their loot from the gas station. They still had chips, sour candy, and M&Ms. So Gray didn't need to stop. He only wanted to.

But stopping would wake Hunter, and the boy had been working like a dog at his parents' farm this summer. Gray's guilt spiraled again, and he worked to tamp it back down. Work wouldn't kill the eleven-year-old, and it was good for his parents to have their grandson around too. Not only both of those things, but Gray was extraordinarily busy at HMC right now, and Hunter didn't have school, so he needed something to keep him occupied and out of trouble.

He did miss his friends though, and on the only weekend Gray had taken off of work so far this summer, he was taking them to Coral Canyon to help Wes move into his new house.

Gray was not at all surprised that Wes had decided to stay in Coral Canyon for a while, nor that he'd bought a house. He still owned the penthouse in the highrise in downtown Denver too, and Gray reminded himself to talk to his brother about selling it. He obviously had no plans to come back to the Denver area, a fact which made Gray a bit sad.

Someone needed to be there to take care of their parents, and he could already hear Colton's solution to that predicament. *Have them move to Coral Canyon.*

Gray could admit he needed a change of scenery. He'd been in the Denver area, and up into the foothills at Ivory Peaks, for his whole life. His thoughts once again zeroed in on Hunter, and all his son would have to give up if Gray made a major move in their lives.

"But maybe now's a good time," he muttered to himself. Hunter would start sixth grade this year, and next year, he'd transition to junior high. Maybe a clean break then would allow him to find new friends at a new school, in a new place....

Gray let the thought linger there, neither committing to it nor dismissing it. He was really good at playing on neutral ground. As a lawyer for the family company, he'd learned that early on. He never took sides. He presented the law and let the big wigs in charge interpret which way to go.

A stitch of excitement pulled through him at the idea of returning to Coral Canyon. He'd been through the quaint, picturesque town before, and he'd enjoyed it. Wes said it was stunning in the summer, and Gray couldn't wait to get out on a river or a lake and catch some fish.

Fishing was how he reset, and how he brought up difficult subjects with Hunter. He'd had something on his mind he wanted to discuss with the boy for a couple of months now, and he had his mother to blame for it.

Dating.

Gray knew he'd get back into the dating pool at some point, but as he'd told his mom several times now, he wanted to don the trunks and rub in the sunscreen on his own timetable. He had more than his own heart to consider, and no matter what his mom said, Hunter wasn't just a cookie-cutter of a human being.

He was a *real* human being, with real feelings, and he deserved the absolute best. Gray did not—would not—introduce anyone into the boy's life who would end up abandoning him. They'd both had more than enough of that for one lifetime, and Gray's fingers tightened around the wheel as he thought about his ex-wife.

Sheila came in and out of their lives on her own whims, and the only thing Gray hadn't been able to deny her was her requests to see their son. He and Hunter had worked out a good system so Gray would know how things were going with simple, everyday phrases, and Hunter had never used any but the positive ones.

His mother fed him, and she didn't leave him home alone. She didn't bring men back to the house while Hunter was there, and he liked going to the beach in Florida. Thankfully, that white sand and sunshine hadn't enticed his son away from him, and Gray cast him another look.

He had no idea how to date with a son. He hadn't even known how to date without a son, and his stomach flipped as he tried to remember how in the world to flirt, to ask a woman out to dinner, or how to kiss someone he liked.

He'd done all of those things previously, but they felt like they'd happened in a different life, to someone else. To someone Gray wasn't anymore.

Eventually, Hunter woke up, complaining of his need to use a bathroom. Gray pulled over at the next gas station, and though they had enough fuel to get to Coral Canyon, he filled the tank and sent Hunter inside for more Red Vines and a fresh soda for both of them.

Once they were all empty in the right places and stocked up in others, they hit the road again.

"Are we goin' fishin' today?" Hunter asked.

"Maybe," Gray said, though he was tired. "We're going to stop by Uncle Colton's and see where Uncle Wes is with his packing. And he might need our help."

"The sun stays out real late," Hunter said, his way of saying he didn't mind if they went fishing in the evening. Gray hoped his energy would last that long, because while he loved a road trip, they could also make a man exhausted—especially the flat, boring drive through Wyoming.

They finally took an exit toward Jackson Hole and Coral Canyon, and the Grand Tetons spread before them.

"Wow, Dad, would you look at that?" Hunter peered through the windshield at the enormous mountains, and Gray felt the voice of God speaking right to his soul. How he loved mountains, especially big ones.

"Pretty amazing, right?" Gray marveled at the mountains too, and he was glad his son had the same feelings he did. "Maybe we should move here."

Hunter looked at him, though Gray didn't meet his son's eyes. The weight of Hunter's gaze on the side of his face was enough, and Gray smiled as he turned toward him. "I mean, Uncle Colt and Uncle Wes live here now."

"But what about Grams, Grandma, and Grandpa?" Hunter asked, his dark brown eyes big and wide. He had such a kind soul, and Gray knew he couldn't really move his son here. Not really.

Fantasies were always different than realities.

"I'm just talking," Gray said. "I don't think we'll move here, buddy."

"Unless they come with us." Hunter picked up his soda and took a long drink. Gray could practically hear the wheels turning in his son's head, and he just waited. Hunter needed silence before he said important things. "Grandpa said he's tired of the farm. Maybe he'd sell it."

Gray held back the scoff. His father wouldn't sell that farm; it had been in the Hammond family as long as the company. Longer, even. "Oh, I don't think Uncle Ames would let him do that," Gray said.

"Maybe Uncle Ames would buy it then," Hunter said.

Gray glanced at his son. "Maybe *we* should buy it."

Hunter's eyes got even bigger, and Gray had his answer. He laughed, glad when Hunter started shaking his head no. "Dad, I like the farm, but it's a lot of work."

"I know, bud." He reached over and tousled his son's hair, but Hunter dodged out from underneath his hand after only a moment.

"Dad," he said, disgusted. "Stop it."

Gray mourned the days when Hunter was younger and loved getting his hair tousled. He liked watching him grow up too, so he couldn't complain too much.

"You're okay out there, though, right?" Gray asked. "You'd tell me if you really hated this summer, wouldn't you?"

"Yeah, of course," Hunter said. "I like it fine. It's just a lot of work, and Grandpa isn't very fast."

"No, he isn't," Gray said, thinking of his aging father. He saw a big sign announcing their arrival in Coral Canyon, and he tipped his cowboy hat toward it. "Here we are."

"Good," Hunter said. "I have to go to the bathroom again."

* * *

The next morning, Gray woke with the sun. He wondered if there would come a day when he didn't, when he could sleep past the morning's rays coming through the slats in the blinds. Maybe after he quit as lead counsel for HMC.

He groaned as he sat up in the guest bed Colton had provided. Wes had been off signing all his mortgage papers when Hunter and Gray had arrived last night, so they had gotten their first fishing expedition in. A beautiful, clear-as-glass, no-boats-allowed lake sat just up the road that led to Whiskey Mountain Lodge, where Gray had stayed before and where Wes worked.

This morning, though, Wes had two moving trucks meeting him at his new place, and he had the keys and garage door opener to get everyone inside the house. It sat only half a mile from Colton's place, and Gray felt another twitch of something, or someone, calling him to come to Coral Canyon too.

He left the bedroom and went down the hall and then the stairs, letting his nose guide him toward the freshly roasted scent of coffee. "Bless you, Colt," he murmured as he entered the kitchen, though he'd never known his younger brother to get up all that early.

Wes did, but the oldest Hammond brother had insisted on sleeping at his new place, though he had no bed. "An air mattress will do," he said, and Gray really didn't want to listen to the almost-fifty-year-old complain about his back that day. Which Wes would totally do. Gray saw a lot of lifting and carrying in his future that day, and he frowned at the line of mugs on the counter.

Colton had never done that before either. It felt like something a woman would do, and Gray would know, because he'd lived with a woman for five years. Not for a while, but what man lined up coffee mugs as if putting together a coffee bar?

Not Colton, that was for sure. And it was only Colt, Gray, and Hunter in the house that morning.

Gray picked up the dark blue mug on the end of the row, noting the line of spoons, the little packets of sugar, and the stirring sticks all neatly laid out. Something was definitely wrong here.

He took the last step to the coffeemaker and poured himself a mug of the dark, steaming liquid, trying to decide if he should go for the raw sugar or the sugar substitute. He wasn't a spring chicken anymore either, but coffee sure did taste better with real sugar....

He'd consumed so much sugar in the car yesterday, and he needed to get on a training diet and regimen for running a marathon. He'd made a goal to run the Boston Marathon, and it was never too soon to start preparing.

So the sugar substitute. He'd just reached for one of the brownish packets when someone said, "Oh, my."

Gray spun around and met the eyes of a beautiful woman with light green eyes, light hair spilling over her shoulders, and holding what looked to be very heavy grocery bags. Her eyes raked down his body, and in that moment, Gray realized how completely underdressed he was.

So underdressed he wasn't wearing a shirt.

The woman's face turned bright red, and she tried to lift her groceries onto the countertop and failed. She grunted as the bottles she carried headed for the ground. Thankfully, they were plastic, and hollow thuds filled the air.

Gray needed to get out of there, fast. Heat filled his own face, and he held his pathetically small cup of coffee in front of his body, as if it would conceal his naked torso and chest.

"Uh," the woman stammered, and Gray should've moved to help her. If he'd been dressed, he would have. Deciding that didn't matter—he had to show this woman he was chivalrous—he practically dove toward her.

He forgot all about the coffee mug in his hand until it shattered on the floor, only a couple of feet away from the woman's shoes.

Chapter Thirteen

Elise Murphy had never seen a man as beautiful as the one standing in Colton's kitchen, and not just because he wasn't wearing a shirt.

"I'm sorry," he said, the first words he'd spoken since their exchange had started a minute ago.

Her arms could barely carry the bottles of flavored coffee creamer as it was, but they'd gone to complete marshmallows at the sight of him.

Steam lifted from the spilled coffee on the floor, and he said, "Give me two seconds, and I'll be right back to clean all of this up." He ran away, his bare feet slapping the tile as he headed for the stairs.

Embarrassment burned in Elise's face, first at her reaction to him, and second at the way she'd dropped the creamer. "He dumped coffee everywhere," she said, reaching for a shard of blue ceramic. "And broke the cutest cup."

She picked up the coffee creamers one by one and put

them on the counter, not moving her feet so she wouldn't step on any other pieces of the broken mug.

"I'm so sorry," he said, rushing back into the kitchen.

He started opening cupboards until she said, "Towels are above the microwave."

He glanced at her, and he now wore a gray T-shirt with the word SUPERDAD across the chest, as well as a cowboy hat. Elise's heart went berserk, no matter how much she'd tried to tell it over the past couple of years that *they didn't like cowboys*.

But this one...oh, she liked this one.

He got out the towels and started mopping up the spilled coffee. "I didn't know someone else was here," he said, his deep voice tickling her eardrums and making her warm all over again. "I get up so early, and I guess I was surprised to see coffee already made."

She picked up the larger pieces of ceramic and tossed them in the nearby garbage can. Elise could barely hold her head up as she said, "Sorry to startle you. I was just bringing in breakfast for everyone. Colton wanted to surprise Wes."

She reached for the paper towels and ripped off a healthy number of them.

"Oh, so you know my brothers."

Elise froze with the paper towels under the running water in the sink. She looked at the sexy cowboy, imagining all that golden skin, those tight muscles in his back and chest. She ducked away again, her face on absolute fire. "Yes," she muttered. "I know them." She squeezed out the water and flattened the paper towels into a wet sheet.

"What are you doing?" he asked as she bent to wipe the floor.

"This gets all the tiny pieces of glass," she said, feeling them catch in the paper towel. "It's a trick I learned from my mother." Satisfied she'd gotten them all and that Colton or anyone else wouldn't step on something sharp, she straightened and turned the paper towels over. "See? You can see all the tiny little pieces of the mug."

He gazed at the paper towel. "Well, I'll be." He looked at her, and oh, Elise could really get lost in stormy, gray eyes like his.

"I'm Gray," he said, extending his hand for her to shake. Elise tossed the paper towels full of tiny spikes in the trash and shook his hand. Tingles ran up her arm and down her back at this man's touch, and that hadn't happened in a very long time. Too long.

"Elise Murphy," she managed to say, wondering what state her hair was in. "I'm a friend of Colton's."

"Elise," Colton boomed as he came into the kitchen, fully clothed, thank goodness. "What have you been up to?" He laughed as he took in the flavored creamers on the counter, the row of mugs, the full coffee pot. He didn't seem to notice Gray standing there at all, which was surreal, because Elise couldn't look away from him.

He smiled, pulled his hand back, and got out of the way as Colton grabbed onto Elise and hugged her. "You're the best best friend in the world."

"Yeah," Elise said, patting him on the back and smiling. "I know I am."

"Seen Wes yet?" he asked, reaching for a mug. "He said he'd be here bright and early."

"Not yet," Elise said. "I was just bringing in the pastries." She ducked around Colton, who'd never made her feel self-conscious though he was twice her size. Gray, on the other hand, made her want to slip into the bathroom and make sure she looked her best.

"I'll help you," he said, his voice much quieter than his brother's.

"Gray," Colton said, as if he'd honestly just realized the man stood there. "Sorry. You've met Elise?"

"Just now," Gray said, smiling diplomatically.

Colton watched him as he lifted his coffee to his lips to sip. Elise turned and walked away, because she'd never been able to hide anything from Colton, and she really didn't want him to know she'd seen his brother half-naked, or that she was really hoping this day wouldn't end without getting his phone number.

Don't be stupid, she told herself. Of the three Hammond brothers she'd met, Gray was by far the most cowboy of them. Not only that, he didn't live in Coral Canyon. He didn't even live in the state.

Elise hurried down the front steps and continued along the sidewalk, aware of Gray's footsteps right behind her. She practically yanked off the back door of her car in her haste to get to the doughnut boxes she'd stacked there.

"Wow," he said. "How many people are we expecting?"

"A lot," she said. "Colton asked all the Whittakers, and all the Everetts, and everyone at the lodge who could be spared."

Gray swallowed. "He really does endear people to him, doesn't he?"

Elise smiled, because Gray seemed to know his brother well. "That he does."

"You two are best friends?"

Elise wanted to deny it, but she didn't see how she could. Or why it would matter. "Yeah," she said. "Me and Bree and Colton. We pal around a little."

"Bree...isn't she Wes's girlfriend?" Gray wore a confused look on his face, and it only made him more attractive to Elise.

"Yes," she said. "She's my cabin mate. We live together up at Whiskey Mountain Lodge."

"You work up there?" He finally bent to duck into her car to take out the doughnuts. He started stacking them on the trunk.

"Yes," she said. "I'm the gardener for the lodge. I do a bit of landscaping for a few people in town too. Colton's one of them."

Gray chuckled, and if he knew what that sound did to a woman, he'd use it against them for sure. "I'll bet he is. He doesn't really like the outdoor work."

"He's told me about your parents' farm," she said, closing the door once he'd pulled out all the doughnut boxes. She picked up three and started back toward the house at a much slower clip.

"Has he?"

"Yes," she said.

"What else has he told you about the family?"

"The usual stuff," she said.

"Did he mention me?"

"Yeah, you're the lawyer," she said, giving him a smile before she went up the steps to the porch. "I just wasn't expecting the cowboy hat."

Gray looked up at her, surprise clearly etched in his expression. "I like the cowboy hat."

Elise had no idea who she was, or where the last words she'd spoken had come from. Nor did she know where, "Me too, Gray," came from. Or the flirty smile she felt parading across her lips. She gave him one last look and headed inside, her skin clammy from the effort it took to flirt with him.

"Thanks, Elise," Colton said, taking the boxes from her. "I could've picked these up, you know."

"Oh, it was on my way." She reached up and wiped the sweat from her brow. She seriously felt like she had a fever, and she had no idea why.

Yes, you do, she told herself. *A cowboy, Elise. He's a cowboy.*

"I saw you looking at Gray," Colton said under his breath.

"Colton," she warned.

"What?" he asked. "I told you he'd be perfect for you."

"You have literally never said that." She rolled her eyes and opened one of the boxes. She really needed some sugar right now—and everyone else who said they'd be coming to show up. Then she wouldn't have to be in this house alone with Colton and Gray.

He finally came inside too, carrying the rest of the boxes. "Got 'em," he said, putting them on the counter beside the others. He had a special ability that allowed him to skip eye contact, though Colton was staring a hole in his brother's face.

"I'm gonna go shower," he said, beelining for the steps.

"All right," Colton said, a little too loudly in Elise's opinion.

Relief rushed through her once Gray had disappeared, and a sigh leaked from her mouth.

"Ah-ha!" Colton said. "What happened before I came into the kitchen?"

"Uh, well." Elise wiped her forehead again, still sweating. What in the world was wrong with her? Maybe she was coming down with the flu. A Gray flu. "He was pouring coffee. He may or may not have been wearing a shirt. Then I dropped the coffee creamer, and he threw his mug at me. Kind of?" She turned away from Colton and paced out of the kitchen. "Then we cleaned up, and he told me he was your brother, and does he work out?" She faced Colton, her heart beating oh so fast.

Colton blinked a couple of times, and then he burst out laughing. Elise realized she'd been babbling, and sure enough, as she usually did, she'd said something to further embarrass herself. Not only that, but she'd said something without censoring herself. That seemed to be one of her biggest problems—not thinking before she just asked if Colton's brother worked out. She couldn't keep her thoughts inside her own head to save her life, that was for sure.

"He's a marathon runner," Colton said, still chuckling. "And wow, you saw him without a shirt on? I didn't realize Gray could be casual." He shuddered like he'd just seen a giant spider. "He's usually so polished and buttoned up. Everything in the right place. He irons T-shirts, for crying out loud." He laughed again, and Elise just looked toward the stairs. What version of Gray Hammond would she get after he'd showered?

She hoped he wouldn't shave, because she liked a little facial hair on a man, and Gray's had been, well, gray. Sexy. *Mature.*

Yes, mature was the right word. The *safe* word Elise was going for.

Colton slung his arm around her, and Elise wondered how long she'd been staring at his stairs. "You know, I could put a bug in his ear about you."

"You do, and you'll be dead to me." Elise glared up at him with everything she had in her five-foot-one-inch frame. "And you won't get your chocolate birthday cake."

"Okay," he said. "Forget I said anything." He grinned down at her. "I've never seen you get worked up over a man."

"You've known me for seven months," she said, pushing him away from her playfully. "I don't think I've met a new man in that time."

Colton looked back to the stairs too. "Yes, well, Gray's... unique, that's for sure."

"We're here," Bree announced, and Elise sighed with relief. Wes's booming voice filled the house too, and it wasn't long before Annie arrived, and then Andrew and Beau Whittaker. With more people in the house, Elise could get lost in the shuffle, something she was very, very good at.

And yet, when Gray came back downstairs with a boy that couldn't be older than twelve or thirteen, he made one sweep of the kitchen and living room, looked past the dozen people who'd shown up for doughnuts and coffee before Wes's big move, and locked eyes with her.

Maybe he'd *want* to give her his number before the end of the day, because Elise had no idea why she'd need it, which meant she wouldn't ask.

Just see how today goes, she told herself. *And if you have to, you can ask Colton for his brother's number.*

Chapter Fourteen

Bree stood in the doorway of Wes's new house, trying not to feel completely inadequate. But of course she did. He'd bought one of the new houses in a brand spanking new subdivision on the northeast side of town.

Rich people lived here.

Which fit, because Wes was indeed, rich.

"Come in," he said. "You don't have to stand in the doorway like a lurker." He grinned at her, and Bree took some of his confidence and pretended it was hers. She smiled back, and let him take her hand in his.

"You've done a lot already," she said, noting the vase of fresh flowers on a tall table in the foyer. Fresh flowers? What universe had she landed in?

"I've done nothing," he said. "For the record. This is all Cindi."

"Oh, the interior decorator."

"Right." He held up his phone. "I do get texts when it's

time to order another vase of flowers or when to change the air filter in my air conditioner." He beamed like getting texts was the most amazing thing ever.

Bree nodded and continued to look around. Yes, she'd been here already. She'd seen the house before Wes had moved in, actually. She'd helped him move. She'd listened to him talk about the amazing backyard where he wanted to house a couple of dogs. Big ones.

"Maybe a horse," he'd said, but Bree didn't think the CCR's of this subdivision would allow horses. He'd just laughed and said he was joking.

"So," he said, slowing as they reached the kitchen. Everything was so clean, and so bright, and so...wonderful. "Just me and you today. Finally." He wrapped both arms around her, and Bree swayed with him, all of her fears and worries evaporating with his touch.

It had been a few weeks since their near-kiss in the stables, and something always seemed to get in their way. First, he'd been paged, then Colton had been on the front steps of his house. When Wes brought Bree lunch, her boss had actually run out into the parking lot after her to ask what Willie's favorite soda was.

She didn't want to kiss Wes in a hot parking lot anyway.

They hadn't gone hiking again as Wes looked for a house, bought one, and then arranged—remotely—to pack and move everything he owned in Denver. He'd taken a quick trip to the city, and his brother, Gray, had dominated this week with talk of selling the penthouse Wes owned to one of their cousins.

To the company, actually. The family company that Wes had headed for fourteen years. HMC.

In one of her worst self-doubt cases yet, Bree had looked up HMC online. What a mistake that had been. They were a huge, global company with profit shares in the billions. They were a Fortune 500 company, and were in fact, in position ten as of last year.

Ten.

Huge conglomerates like Walmart and Apple and Amazon were higher than them, but that was about it. And he'd run the whole thing.

Bree had no idea what he was doing with her.

"Are you ready to go?" he asked. "I've been hearing about this elk poutine for far too long, and I'm dying to try it."

Oh, right—she was going to Jackson Hole with him today. They were riding the gondola to the top of the world and eating dinner at the steakhouse with the delicious elk poutine. "Yes," she said. "I'm ready."

But she wasn't sure if she really was or not. She wanted to be. Hoped she could hold the interest of a man like Wes. He seemed happy with her, and they never really ran out of things to talk about.

His phone chimed, and he glanced at it. "It's Colt. He wants to know if you'll walk with me down the aisle next weekend."

Bree's heart seized. "What?"

Wes grinned as he turned his phone toward her. "He and Annie are finalizing everything. Gray's over there right now, before he heads home." He looked at his phone again. "I don't know why he just doesn't stay, but he says he has to work."

"He's bringing your parents too," Bree reminded him. Meeting Wes's parents had her stomach in knots, but he claimed his mother would be thrilled. Simply *thrilled*. He even said she'd probably start crying.

Bree thought her tears would probably be about what a poor choice Wes had made in a girlfriend. After all, Bree had nothing to offer him.

Yes, you do, she told herself, trying to press against the ugly thoughts. She was smart. She did work hard. And why was her love worth any less than someone else's?

Wes finished texting Colton and turned around in a full circle. "My jacket...we do still need jackets, right?"

"It's very windy on top of the mountain," Bree said. "But it's up to you."

"I got it out...ah-ha." He spied it on the back of the couch and walked toward it. "I told Colton you'd *love* to walk down the aisle with me. I mean, you're one of Annie's bridesmaids. I'm Colton's best man. It makes sense." He met her eyes, and Bree put a smile on her face.

"Yes," she said. "I'd *love* to." And she wasn't lying, so the giggle that followed was real. Easy. She just needed to get outside of her own head and enjoy her time with Wes.

They loaded into his truck, and Wes told her more about his father and grandmother on the hour-long drive to Jackson Hole. "I've never been here," he said, peering out the windows and windshield. "There's people everywhere."

"It's a big tourist town," she said. "This is downtown. It'll clear up as we go up to the resort where the gondola is."

"Did you grow up in Coral Canyon?" Wes asked, and Bree stiffened. He'd never asked about her family again, and she suspected Colton had said something to him about her resistance to divulge much about them.

But Colton wouldn't confess to that, and Wes seemed completely at ease in the truck.

"No," she said. "I'm from a tiny little town in Vermont."

"Oh, wow," he said. "Is that like here?"

"It gets cold there," she said, her mind wandering along forbidden paths. "I don't mind the cold."

"Neither do I," Wes said. "When I stopped working at HMC, I thought really hard about where I wanted to go. The beach doesn't call to me."

She watched him as he looked at his phone and turned where the map program told him to. They left the hustle and bustle of downtown Jackson Hole behind, and Wes went further into the mountains.

He didn't ask her anything else about her family, and Bree found herself wanting to tell him. She trusted him.

Immediately, she pulled back on the word vomit about to come out of her mouth. She didn't trust herself, so how could she know if she could really trust him? Maybe she'd fallen for his good looks, his charm, his money, his family, just everything that made him so wonderful.

She bit her bottom lip and looked out her own window, a sense of awkwardness falling over her. "Look," she said suddenly. "There's a moose out there."

Wes looked, his face brightening as if he'd just learned he'd get an extra birthday this year. "Look at that."

Bree grinned at him as he came up to where everyone had parked and was getting out of their cars to look at the moose. Normally, she'd have wanted to as well, but they had an appointment for their gondola ride, and they couldn't miss it.

"Do we have time?" Wes asked, pressing on the brake.

"I don't think so," she said, watching the magnificent moose as it lumbered slowly along out in the field. "Maybe it'll still be there when we get done." But she knew it wouldn't be. But being as close to Yellowstone National Park as they were, they could make another day trip to see wildlife.

"I don't want to miss the gondola," he said.

"I know." She reached for his hand and squeezed it when he gave it to her to hold. "You've been talking about it for *weeks*."

"Oh, come on," he said with a laugh. "We just planned this a few days ago."

"Two weeks ago, Wes," she said, laughing too.

"Is that right?" He grinned and shook his head. "I suppose so. The days just sort of fly by, don't they?" He looked to her for confirmation, and Bree could only agree with him.

"It's right here," she said a minute later, and he turned into the parking lot for the Snake River Resort. "See it?"

"Ho-ly cow," he said, stopping right there in the middle of the aisle and looking up, up, up through his windshield. "I can't even see the top of that mountain."

"You're gonna stand on it, cowboy," she said. "Now work your magic and find us somewhere close to park."

He grinned and did just that, though there wasn't anywhere close to park. He did eventually find a spot, and they took their jackets and one backpack with them toward the ticket counter.

"I used to work near here," she said while they waited to board one of the huge gondolas. They held dozens of people, and it looked like it would be a full house today.

"Yeah? Tell me about that."

"I bought a flower shop," she said. "If you can believe that."

"Oh, I believe it." He tucked her close to his side as someone squeezed by them. "You didn't like it?"

"Uh, it was okay," she said. "I'd taken some floral arranging classes at a vocational college and liked those. Running a business was a different matter."

"Yeah, I get that," he said, his voice turning down a notch.

She looked up at him and found him with a thoughtful, contemplative expression on his face. "Anyway, I sold that and started doing some outdoor tours. I worked at Jenny Lake, and then as part of the staff at the Bar J Wranglers."

"You're kidding." He smiled so wide. "My grandfather loved them."

"I worked on the ranch too. They have a real working cattle ranch too. Did you know that?"

"No, ma'am, I did not."

"We passed it on the way here."

"Really?"

Bree laughed and nodded. "I'll show you on the way back." People started loading the gondola, and Bree's excitement grew. She'd ridden the aerial tram at least a dozen times, but it was exciting every single time.

"We'll be up there in twelve minutes, folks," the man near the door said. "Watch your step. Find a spot. You can move around on the tram, but there's a lot of us."

"I'm so excited," Wes said, and Bree sure did like this version of him. The man who radiated giddiness at doing something new. He looked and felt so young to her then, that their age difference didn't matter.

Not that it had mattered before, but Bree did enjoy this fun-loving, free-spirited side of Wes.

They managed to get a spot along one of the windows, and he simply stared out at the land below. "This is incredible," he said.

Bree wanted to tell him to wait until they got to the top of Rendezvous Mountain, but she didn't. He'd see when he got there.

When they stepped off the tram, the wind whipped, just as she'd thought it would. She already had her jacket on, but many others hurried to put theirs on, and one teenage girl complained to her dad that she didn't know it would be cold. But the rest of the family had jackets on, so Bree was betting she'd been told and had just ignored her parents.

That was what Bree would've done.

Thick, loud memories rushed at her, and she remembered the day Bronson had died in a single instant. Her mother had told her not to go to Duck Lake. She'd gone anyway.

Sharp regret lanced through her, and she worked to keep from breaking down right then and there.

"Hey," Wes said, guiding her out of the flow of traffic. "Are you okay?"

"Yeah." She swallowed, trying to find her bearings. There was no lake here. No ice. No snow-covered pine trees, and no hole where her brother had disappeared. "Yeah, I'm okay."

Wes continued to peer at her. "Bree," he said. "Tell me what just happened."

"What happened?" she asked.

"You sort of froze up, and then you turned around like you'd get back on the gondola, but the guy wouldn't let you. I called your name, and you didn't even hear me." He wore nothing but concern in his face, and compassion in his eyes, and Bree couldn't help the tears that pooled in her eyes.

She looked away from him, because she'd never had someone be so kind to her. Fine, maybe Colton, but Wes was different. Wes made her heart thump strangely, and Wes made her think about getting married and having his kids and growing old with him.

"I...." She didn't know how to tell him.

"You have to get off the cement pad," a man called, and Wes took her by the elbow and led her away from the restricted area. They followed the path around and up to the highest point, where the others on the tram had already gone. It was quite steep, and Bree's breath came in huffs and puffs by the time she stood next to Wes at the top of the world.

"Wow," Wes said, and that summed it up. Everyone stood still and quiet as they gazed out over the Jackson Hole Valley, along with the unfettered view of the Grand Tetons.

"I can't even," Wes said. "I've never seen anything like

this." He swept his arm around Bree's waist and pulled her into his side. "Thank you for bringing me here. Thank you so much."

Bree wrapped her arms around him too and leaned into the strength of his body. She was going to have to tell him about her brother, her parents, and all the horrible things she'd done in the past twenty-one years.

She felt herself tethering to him, and he to her, and the secrets could consume them both. She didn't want to hurt Wes. She didn't.

Bree tipped her head back to look up at him, finding wonder and awe in his expression. That quickly changed to what Bree could only classify as love and adoration, and before she knew it, Wes leaned down and kissed her.

Chapter Fifteen

Wes had known kissing Bree would be the most amazing thing he'd ever done in his life. Better than taking his two billion and turning it into four by the time he was twenty-five. Better than securing the three hundred-million-dollar deal that had finally made his father see him as a real CEO. Better than the views of the valley and mountains he'd just seen.

Better than *anything*.

He kissed her as sparks flowed between them, as she kissed him back with as much passion in her touch as he felt pounding through his veins. He didn't care that someone was probably watching. If he'd known—truly known—what kissing Bree would feel like, he'd have done it in the stables weeks ago, the public page notwithstanding.

He'd have kissed her in front of his brother. In front of *any*one, *any*where.

Wes finally regained some control of himself and pulled

away, the chill from the wind returning. During the kiss, he'd been immune to everything around him.

A chuckle started in his chest, and he let it tickle his vocal cords. "That was a double wow," he murmured, drawing her into his chest and holding her as close as he could. "I just...." He wanted to say what was in his heart, but he was afraid. Afraid she wouldn't feel the same way he did. Afraid he'd fallen too fast. Afraid she'd get scared and put distance between them.

She held him too, and they eventually shifted to look out over the valley again. "We can't stay up here forever," she finally said. "If we don't get on the next gondola, we won't make our reservation at Charlie's."

"Always the taskmaster," he said with a smile. He looked around. "What else is up here?"

"Just that shack with the waffles," she said. "There's a few souvenirs in there too."

He'd just kissed Bree, and that was all the souvenir he needed. He certainly wouldn't be forgetting that any time soon. He wouldn't forget it ever.

They wandered back down the path and joined the line of people to get on the next tram. The ride down to the base of the mountain had them all piling on the right side of the tram as the guide said he saw a black bear over there.

Wes saw it, but Bree didn't even come over. When he looked at her, she wore a look of fear on her face, and he quickly stepped back over to her. "Scared of tipping?"

"We're leaning so far," she said. "Can't they feel it?"

Wes put his arm around her shoulders and chuckled. "I don't think we can tip this," he said.

"You'd be surprised," she said. "There's a first time for everything."

He pressed his lips to her temple, and thoroughly enjoyed it. The whole day held magic and possibilities, and Wes hadn't felt like that in such a long time.

They walked over to the steakhouse and were promptly ushered to a table for two in a dim corner. "How romantic," Bree said, glancing around at the candles on the table and the low lighting above it.

"You've been here before," Wes said, taking his napkin and spreading it across his lap. "Did you bring your other boyfriends?"

"A couple," she said airily. "The ones who could pay for their own meals." She grinned at him and burst out laughing, and Wes just smiled and shook his head. She did seem to be over Alex, who'd caused her to get a second job and have balances on her credit cards.

He marveled at that, because Wes didn't think he had a very forgiving heart. If someone wronged him, he held onto it for a long time. Bree sobered quickly, and their eyes met. He had a dozen things he wanted to ask her, but he kept his mouth shut.

"Tell me something," he said instead. "In that gorgeous voice of yours."

Bree rolled her eyes, but a glow came from within her now, and Wes sure did like basking in it. "I don't have anything to tell."

"You'll think of something." He glanced up as the waiter arrived at the table.

"Drinks?"

"Diet Coke," he said.

"Same," Bree said. "And we want the elk poutine to start. As soon as possible."

"No problem." The waiter left, and Wes focused on the menu.

"What else do you eat here?"

"Oh, I've only ever gotten the poutine," she said.

He looked up at her. "Really? Just an appetizer?"

"Maybe my dates weren't as rich as I thought." She giggled then, and Wes could only grin at her.

"Well, your date tonight is," he said lightly, looking for something like surf and turf—one of his favorite meals. "So order whatever you want."

"I'm going to do just that," Bree said, a teasing quality in her voice. "You might regret it."

Wes looked at her, deciding to let one serious thing come out of his mouth today. "I don't regret anything between us, Bree."

She sobered too, her eyes rounding, and a bit of fear entering her expression. In the next moment, she ducked her head and studied the menu. "Oh, look," she said a moment later. "They have baby back ribs. I'm going to get those."

* * *

A week later, Wes stood in front of the mirror, adjusting the bow tie around his neck. He'd done this once before for Colton, and his brother hadn't made it to the I-do. But today, he was going to.

Number one, Wes had already seen Annie, and she was already dressed in her wedding gown. He supposed she could make a break for it at any moment, the way Priscilla had, but he'd seen her look at his brother. She loved him. He loved her.

Wes sighed without meaning to, the last seven days with Bree marching through his mind. He'd kissed her every single one of those days, and he'd fallen more and more in love with her each time they spoke or saw one another.

Gray had arrived late last night, and his parents and grandmother had gone straight to bed. Bree had already left Wes's house, and he hadn't had a chance to introduce them to her yet. He'd told his mother he had someone special for her to meet, and surprisingly, she'd never brought it up again.

He suspected Gray or Colton had told her all about Bree already, and that made a frown tug at his lips.

"We're ready," Cy said, and Wes turned from the mirror. He and his brothers had been given a bedroom in Annie's house to get changed and ready, and the wedding would take place in her backyard. Most of her belongings had already been moved into Colton's house, but the two of them were leaving tomorrow morning for an Alaskan adventure. That was what Colton had called it, at least.

As Wes had never been to Alaska, he was a bit jealous, and he wondered if he could steal Bree away from her life here, and they could go to the remaining ten states he hadn't seen yet.

He knew she wouldn't go, just like she wouldn't allow him to pay off her credit card debt. He still thought about that, though the pastor had pointed him toward the health clinic in town, which was always looking for volunteers. He wondered if the continued thoughts of Bree meant the Lord was trying to tell him to bring up paying her debts again.

There were so many things he wanted to ask, but didn't dare to vocalize. Frustration built inside him as he followed Ames and Cy out into the hall. He couldn't wait to see Colton's face when he saw the twins. He'd probably glare and then roll his eyes.

Cy had offered to get his wardrobe approved, and Colton had said, "It's my wedding. I trust you'll use your best judgement."

If leather pants were Cy's best judgement, Wes didn't want to know what his bad judgement looked like. In reality, Wes knew Cy was a good man. He did amazing things for veterans, and he donated a ton of money to charities around the world. He just didn't want anyone to know that.

He loved playing the bad boy, but someone probably should've warned him that his black leather pants sort of squeaked when he walked. Nothing "bad" about that.

Ames waited in the kitchen, and he wore a leather jacket and a top hat. Wes grinned at him and reached up as if he'd knock the hat off his brother's head.

"Don't," Ames growled, jerking backward.

"Oh, come on, *Abe*," Wes said, looking at the top hat. "Why are you wearing that?"

"Colton made a point on the family text that hats were required," Ames said.

"Yeah," Gray said dryly, never amused by the antics of the twins. "Cowboy hats, you moron."

"Colton didn't specify," Ames said, grinning.

"And we offered to run our outfits by him," Cy said.

"Just the fact that you used the word *outfits* is disturbing," Wes said, but he was smiling too. Colton knew who the twins were, and he wouldn't be surprised at their "outfit" choices at all.

The scent of roses entered the room, and all four Hammond brothers turned to find the women coming into the kitchen. He stilled completely at the sight of Bree, all done up with her dark hair in curls pinned to her head. She wore the same pale blue dress as everyone else, but she wore it better than anyone.

His mouth turned dry, and Wes decidedly fell a bit more toward loving her.

"You're stunning," he said right out loud, and Cy snickered.

"You're not alone," Ames said, nudging Wes. That seemed to break his trance, and heat rushed into his face.

He ducked his head too, so glad he'd chosen the appropriate headgear for the wedding—a cowboy hat with a wide brim to hide his embarrassment.

"Well, don't y'all clean up nice," Sophia said, a real cowgirl twang in her voice. Wes just blinked at her, but Bree and Elise burst out laughing. Amidst their giggles, Sophia added, "Which one of you is Ames?"

"That would be Abe Lincoln over there," Wes said, grinning at his brother.

Sophia looked him up and down, down and up, clear displeasure in her expression. "Hmm. You sure you want to wear that hat?"

Ames swiped it right off his head, but his hair wasn't much better. "No, ma'am."

Gray leaned in close to Wes. "No, ma'am."

They chuckled together, and there was enough commotion that Ames didn't notice. In fact, he couldn't seem to look away from Sophia at all.

"That would make you Cy," Patsy said, stepping over to the man in the leather pants. She said nothing of his attire, and instead introduced herself in her normal, brusque way. Cy grinned at her like he was impressed, though Wes knew he disliked authority on principle alone.

"I'm with you, Gray," Elise said, her voice barely loud enough to reach Wes's ears. They switched places, as Wes was leading the wedding party down the aisle to the altar, but he sure did notice the way Gray's whole face had turned a shade of red he'd never seen before.

Gray leaned closer to Elise and said something in such a low voice that Wes couldn't hear it. When he turned and looked at them, they already had their arms linked, and Elise was looking up at Gray like she'd just seen an angel from heaven.

"Holy cow," Wes whispered.

"What?" Bree leaned toward him, but her eyes were

trained out the door and into the backyard. "Do you see Colton?"

Wes pulled himself together, though he'd never thought Gray would open his heart to another woman. Hadn't he been telling their mother to back off for years? Yes, yes, he had.

And tiny, barely five-feet-tall Elise had charmed him already. As far as Wes knew, they'd only met the one time, when everyone from the lodge, as well as all the Whittakers and Whittakers-by-association, had helped him move into his new house a couple of weeks ago.

"Oh, there he is," Bree said, and Wes focused on the wedding. His brother stepped up to the altar with Mom and Dad, giving them both a quick kiss on the cheek before they sat in the front row.

Then he immediately looked to the back door, which Wes and Bree filled. He wore nothing but panic in his face, and Wes wanted to reassure him that everything would be fine. Annie was still here.

In fact, she entered the kitchen a moment later, saying, "My father hurt his foot. We need a few minutes. Is everyone okay to wait?"

Colton wasn't, but Wes didn't say anything. He just nodded with everyone else, and the bride hurried out of the kitchen, muttering something under her breath.

"He's going to pass out," Bree said, tightening her grip on Wes's arm. He looked down at her, unsurprised by the worry she had for Colton. They were good friends, and he'd learned that the three of them had been dubbed the Three Musketeers by the Whittakers and others at the lodge.

"Look at him," she said, and Wes found Colton leaning on the altar while a vast majority of the audience had twisted to look at them. "He's panicking. He's going to run." Bree turned and reached for Elise. "Elise, get up here. Sorry, Wes, can you move?"

Elise squeezed between them, and Wes had no choice in the matter. He fell back a step, running into Gray, who moved too. Cy made a big deal about Gray touching him, and then Ames got all bent out of shape too, saying, "What is going on up there?" in a voice that was much too loud.

Annoyance ran through Wes at his youngest brothers, and he wanted to tell them not everything was about them. But he didn't want to add to the tension and nerves of this wedding, so he said nothing.

Not only that, but Bree and Elise had started some sort of elaborate signing with their hands and arms—even their faces. He stared at them, trying to figure out what in the world they could be telling Colton.

He motioned back to them, and Elise giggled and shook her head.

"What are you saying?" Gray asked, and Wes was glad he'd asked.

"Oh, nothing," Elise said through her laughter. "We're just distracting him."

It seemed to be working, as Colton had straightened, and he even tugged on the bottom of his tuxedo jacket to get it lying flat again.

"He's going to stay," Bree said in a satisfied voice. "Good work, Elise."

"Well done to you too," she said, stepping back to Gray's side with a wide smile. Gray couldn't seem to look away from her, and Wes knew exactly how he felt. Bree met his eye, and she wore such a light in hers that Wes wanted to commit what true joy looked like to his memory.

He reached for her instead and leaned real close to her ear. He even let his lips brush against her earlobe as he said, "I think you're incredible."

She stiffened next to him, as she'd told him she wasn't used to getting compliments like that. But she *was* incredible, and Wes wanted her to know it. He'd tell her every day if he could.

"Okay," Annie said behind them, her voice on the outer edges of panic. "We're here. We're ready."

Wes turned to see her brushing her hands down the front of her dress and then smiling at her aged father. He'd probably been taller than her at some point, but he wasn't now. He wore a nice suit though, and a wide smile, and Wes could feel the familial love they shared.

"We're ready, Hunter," Gray said into his phone, and then he pocketed it again. Eleven-year-old Hunter was in charge of the music, because Colton had wanted everyone in the family to play a part in the wedding, but Hunter didn't want to walk down the aisle carrying petals or the ring.

"That's lame, Uncle Colton," he'd said. In the end, Annie had suggested Hunter could press the play button as easily as her sister, and Hunter had taken over the job of the music.

Colton had coached him on what to say too, and Hunter had practiced a dozen times. So Wes expected the wedding march to start blaring from the speaker system he'd helped rig up the previous night.

He waited...and waited...and waited. He knew not to take a step until that music played, and he glanced over his shoulder to Gray. "What's—?"

Deafening applause filled the backyard, and Wes emitted a startled yelp, glad he wasn't the only one.

"Wrong one, bud," Gray muttered while a few people twittered in the yard.

"Sorry, Uncle Colton," Hunter said over the speaker system. "Here's the right one."

"Say the thing," Colton called, and more people laughed, including Wes. He loved Hunter, and the boy would beat himself up for not getting it right when he'd worked so hard on it just last night.

"Oh, right. Welcome to the wedding of Colton Hammond and Annie Pruitt. The bride and groom are *so* pleased to have you here this afternoon, and we pray for blessings upon us all."

Behind him, Gray chuckled and said, "Well, he did it."

"He did great," Elise said. "He's the best boy, Gray."

"He is great," Wes agreed, glancing over his shoulder to the two of them. They hadn't heard him speak at all, as they looked longingly into each other's eyes. Wes cleared his throat, and Gray jerked his head forward, breaking the connection between him and Elise.

"We have pictures after this," Wes said, nonverbally reminding Gray he didn't want to have a beet-red face in all of them. But he was clearly smitten by Elise, and Wes needed to talk to Bree about it as soon as possible.

The wedding march started, and Wes took his first step down the aisle, Bree right in sync with him. He smiled at the guests, most of whom he didn't know. It didn't matter. In Coral Canyon, he felt like he belonged to the community, and they belonged to him.

He did recognize Annie's daughters, and all the Whittakers, and a couple of suppliers that brought goods up to the lodge.

At the front, near the altar, he kissed Bree's hand and went to the right while she went to the left. He took his brother in a tight hug, clapped him on the back, and took his spot on the far side. Gray did the same, joining him. Then Cy, then Ames. With the four of them standing there, and four of Annie's close friends on her side, everyone looked to the back door.

And waited.

Chapter Sixteen

Colton seriously thought Annie was never going to come out. What was taking so long? Why hadn't she been ready ten minutes ago, when the wedding was supposed to start? He didn't know, and he felt like he was going to throw up.

Then, suddenly, Annie appeared, pulling her puffy dress through the doorway with a big smile. She waited for her father to come through, and she laced her arm through his.

Emily and Eden got up and walked down the aisle to their mother, and they linked arms too. Then the four of them came toward him, and Colton's pulse increased and increased with every step they took.

He was getting all of them, and he couldn't be happier.

"Love you, Mom," Eden said, and she went back to her seat while Emily hugged Annie too. When it was just her dad left, he kissed her cheek and passed her hand to the crook of Colton's elbow.

He grinned at her father, and then pressed a kiss to Annie's cheek. "Hey, pretty lady."

Annie could only smile, and a rush of joy moved through Colton. They faced Pastor Clemens, who indicated they should move closer to the altar. Colton couldn't believe he was here again, and in such a short time too.

But Annie knew what—and who—she wanted, and Colton did too. He'd seen no reason to wait, and they'd ended up getting married before Emily.

Colton paid attention to every word the pastor said, wanting to hold onto these moments for the rest of his life. Pastor Clemens said, "It is a miracle when two people find each other the way you two have."

He really believed the pastor too. He'd shown up at the lodge during Annie's birthday party, and he'd been stuck at the lodge during the worst snowstorm Wyoming had seen in a decade. If that wasn't God's hand bringing him and Annie together, Colton didn't know what would be.

He glanced at Annie, and she had a single tear sliding down her cheek. She wiped it quickly and met his eye. His love for her grew tenfold in that moment, and together, they looked back at the pastor.

"It's a beautiful thing to pledge oneself to another person. Try to remember who you are, as well as think about what your partner needs to be happy. Work to improve yourself, and strive to support each other too."

Colton wanted to do all of that, and he was eternally grateful he didn't have to do it alone anymore. He couldn't believe he'd made it forty-three years by himself, and he was glad he didn't have to go one more day alone.

"I know neither of you want me to go on and on, so I'll get to the good stuff," Pastor Clemens said with a smile. "Love each other. Cherish one another. Keep the Lord with you, and I promise you'll always be led toward happiness."

With that, he allowed Colton to step away from Annie and pull the paper with his vows out of his pocket. "Annie," he said. "You captured my heart in only a few days, when it was wounded and barely beating. You healed it, and then you waited for me to figure out that it was ready to love again. I love you, and I'm thrilled we'll get to spend the rest of our lives together."

He hadn't looked at the paper once, and he laid it on the altar. "Guess I didn't need that." He chuckled, glad when his brothers behind him did too.

Then Hunter played the laugh track, and the fake laughter filled the backyard. Colton turned and looked at the house, laughing when he saw Hunter's wide grin. The sound cut off, and Annie shook her head. "You two."

"That was a good one," Colton said. "And it's your turn, sweetheart."

"I don't have anything that good," she said. "And I didn't write anything down."

"I'm sure it'll be fine." Colton beamed at her, suddenly anxious about what she might say.

"I've never told anyone this," she said. "But that night we first met, at my birthday party, when Celia told me to make a wish, I wished for a cowboy billionaire of my own to fall in love with. Not five minutes later, you walked in, wearing this huge, puffy...monstrosity of a coat." She giggled, and Colton had heard about his coat plenty of times.

He rolled his eyes while she laughed, and he laughed along with her.

"We didn't play games with each other, and I count myself one of the luckiest women in the world to be yours."

"So you kinda like me," he said. "I didn't hear that in there."

"Yeah, cowboy," she said. "I'm kind of in love with you."

He cued Hunter, who was now in rare form as he played a sound clip of several people going, "Awww."

Annie shook her head, and she looked back at Colton. "That's it. Those are my vows."

"Great, let's get this done," Colton said, looking at the pastor.

He asked Annie if she'd be Colton's, and she said yes. He asked Colton if he'd be Annie's, and he said yes.

"I now pronounce you husband and wife," Pastor Clemens said, and Colton grinned at his new wife.

"Colton," she warned, but he whooped and threw his cowboy hat into the air as Hunter played the applause track again, and everyone in the audience joined in with real clapping.

Colton took Annie into his arms, and without his cowboy hat, he could easily kiss her. So he did, buoyed by the loud cheering and whooping from his brothers.

He righted Annie as they laughed together, and they faced

the crowd of friends and family and lifted their joined hands into the air.

The applause track ended, but the real clapping and cheering continued, and Annie led Colton down the aisle and toward the house. He paused before going into the kitchen with her to knock knuckles with Hunter, the two of them laughing together for a couple of seconds.

Then he stepped into the kitchen and into the arms of his new wife.

Chapter Seventeen

Bree squinted at the computer screen, not about to make an appointment with the optometrist, though she was having a harder time seeing tiny things. Especially on a computer screen.

But getting glasses made her feel old, and Bree wasn't ready to go there yet. With the squinting, she could see the numbers, and she clicked to the next tab and typed them in.

A sense of pride and relief filled her as she sat back, still looking at the numbers she'd filled in. "That'll pay that credit card off," she said to her empty bedroom. After this, she only had two more to go, and they were both below fifty percent. Her credit should start to get better, and for the first time in months, Bree could see the light at the end of this tunnel.

"Thank you, Lord," she said as she clicked the PAY button at the bottom of the screen. She'd moved into the technology era along with most everyone, and she loved paying her bills online. Twenty minutes every two weeks, and she was done.

She immediately thought of Wes, because she wanted to share this victory with him. At the same time, she didn't want to bring up her money issues with him, because he'd simply offer to pay her credit cards off completely.

And she could admit that would be a huge blessing and relief in her life. She'd thought about it long and hard after he'd offered, though she'd shot him down quickly. But her pride wouldn't allow her to take charity from him. She could pay back what she owed. In four more months, she'd be debt-free again, and a year of sacrifice was a small price to pay for a few mistakes and bad choices.

Bree was willing to pay that price.

A sense of peace came over her, and she felt enveloped in the love of God. She wasn't sure why. She'd been going to church the same way she always did. She was mindful of the things she did and said, as more often than not, one of the Whittakers would pray for them all to remember who they represented. Bree wanted to be a light in the world, a calm place people could come if they needed help.

The problem was, she still had some darkness inside her, and she didn't know how to root it out and get rid of it completely.

She stood up and tried to push the thoughts away. She knew where the darkness came from, and she wasn't willing to open that part of her heart and mind. She'd have to acknowledge decades-old mistakes that she'd perpetuated over the past twenty years, and she knew it would be painful.

Very painful.

She left her bedroom and went into the kitchen, where

Elise sat at the table, a smile on her face and her bowl of breakfast cereal forgotten in front of her.

"Texting Gray again?" Bree asked, delighted that Elise seemed to have found a cowboy she liked.

Elise startled, as if she'd forgotten she didn't live alone, and looked up. A hint of redness crept into her normally pale skin, and she looked at Bree. She reached for her spoon, realized how soggy her cereal was, and got up to dump it in the sink. "Maybe."

"Maybe." Bree scoffed. "Come on, Elise. I know you're texting him."

"How do you know it's him?" she asked. "It could be my mom."

"I've never seen you smile at your phone like that when you're talking to your mom." Bree reached up to get a mug out of the cupboard. "Besides, Wes told me that Gray told him that—"

"I don't want to hear it," Elise said loudly over her. "I can't believe he tells his brother anything." She lifted her phone. "I'm going to tell him to stop that."

"Ah-ha! So you are texting him right now."

"Maybe," Elise said again, her fingers flying over her screen.

"It wasn't anything bad," Bree said. "Wes just said that Gray told him he was talking to you. I guess it's a big deal for him."

Elise put her phone down and turned away from the sink as Bree poured herself a cup of coffee. "It's a big deal for him?"

"I guess," Bree said, glancing at her best friend and roommate. "I don't know. We didn't talk about it very long. I knew you wouldn't like it, and I—we—had other things to do." She didn't need to go into the details of how she'd kissed Wes after the one time they'd talked about Elise and Gray.

Elise gave an enormous sigh and sank into the chair at the kitchen table again. Bree joined her and just watched for a few moments. Elise usually said what was on her mind, but it sometimes took her a second to organize everything.

"I do like him," she finally said. "A lot. He's funny, and kind, and serious too. But."

Bree swallowed her coffee. Waited. When Elise didn't continue, she asked, "But what?"

"But he has Hunter, and he's...I don't know. Very hung up on Hunter."

"What does that mean? Hung up on him?"

"He's very protective of Hunter. He didn't even introduce me to him when they were here for the wedding." She wore a look of misery on her face, and Bree reached over and patted her hand.

"There must be a reason why," she said. "So you'll find that out, and Gray will work through it, and everything will be fine." Even as she spoke, Bree felt a rush of hypocrisy move through her. She would do anything to keep her family secrets, and maybe Gray was the same way. Maybe Gray didn't want to share all his dirty laundry with Elise. Maybe he wasn't ready to work through it.

Maybe everything wouldn't be fine.

Bree took another sip of coffee, but the liquid was far too bitter now, and she set her mug on the table. "I have to get going." She wasn't sure why she didn't want to continue this conversation with Elise. "Lots to plan today."

"I'll walk over to the lodge with you," she said. "I'm getting eight new rose bushes delivered today, and I have a ton to do too."

They left the cabin together, and thankfully, Elise didn't press Bree for more advice. She did say, "He doesn't want to relocate right now. Hunter has a strong friendship foundation —as well as his grandparents—in Colorado."

"I see," Bree said. She took a deep breath of the fresh summer air, the crispness of it refreshing now that September had arrived in the mountains. Soon enough, it would rain and snow, and Bree would be walking under an umbrella to get her chores done in the stable or to get to the lodge for the next activity she'd planned.

"What about you moving there?" she asked. "I mean, I know you love it here, but you're not really tied here." She looked at Elise, who walked with her head bent down.

She nodded slightly. "Yeah." She didn't say anything else, and Bree thought she probably knew how Elise felt. No, she didn't have family here. She didn't have children or a boyfriend. But she felt tied to Coral Canyon and Whiskey Mountain Lodge nonetheless, because the Whittakers treated everyone like family.

Elise did have a core group here she belonged to, and it included Bree. Patsy and Sophia. Annie, and Celia, and Amanda. The women in Coral Canyon watched out for each other, and if Elise left, she'd create a hole in Bree's life, as well as many others.

She'd be alone in Colorado, and Bree knew Elise didn't like being alone for very long.

Bree reached over and laced her arm through Elise's. "I'd miss you if you left."

Elise finally looked up, her light green eyes so innocent and so wide. "I'm not going to leave," she said. "I've already followed a man a thousand miles to be with him, and look how that ended up." She drew in a deep breath. "No, I'm not going to chase after Gray. Maybe we'll just be friends. Maybe the time just isn't right."

"Maybe you like living with me," Bree teased, hoping to lighten the moment.

"I'd definitely miss you too," Elise said soberly. "I'd miss this lodge, and everyone we work with here. I'd even miss the loud brothers." She grinned then, and all the melancholy that had been accompanying her fled.

Bree giggled with her. "They are loud, aren't they?"

"Yeah," Elise said. "But I do love them."

"Me too," Bree said, thinking of another set of brothers that had recently gotten together for a big celebration. "But you know, Colton's here. And Wes too. Maybe Gray will come to Coral Canyon. You never know."

"Not for a while," Elise said. "He's still lead counsel for the company until the end of the year. And then Hunter will be halfway through a school year...." She let her voice trail off.

Bree took a few steps without jumping into the next sentence. "Anything is possible, Elise."

"Especially with God," Elise added.

"So maybe just make sure He knows how you feel and

what you want, and maybe He'll work on Gray's heart." Bree gave her friend a smile, and Elise returned it.

"Thanks, Bree. So let's talk about you and Wes."

"Oh, I don't think so," Bree said with a light laugh.

"At least he doesn't make you pay for things," Elise said. "We can say that much, right?"

"Yes," Bree said with a grin. "We can say that much."

"Have you kissed him yet?"

Bree's first inclination was to tell Elise she didn't want to discuss personal things about her relationship with Wes. But she had in other relationships. This one felt different, though, and a dose of fear catapulted through her whole body.

"Yes," she finally said. "We've kissed."

Elise squealed, and Bree shook her head. "It's not a big deal. He's like, the twelfth boyfriend I've had this year."

"Oh, that's not true," Elise said, swatting at Bree's upper arm. "But maybe he'll last longer than six months."

"Well, it's only been two, so I guess we'll see about Christmastime how things are going."

They reached the lodge, and that meant more people, more ears to overhear delicate conversations. Bree had never been happier. She knew Elise wouldn't intentionally hurt her feelings, because Elise was the kindest person on the planet. But her remark about Bree's relationships only lasting six months stung. She also wasn't wrong, so Bree didn't have an argument to give.

It felt like she'd known Wes longer than two months, and of course, she had. She'd known him for nine months, since they started talking last Christmas. So maybe, just maybe, she *could* have a romantic relationship with a man that lasted longer than six months.

The noise from inside the lodge leaked out when Elise opened the door, and Bree sighed. "Here we go."

"I didn't think we were doing anything crazy today," Elise said. "I wonder who's here." They went down the hall and around the corner to where everyone in the lodge always gathered: the kitchen.

Celia wasn't there. No sweet smell hung in the air.

But someone had definitely made coffee and someone had brought breakfast sandwiches from town.

As soon as Bree looked into the dining half of the kitchen, she knew who.

Wes.

He sat at the table with half a dozen pieces of paper spread in front of him, talking animatedly about something while all four Whittaker brothers, Patsy, Sophia, Annie, and Colton listened intently.

The man oozed charm and charisma, and while Bree could hear what he was saying about group rentals and specific vacation packages, she didn't comprehend his words. All she could see was him.

His dark hair, that chiseled jaw, those blazing eyes like coal. He lit up when he talked business, and Bree realized she'd only seen a fraction of the man Wes actually was.

"And there you have it," he said, leaning back.

A moment of silence descended on the kitchen, and then everyone started talking at once. Graham asked questions, and Patsy said, "That will never work," and folded her arms. Even

Sophia had something to say, and all she did at the lodge was cook.

Wes sat in the middle of it all, grinning as if he'd eventually win everyone over to his side. Which, of course, he would. One didn't run a multi-billion-dollar company for fourteen years and not have some skills in getting people to see things his way.

Bree leaned against the wall while Elise joined the fray of people. She just watched Wes, because he was glorious to behold. A few seconds later, he noticed that she'd arrived. He jumped to his feet, gathered his papers into a stack, and handed them to Graham.

"All right, guys," he said. "We can talk more later."

"Later?" Beau asked. "Where are you going?"

"We just got started," Andrew said. "Did you hear what he said about the private boat tours? I actually really liked that."

"This guy's crazy," Eli said. "But in a good way."

Graham looked up from the pages as Wes tried to get out from behind the table where he'd been sitting. "He might actually be on to something here."

Wes finally freed himself from the fray of bodies and chairs, and he approached her with pure joy on his face. "Hey, gorgeous." He swept her into a hug and kissed her quickly. "What are you doing this morning? Can I tag along?"

"I think you might have a riot if you try to leave," she said, indicating the mass of people behind him, still talking and asking questions.

"Oh, they'll be fine," he said. "They have the proposal."

"What proposal?"

He laced his fingers through hers, and they went into the much quieter living room. "I guess I can't leave. I have check-out in fifteen minutes." As if drawn by his words, a couple started down the steps, their suitcase thumping on every one.

"Let me," Wes said, springing into action. Bree watched him help them with their luggage, grab the tablet, and start the check-out process. He turned back to her. "Andrew and Graham wanted me to do a little consulting on the lodge. It kept getting put off, but the past couple of weeks, I made a proposal for what they might do to bring in more business or charge more for what they already have. And I presented it this morning."

"What about the boat tours?"

"There's a great lake just down the road from here," he said. "Gray took Hunter fishing there when they came. No motors allowed on the lake, and you can rent paddleboats and fishing boats. So I thought—why don't they offer fishing weekends? Or midweek activities? Guy's getaways for fathers and sons? They could rent every boat at that lake, and essentially be renting the whole lake. Bam. Private lake tour."

Bree simply looked at him, because he emanated happiness, and power, and perfection. "That's a great idea," she said.

"Right?" Graham grinned and turned when someone else started down the steps. Up he went again, seemingly spurred on with energy from his presentation. Bree wondered how long he'd last here at the lodge, carrying people's bags up and down the steps, checking them in and out on a tablet.

It didn't fit his personality at all. Wes was made for lucrative deals. Big boardrooms. The spotlight.

Which left her wondering, once again, what in the world he was doing here in Coral Canyon, at this lodge, with this job.

And what had he been thinking when he'd started a relationship with *her*?

Chapter Eighteen

Wes waved to Bree when she indicated she was going to head outside, but he was with guests, so he couldn't go with her. Something pumped in his blood he hadn't felt in a long time, and he knew exactly what it was.

The high of a presentation. Adrenaline over talking about business.

Wes *loved* business, and making deals, and trying to push his mind outside of the box it was in. And hey, Graham and Andrew had asked him to do that. He'd noticed Patsy's reluctance, the way her eyebrows drew down, and her statement about how something would never work.

He'd worked with plenty of people like her. Their businesses eventually went bankrupt or closed their doors. He knew from a vast number of experiences that it wasn't until he allowed himself to think absolutely crazy things that he would find one idea that could change the course of the whole business.

"Thanks," he said as someone handed him a five-dollar bill. He'd been saving all of his tips for the past two months in a jar, of all things. Wes usually didn't even handle cash, and he certainly didn't keep it in a pickle jar on his nightstand.

But he was right now, because he was going to give the whole thing to Bree for her birthday. No, she had not told him when it was, but Annie had mentioned it when Wes was at Colton's house for dinner earlier this week.

In fact, he was going to ask her out on her birthday and see what she said. Wes had no more barriers up when it came to Bree, but he could still feel a wall coming from her. He knew it surrounded personal things, like her family and her birthday, and he was determined to chip away at it one day at a time.

He almost felt like he was doing something wrong, but he'd been praying about Bree, and the Lord hadn't told him to back away yet. But he didn't want to pursue her if she wasn't as interested in a relationship with him.

"Maybe better stop kissing her then," he muttered, but he didn't want to do that either. Bree genuinely seemed to like spending time with him. She liked kissing him, from all he could gather. They saw one another every day, and she even texted him at night. She'd given no indication that she didn't want him to chip away at her walls.

Except for her complete silence about her family and a few other personal details. Wes didn't know if she just had a different personality than he did—which she obviously did—or if it was something he should be concerned about.

When the last guest had checked out, he texted her. *Where are you? I wanted to see you before I left for today.*

Not doing check-in? she messaged back.

Nope. Afternoon off. What are you doing? Want to go to Yellowstone today?

Bree didn't answer. Wes sat on the steps just across from the giant front doors of the lodge and waited. She didn't work in town on weekends, and surely she was around the lodge somewhere. She sometimes helped Elise with the grounds, and she sometimes ran classes if there were a lot of guests staying through the weekend.

Wes had checked out half the guests today though, so if Bree was doing something, it wouldn't be with very many people. She didn't normally plan activities for only a dozen or so people, so he'd be surprised if she didn't have the afternoon ahead of her with not much to do.

He looked up when the front door opened, and Bree walked in. "Hey." He grinned at her and stood up. "There you are."

She folded herself neatly into his arms, wrapping hers around him and holding him tight. Everything inside him sang, and he put this moment in his memory so he could remind himself that yes, Bree Richards liked him.

She eased back a little and looked up at him. "Yellowstone is a two-hour drive."

"Okay," he said.

"One way. It's noon already."

"So maybe we'll stay overnight," he said. "I'm not doing check-in tomorrow, so I have a while off. You're not working at the office. What are you doing around here?"

"Not much, I guess," she said, stepping out of his embrace completely. "You want to stay overnight?"

"We'd get two rooms," he said, thinking she was probably worried about that.

"You have guitar lessons this afternoon."

"Do you not want to go?" he asked. "If you don't want to go, just say you don't want to go."

Bree looked at him with those dark, brownish-hazel eyes he loved so much. He hadn't meant to sound harsh, and he realized he'd reverted back to his CEO-ways. Just state the facts. Don't make anything about how you feel.

"Sorry," he said quickly. "It just feels like you don't want to go."

"I do," she said. "I love Yellowstone."

"Great," he said. "I've never been, and I'd love to go with you. So let's go."

She gave him a soft smile, and the tense dam inside Wes broke. "You need to get a place to stay before we just go," she said. "You realize people make reservations for Yellowstone a year in advance, right?"

"I...did not know that," he said. "I'll do it right now." He sat down on the steps again and got busy on his phone, searching and finding a place right in the park where they could stay.

But the room he was looking at had communal bathrooms. *No, thank you*, he thought. He had enough money to find a place with a private bathroom. "Oh," he said. "We could get a two-queen suite, private bathroom, Old Faithful Inn."

He looked at Bree. "Doable? Or do you require your own room-own room-room?"

"Own room-room?" she teased. "My own bed should be okay."

"It's a suite. We can move one of the beds into the other area, and create two bedrooms." He tapped to book that one, not even looking at the price.

Bree sat beside him and looked over his arm. "Wes, that suite is twelve hundred dollars."

"Yeah." Wes kept tapping to reserve. He had his credit card number memorized, and he wouldn't miss twelve hundred dollars.

"Wes," she said.

"What?"

"Are you serious?"

"Sure," he said. "I don't want to camp, and this is right by Old Faithful. It's in the park. It has what we want and need." He looked at her. "It's no big deal."

"All right," she said, but she sounded like she doubted him.

Wes went ahead with the booking and tucked his phone into his back pocket. "Okay, so we need to pack. And then we can go. Yeah?" He smiled at her and leaned toward her, glad when she met him halfway for a real kiss. Nothing too quick or too rushed.

Wow, he loved kissing her.

"I wanted to ask you something else," he said, pulling away. "Dinner this next week, on Wednesday. You and me. What do you say?"

"Wednesday?"

He watched something parade across her face, and he knew it came from realizing that Wednesday was her birthday.

"Yeah," he said. "I'm not working that day at all, and I thought I'd do a little hiking in the morning. I could take you to lunch instead, if you wanted. I'm going to move my guitar lesson to that afternoon. And dinner."

He had a lot more plans than that, but he didn't need to spill the beans quite yet.

"Sure," she said. "I can do dinner on Wednesday."

"Great." He stood up and extended his hand to pull her up too. He took her right into his arms, his heart pounding beneath his ribs. "I'll make sure we have a big birthday cake too."

She stiffened in his arms and pulled back enough to look at him, her eyes wide. "You know it's my birthday."

"That's right," he said, smiling. He would not let the fact that she hadn't told him upset him. But she had kind of failed the test.

"Who told you?"

"Your BFF."

"Colton," she said under her breath. "I should've known."

"Annie's making the cake," Wes said. "And why couldn't you tell me it's your birthday?"

She sighed and stepped away from him, and Wes suddenly felt tired. The two hours to Yellowstone felt like a chore—or something he'd do himself, and then he'd continue to Idaho, Montana, and all the other states he hadn't visited yet. Alone.

Without Bree.

The very thought made him recoil from himself, and he cleared his mind as Bree turned back to him.

"Because, Wes," she said. "If you know it's my birthday, you'll spoil me rotten."

Confusion knitted through him. "And...you don't want your boyfriend to spoil you rotten on your birthday?"

She smiled, and she was so beautiful. "I mean, I guess so."

"You guess so." Wes wasn't sure what to do now.

"I do," she said.

"But you didn't tell me."

"I don't want you to spend a lot of money on me," she said.

Wes wanted to argue with her. Tell her he *had* a lot of money, and who better to spend it on? Instead, he nodded. "Okay. Dinner. Cake. One present. Is that acceptable to you?"

"One present," she mused, inching a little closer to him. "It can't be a car."

"I will not buy you a car," he vowed.

"Or a house." Bree grinned up at him and stepped back into his arms. "Or anything bigger than a shoebox. Or any jewelry."

"Okay, now you're just being ridiculous," he said. He smiled too, but he wasn't feeling very happy inside. "You can't tell me what I can and can't buy you."

"Why not?"

"Would you object to a vacuum cleaner?" he asked. "That comes in a box bigger than a shoebox."

"If you buy me a vacuum cleaner for my birthday, it's over between us."

Wes burst out laughing, glad when Bree did too. "But you just said no jewelry, and what if I want to buy you something sparkly? That's smaller than a shoebox, *and* it's meaningful." He swayed with her, liking this new direction the conversation had taken.

"It's too expensive," she whispered.

"Bree," he whispered back. "When are you going to accept that nothing is too expensive for me? Not when it comes to you."

"I don't know," she said.

"Work on it, okay?" Wes leaned down and kissed her again, hoping she could feel how very real his feelings for her were. "And I'm buying you whatever I want for your birthday," he said, his lips still touching hers. "But I will concede to no car, and no house."

"And no vacuum cleaner," she added before claiming his lips again.

He could live with that, and he could *definitely* feel how she felt about him when she kissed him.

* * *

"Pull over here," Bree said. "They're looking at something up there."

Wes did what she said, because he'd missed the moose in Jackson Hole, and he wanted a legit wildlife sighting. He put the truck in park, cut the ignition, and got out. "What do you think it is?"

"No idea," she said. "People pull over for everything in Yellowstone."

"I hope we can see it," he said, taking her hand in his. They'd packed quickly and hit the road within an hour after he'd agreed not to buy her a car, a house, or a vacuum cleaner for her birthday. The drive had been pleasant, without any tension even during the silent bouts.

"It's a bear," she said, slowing for a moment. A couple was headed back to their car, and she asked, "It's a bear, right?"

"Three of them," the man said. "Not too far away either."

"Three bears," Wes said, in complete awe. Maybe if he'd spent more time in the mountains and canyons surrounding Denver, he wouldn't feel so filled with wonder. But a wild animal to a CEO was someone who shows up in the office in jeans instead of a pair of pressed slacks.

He was tall enough that he could see past a lot of the crowd, and sure enough, with just a few more steps, he could see what everyone had pulled over for. "There they are," he said, pausing.

"Let's go a little closer," she said. "I can't see them yet." They dodged through other people, going out to the right where they wouldn't block anyone, and Bree paused too. "Oh, wow."

The three bears were probably a few hundred yards away, and at least four forest rangers stood at the front of the crowd to make sure no one got too close. One bear was standing, his head down, and the other two, smaller bears, were several feet away from the first.

"Is it a mother and cubs?" Wes wondered. The smaller

bears weren't *that* much smaller, but if they'd been born in the springtime, they could still be cubs.

"No idea," Bree said, and her voice held wonder too. "They're amazing, though."

The general attitude among the crowd was the same thing, and no one spoke in too loud of a voice or tried to get past the rangers. Wes and Bree stayed for a long time, until finally she said, "Should we go?"

"Yeah," Wes said, finally tearing his eyes from the trio of bears. "That was amazing." Back in the truck, he added, "A real wild animal sighting. So exciting." He grinned for all he was worth, and Bree laughed at him and took his hand in hers.

"I like it when you get excited about simple things," she said. "It reminds me that you're just a little boy in a big body."

"Oh-ho," he said, still chuckling. "Is that right?"

"It's just...you have a lot of money. You wouldn't think that a few black bears would be that exciting. You could probably buy them as pets."

Wes glanced at her. "I would like a dog. Not a bear."

She shook her head, though her smile remained in place. "You know what I mean."

"Having money isn't that exciting," he said.

"I would be excited about it."

"It wears off quickly."

"This will too."

"I don't know," Wes said, navigating them toward the inn. "That was pretty awesome. I got a lot of pictures, and I hope we see more wildlife while we're here."

"I'm sure we will," she said. "I looked it up, and they've had a ton of animals down where the public is this year."

"So hopefully, we'll get lucky." He didn't care what she said—seeing the black bears was exciting. Of course, making his first billion had been too. But honestly, Wes had been given two billion to start with. Sure, he'd worked hard, but he'd never wondered if he'd have to go without. He'd never worked two jobs because he had to. He'd never really had to think that hard about how he'd pay for the things he needed—and everything he wanted too.

So he could understand Bree's point of view. He just hoped that one day—and one day soon—she'd stop thinking about his money as what defined him.

He wanted to be more than that.

He already *was* more than that. He glanced at her. Maybe she didn't see that in him yet.

What do I need to do to show her there's more to me than a bank account? he asked the Lord. *Help me provide for her what she needs, whether that's money or something else.*

He kept the prayer going as he drove through the more crowded parts of Yellowstone National Park to get to the inn, stalling on one question he really wished God would answer for him.

Do I love her?

Will You please let me know if I'm in love with her the way she deserves to be loved?

Wes had been in love before—or so he'd thought. He'd asked two women to marry him, and that certainly took some measure of love to think he could join himself to them for the rest of his life.

In the end, he hadn't been able to do that, and they'd broken up. He hadn't mourned those break-ups for very long, so maybe he hadn't truly been in love with Claire or Lauren.

He tried to imagine his life without Bree in it, and everything seemed dull, sad, and gray. In fact, he'd lived through six months exactly like that, and he hadn't enjoyed them all that much.

So am I in love with her? he begged the Lord. *And how will I know when I am?*

Chapter Nineteen

Bree heard Wes's alarm go off in the other room, and she rolled over in the very uncomfortable bed. The suite was in the original part of the inn, and had been built over a hundred years ago. She'd liked the charm of the old building, and they'd managed to find some good food in the adjoining restaurant.

They were going on a hike this morning, and then driving around the park, hoping to run into a herd of bison or see an eagle soaring or something equally as wild. Wes's words.

Bree stayed in bed though she heard Wes get up. He groaned in the other room, and she stifled her giggle until he went into the bathroom. She probably should've warned him that anywhere they stayed near or in Yellowstone wouldn't have a nice bed. She knew, because she'd rented the cabins around the park; she'd slept in a tent in one of the campgrounds; she'd even gone with her old floral friends once and they'd rented a condo about a half-hour from the park. Nothing was ever comfortable.

Wes was probably used to the highest thread counts on his sheets too, with downy pillow tops on his king-sized mattresses.

Bree knew she was being cruel and sarcastic, and a vein of regret ran through her. There was nothing wrong with wanting a nice bed to sleep in. Bree wanted one right now, and she groaned too when she sat up.

Wes got ready fast, and he slid open the door separating the bedroom from the sitting area, where he'd moved her bed. "Hey, you're up." If she hadn't heard him groan, she wouldn't have known he hadn't slept wonderfully. "I'm out of the bathroom, if you want to shower or anything."

"Sure," she said.

"I'm going to go find coffee and something to eat." He picked up his wallet from the countertop that held a microwave and had a small sink in it. "You like cream and sugar, right?"

"Yes, please," she said, admiring him without the cowboy hat he usually wore on his head. He had less gray hair than Colton, and she found herself wanting to curl her fingers through it. She had before, when he'd taken off his hat to kiss her, but that somehow wasn't enough.

"And nothing with raisins." He lifted his eyebrows at her as he reached for his cowboy hat. Bree watched as he put it on, taking an extra moment to settle it just-so. "Did you want to come with me?"

"No," she said, blinking her way out of the trance she'd

fallen into. "I'll shower while you're gone. Nothing with raisins." She smiled at him, and Wes's whole face softened. He swept one arm around her and leaned down to kiss her, his mouth already formed into a smile.

Bree giggled against his lips and put both hands on his chest, turning her head as she laughed. He growled and dropped his lips to her neck, and Bree laughed harder. "Oh, go on," she said, pushing him away. She couldn't really get a man of Wes's size to move, but he fell back a couple of steps anyway, laughing with her.

He tipped his hat and stepped through the door, and Bree turned in a full circle, her heartbeat sprinting in her chest. That man made her feel more alive than any other, and with that realization came a heavy dose of fear.

She collected her thoughts and reached for her bag before going into the bathroom. She showered and dressed and dried her hair before Wes returned. She had her mascara wand in her hand when the door opened, and he said, "I found some amazing apple fritters, sweetheart."

"Okay," she called. "I'll be right out." She finished her minimal makeup quickly and zipped everything back into her bag. She took it with her into the sitting area, where she found Wes getting ready to push her bed back into the bedroom. "How'd you sleep?" she asked.

He just groaned as he leaned his weight into the bed and moved it. The task done, he said, "I've slept in better beds."

Bree smiled at him. "So have I."

"So we won't stay here again."

"I wouldn't advise it." She reached for the white pastry bag he'd brought back with him. "But these look amazing." She pulled out the two apple fritters and then looked at the coffee cups. "Which one's mine?"

"The one that's not half empty," he said. "I'm gonna need more of that. I don't think I slept for more than an hour last night."

"I heard you snoring," she said. "You slept for longer than an hour."

"At a time," he said. "I had to move so much." He stretched his back. "Maybe we should just go back to Coral Canyon."

"Nope," Bree said. "I have a good feeling about today, and we're sticking to the plan."

"Fine." Wes wore a smile when he looked at her again. They ate their breakfast and hauled their bags out to his truck. He set out on the main road, which wasn't too busy yet because it was fairly early in the morning on a Sunday.

"Oh, wow," he said as they came up on a patch of fog. All at once, he hit the brakes, and Bree braced herself against the dashboard.

"Buffalo," she said in the next moment.

Wes reached out and pressed a button that turned on his hazard lights, both of them flashing. "Hopefully no one will come up behind us and hit us."

Bree glanced in her rearview mirror, and another car had already joined them in the fog.

"Buffalo in the mist," he said as a whole herd of them crossed the road right in front of them. He rolled his window down, and then hers, and Bree could hear their snuffling as they breathed, their hooves on the pavement, and a groan from them every now and then.

The moment felt made of magic, and like she and Wes were the only people on the earth in that moment, alone with these wild animals.

She looked at him, and he looked at her, and she reached for his hand. Nothing was said, but so much communicated, and Bree felt absolute peace and comfort in that moment. Pure love flowed through her as well, and she let it cleanse out some of her self-doubt about why Wes was with her.

He lifted her hand to his lips and kissed her skin, and Bree looked out the window at the bison. "This is incredible," she said.

"I think you're incredible," Wes said. He released her hand and eased up on the brake, as the last of the buffalo crossed in front of them. They continued toward their hike, seeing a few elk but nothing more.

Bree stayed inside her own mind, trying to figure out how she truly felt about Wes. He seemed genuine in everything he did, and she wanted to believe that he'd shown his real self to her.

"Ready?" he asked, and she realized they'd reached their hike trailhead.

"Yes." She got out of the truck and opened the back door to get her backpack. They'd only bring one today, as it was a short hike—in to an overlook above a canyon in the park—and then back to the truck. "What do you want in this?"

"Just water," he said. "And my sunglasses." He reached back into the truck for those and settled them on his face. He grinned, and though she couldn't see his eyes, he was the sexiest man she'd ever laid eyes on.

She stuck a couple of bottles of water in the backpack, made sure she had sunscreen, and her usual granola bars, just in case, and then joined him at the front of the truck. She wrapped her arm around his waist, and he looked down at her. "I sure do like you, Wes," she said, almost a whisper.

"Yeah?"

She nudged him with her hip. "Obviously."

"Oh, I think sometimes it's not that obvious to a man," he said. They started down the trail, which was well-maintained and clear, and Wes added, "Tell me what you like about me."

"Oh, boy," Bree said. "I didn't think you lacked confidence."

"I don't," he said. "Except when it comes to you."

"What does that mean?" Bree walked behind Wes on the single-file trail, and she couldn't see his face.

"It means that you don't make it easy for me to know how you feel. You don't say it very often, and I don't know. I like you too, and I'm trying to be the best version of me."

"Do you have a bad version?"

"Everyone does," he said. "I get mad sometimes." He chuckled. "Heck, Colton used to call me Wesley the Wolf at work. I could, uh, be a little blunt during meetings."

"Oh, I can see that," she said. "But you're not hiding another girlfriend somewhere, right?"

"Of course not."

"You don't smoke or drink in secret."

"Nope."

"I know your real name," she said. "You pay your own bills. You think my hair looks good short. So I think you're pretty amazing."

"Those are some low expectations," he said. "I want to be better than that."

"Wes, you already are."

He paused and turned around. "Okay, if that's true, tell me what you like about me."

She searched his face, trying to find what he wanted from her. "I think you're gorgeous," she said, her mouth suddenly dry. "I think you're smart. Funny. Personable. I think you're kind, and faithful, and just wonderful." She drew in a breath. "You must know how to work hard, though I haven't seen you do more than carry a few suitcases, but you do that really well."

He finally smiled, and Bree relaxed a little bit. "You love your brothers and your parents. You have dreams you want to accomplish. I don't know." Bree looked out at the rock wall across the river from where they were hiking. "I like that you take care of me. That you're concerned about me. That you want to spend time with me, doing things I like to do. I like your heart."

She needed to stop talking, and she pressed her lips together to force herself to do that. She couldn't see Wes's eyes because of those sunglasses, but she saw him take a deep breath and then reach for her.

He kissed her then, and this was unlike any other kiss they'd shared. He demanded more from her, and she gave it to him willingly, hopefully saying even more than the words she'd already vocalized.

"I'm falling in love with you," he said huskily, pressing his forehead to hers. "I know that scares you. Heck, it scares me too. But I feel it, and I wanted to say it so you knew. Okay?"

Bree nodded, breathing in the scent of him and trying not to spiral into a dark place. No one had ever told her they loved her, and Bree didn't know how to process something that heavy. That wonderful.

"Okay." Wes drew in another breath and stepped away, turning to continue down the trail. Bree could barely stand without him to hold onto, and she watched him take several steps without her, putting more and more distance between them.

Then she looked up into the sky and whispered, "Dear Lord, help me to not mess this up." She had a feeling the status of their relationship sat squarely on her shoulders, and she did not want to lose Wes. He was the single best thing in her life. "Please don't let me ruin this. Guide me."

"Bree," he called. "Come see this."

She looked back to where he stood several yards down the trail. "There's an eagle over there." He pointed around the bend she hadn't reached yet, and she took off to go have another amazing experience with him.

* * *

Days passed, as they were wont to do, and Bree woke a few mornings later in her bedroom in her cabin.

Wednesday.

Her birthday.

Most people probably liked their birthdays. They looked forward to getting cards in the mail, and gifts from friends, and eating their favorite foods and lots of birthday cake.

Bree usually did get a card, but she hadn't seen anything from Vermont yet. Honestly, they made her guilt grow barbs and sting her for weeks after she opened the card and saw her mother's slanted handwriting. One year, she'd lifted the fifty-dollar bill that had fallen from the card to her nose, and she'd smelled her father's cologne.

She'd burst into tears and called in sick at the lodge. Thankfully, she hadn't had a roommate at the time; she hadn't lived in the cabin where she lived now.

Nerves ran through her, because she had a bigger audience now than she'd had a few years ago.

Warmth ran through her as she lay in bed, and she finally swung her legs over the edge of the mattress and reached for her phone.

She had one text message, and she wasn't surprised that it was from Wes. *Happy birthday, gorgeous! Can't wait to see you tonight.*

He'd texted at five minutes past midnight, and Bree smiled at her device. A rush of love moved through her, and she almost couldn't believe it. It was the *almost* that surprised her the most, because even a couple of weeks ago, she wouldn't have believed it at all.

She got up and padded to the door, opening it and startling as a bunch of blue balloons came into the room with her as she pulled the door toward her. "Oh." The balloons had been tied to her doorknob, and they all had variations of "happy birthday" printed on them.

A laugh started low in her throat, because she knew who was behind this. Wes.

A card flapped on the strings of the balloons, and she reached for it. A couple of dogs sat on the front of the card, and Wes had written inside, *I'm glad you were born, Bree. You make me so happy. Happy birthday.*

She pressed the card to her chest, because she wasn't sure she'd ever made anyone happy. At least not long term. Maybe she made Colton happy when she made chocolate cake. Or maybe she made the guests at the lodge happy when she did an amazing horseback riding tour. But to be the actual cause of true happiness for someone? Bree had never been told that before.

She went down the hallway to the kitchen, where she found a silver tray sitting on the table. It held a giant-sized box of her favorite cold cereal, a bag of her favorite coffee, a new mug with a red bow tied around it, and a bowl big enough to hold the whole box of cereal.

She giggled again when she picked up a little card that said, *Milk's in the fridge, sweetheart. Enjoy your birthday breakfast. ~Wes*

"That man has got it bad for you," Elise said as she entered the kitchen.

"Yeah," Bree said, not even bothering to deny it. She smiled at her best friend. "Did you let him in the cabin?"

"Yes," she said. "And it was late, too, so he owes me big time."

Bree laughed as she stepped over to the fridge to get her milk. "What are you going to have him do to pay you back?"

"I haven't decided yet." Elise started making coffee with their regular grounds. "But it's going to be something huge." She grinned at Bree and set the coffee pot in its place before she hugged Bree. "Happy birthday, my friend."

"Thanks, Elise." She held tightly to her friend, hoping with everything in her that today would be the best birthday of her life.

That darkness teemed inside her, and she decided maybe she'd let a little bit of it out. "Have you gotten the mail in the past couple of days?"

"Yeah, I got it yesterday," she said, nodding toward the living room through the doorway. "It's on the table where we always put it."

"Thanks." Bree sat down to eat her cereal, the call of the mail intensifying with every minute that went by. But she wanted to see if she had a birthday card from her parents without Elise in the cabin, and Elise took her time nursing her cup of coffee.

Finally, she said, "I'll see you later. I have to run to the nursery for some new shrubs this morning."

"Good luck," Bree said, and she waited until Elise closed the front door behind her before she practically leapt from her chair and strode into the living room. Sure enough, a pile of mail sat on the table where they usually put packages and bills and receipts.

Bree started sifting through it, though she spotted the dull rose-colored envelope in the stack poking above the other legal-sized mail. She got to it eventually, and she saw her mother's handwriting.

Her heart squeezed tight, and her lungs tightened. She flipped the envelope over and slid her fingernail under the flap. It popped open easily, and she pulled out the card. Flowers covered the front, and Bree's emotions knotted.

Still, she flipped open the card. The first tears appeared in her eyes when she saw more of her mother's handwriting. The familiar cash, placed there from her father. She sucked in a breath and set the card on the table, as if she'd display it for the foreseeable future for all who came to the cabin to see.

She wouldn't, and she picked up the card and took it to her bedroom, opening the drawer in her dresser where she kept anything that had come from Vermont. She lovingly placed the card on top of last year's and looked down at everything that represented a sliver of herself she didn't allow to bloom. After a few moments, she closed the drawer and contained the darkness.

She wanted this birthday to be amazing, and she couldn't deal with twenty years of emotions in a single morning. She knew she needed to deal with it soon, though, as the turmoil inside her had been boiling for weeks now.

But not on her birthday.

Chapter Twenty

Wes put his fingers on the strings where his instructor had shown him. "I can't hear it," he said, strumming the guitar.

"You *feel* it," Gentry said. "Your fingers will know it's right."

Wes wanted to be able to hear that it was right, though. He kept strumming, and he hummed along with the song she'd given him for homework last week. When he got to the riff, his fingers stumbled, and Gentry held up her hand.

"Here, you have to pick the strings," she said. "You can't just slide along the strings."

"I need to learn how to do that."

Gentry picked up her guitar and showed him, but Wes didn't think his thick fingers could do what her more slender ones could. He tried, and he realized he was going to need a lot more practice in order to pick like that.

"You'll get it," she said, smiling at him. "Remember,

you're two months into lessons. You've made a lot of great progress, Wes." She set her guitar in the stand and stood up. "I'm going to keep you on this song for the week, and I want you to review last week's pages too." She wrote in her notebook, and then added, "I'm giving four more pages in your book too. You should be able to do them, since there's no new notes. Just trickier rhythms."

"All right," Wes said. He laid his guitar in its case and buckled it closed. He accepted his notebook from Gentry, thanked her for her lesson, and headed outside. The leaves had started to turn into glorious shades of red, orange, and yellow, and Wes absolutely adored autumn.

But he didn't have time to admire the beauty of it today. He had dinner to pick up, and a table-for-two to set, and an obsessive need to lay out Bree's presents exactly right. He went home first and scrubbed the kitchen from top to bottom, loaded his dishwasher and started it, and draped a white cloth over the dining room table he'd bought when he moved into this house.

He set silverware and plates, put unlit candles on the table that he'd light later, and a couple of blood-red napkins. A vase of red roses went in the middle of the table, and he'd move those once he and Bree sat down to eat, because he wouldn't be able to see her past them.

With that done, he got out the things he'd bought for her birthday. The pickle jar full of his tip money got a bright purple Christmas bow stuck to the top of it, and he set it at Bree's place at the table.

The other gift was definitely smaller than a shoebox, and

Wes cracked open the jewelry box to look at the pendant one more time. The silver chain held a teardrop-shaped gem in a gloriously bright pink—a pink sapphire. He'd paid a lot for it, but he'd already removed the price tag from the chain so Bree wouldn't see it.

She loved pink, and he couldn't wait to see this gem resting against her collarbone.

He closed the box and put the black velvet into a bigger box, taped it closed, and wrapped that one in silver paper. He tied a pink bow around it, wondering why his fingers were so clumsy.

After far too long, he got the bow to lay semi-decently, and he put the box on Bree's plate on the table.

"Time to get the food." Wes drove to town to do just that, taking the foil trays back to his house and sliding them into the oven at the temperature he'd been instructed to use. Then, though he'd showered that morning, he jumped in again to be his freshest for Bree.

As he washed his hair, he couldn't believe the lengths he was going to for this woman. He'd like to think he treated all of his girlfriends with as much care and thought, but he knew that would be somewhat of a lie.

Bree was special, and Wes had been praying for the past few days to know precisely how he felt about her, and that he'd be able to act on those feelings. She wouldn't allow him to drive up the canyon to pick her up, and instead, she was coming to his house at six.

Freshly showered, shaved, deodorized, and in his best jeans and a dark blue polo, Wes reached for his cowboy hat.

Bree had told him on Sunday that she loved him in his cowboy hat.

Loved him.

But then she'd said that she sure did like seeing his hair too. So he hesitated before putting on the hat, then decided he wanted to wear it, at least in the beginning. He could take it off to kiss her hello and then hang it by the front door.

Satisfied with his plan, he went down the hall to the kitchen, where everything seemed to be ready. He pulled the food out of the oven and set it on the stovetop, then turned around, searching for the next thing to be done.

But there was nothing to be done. So he went out to the front porch and sat in a chair he'd put there. Actually, Cindi, his interior designer had put the patio set on the front porch, and Wes couldn't say he hated it. He'd sat there plenty of times in the month he'd lived in the house, as it had quickly become one of his favorite places to think.

Bree's car pulled into his driveway a few minutes before six, and Wes couldn't help the smile in his whole soul. He knew in that moment that he was all the way in love with her, and that knowledge kept him solidly in his seat.

She primped for a moment, then turned off the car and got out. "I see you up there," she called to him, and Wes chuckled as he stood.

"I wasn't trying to hide."

"Yeah, okay." She came toward him, and he simply drank her in. She wore a cute dress with a bright, splashy floral pattern in pink, purple, and blue against a white background.

She wore a tight, white shirt under the spaghetti straps of the dress to cover her shoulders, and Wes mourned that.

He met her at the top of the steps and took her face in both of his hands. "Oh, you are exactly what my soul needed today." He took off the cowboy hat and handed it to her. "I think you liked me without this."

She took the hat. "Is that your gift to me?" She grinned at the hat and then him, plenty of flirtatiousness coming through in those pretty eyes.

"Not even close," he said, lowering his head so he could kiss her. He poured everything he had into this kiss, and he hoped she could feel it. "Happy birthday, baby," he whispered.

"Thank you," she said, her mouth very close to his still. "But not baby, okay? That's not a good endearment for me. I mean, I'm thirty-seven today. Not anywhere near a baby."

Wes chuckled and drew her into his chest, wondering if he could tell her now that he loved her. "How about gorgeous?"

"Yes, I think we've established that I like that one." She stepped out of his arms. "Are we going to dinner?"

"Nope," he said, leading her toward the front door. "I brought dinner to us." He opened the door and let her go inside first.

"Ooh, fancy," she said in a false accent as she went inside. "Something smells good."

"It's your favorite," he said. "Italian." He followed her through the living room, thinking he'd follow her anywhere. "But let's do presents first. They're on the table there. I think you'll know your spot."

She stopped a few feet away from the table, and Wes sidled up beside her. "What's in the jar?" she asked.

"My tips," he said. "From the lodge."

"Wes, I said—"

"You said no car, no house, and no vacuum cleaner." He leaned closer to her. "I've been planning that one for months, Bree. You can't refuse it. I've been keeping it in a pickle jar, for crying out loud."

She looked at him, but he kept his focus on the purple bow on top of the jar. "How much is in it?"

"I have no idea," he said. "Whatever people gave me for carrying their suitcases. Since you said that's all you've seen of my hard work, that should tell you how hardworking I am."

"Wes, that's not what I meant."

"I know." He grinned. "It's yours. Don't you want to open the box?"

She did, he could tell. She walked toward the table and picked up the silver-wrapped package. "I love pink," she said, untying the pink bow in only a few seconds. He watched his hard work disintegrate into a ribbon, and then delight spread through him as she tore the paper off the box and found a bland, shipping container.

She glanced at him, and Wes inched closer so he could see her better. She un-taped the top of the box and then giggled. "You disguised a jewelry box."

"Guilty," he said.

She pulled out the black velvet box and shot him a nervous look. She didn't ask what it was though, and she cracked the lid. She sucked in a breath and held it. "Wes."

"It's pink," he said, enjoying the delight in her eyes. She looked at him, a bit of shock in her expression too. "A pink sapphire, in fact. They're very rare." He took the box gently from her. "Like you." He removed the pendant and said, "It'll look great with this dress. You want to put it on?"

"Yes, please," she said, brushing her hair off the back of her neck. Wes gently lifted the gem over her head, his pulse hammering as his thick fingers worked the clasp at the back of her neck.

He finally got it, and relief streamed through him. "Got it."

She turned, and Wes looked at the pretty gem resting against her chest. She reached up and touched it. "I love it."

"It's beautiful," he said.

"Thank you, Wes." Bree's voice held so much emotion, and he lifted his eyes to hers.

"Happy birthday."

"This is the best birthday I've ever had."

"Is it?"

She nodded and embraced him, holding him so tightly that Wes felt loved and cherished and *needed*. And Wes hadn't really been needed for a while now, and it sure did feel nice to be useful again.

"Okay, dinner," she said, stepping back and brushing at her eyes. "I could use some pasta about now."

"There's garlic bread too," Wes said, covering over his own emotions with wit. He spun toward the stove and got the food uncovered. "You wanna bring over the plates?"

"Yes," Bree said, and she appeared at his side a few seconds later. "You got fettuccini Alfredo."

"With a side of marinara," he said. "Because you like the half and half mix." He served her what he knew she liked, and she took the plate from him. But she didn't go back to the table.

"Wes, I think you're as close to perfect as a man can get."

He put a piece of garlic bread on his plate. "That's because I've been hiding all my flaws from you." He grinned at her and added another meatball to his spaghetti.

"You told me you wouldn't hide things from me," she teased as they walked back to the table together. He put his plate down and turned back for the matches. He lit the candles and turned out most of the other lights to set the mood.

"You know my real name," he said. "And everything worth knowing about me. So I've kept it a secret that I don't do my dishes every day. Trust me, this is stuff you don't want to know until you're helplessly in love with me." He laughed. "Then the dirty dishes won't matter as much."

Bree shook her head as she laughed with him. They started eating, and Wes asked her what else she'd done for her birthday, if she liked her cereal he'd left for her, and why this birthday had been better than the others.

She'd sent him pictures of her with the cereal and with the balloons, so he already knew she'd liked them and appreciated them. In fact, he'd never seen her so happy before.

She talked about the cupcakes Willie had brought in to the employment office, and that they'd gone to ChixPix for lunch before she went up to the lodge. Sophia had made a cake for

Bree, and everyone at the lodge had sung to her and given her gifts too.

"You have a good support system here," Wes said. "I'm glad about that." He really wanted to ask her about her family, and maybe now was the time. She certainly seemed like she was in a good mood and might actually answer him.

"It's nice to have friends," she said.

"And what about your family?" he asked. "Do they, uh, send anything for your birthday?"

Bree's expression flashed with alarm, but she barely hesitated before saying, "My parents sent a card."

"That's great," he said. "Siblings?"

She shook her head, but her mouth had tightened into a very tight line. She hadn't lied to him in the past, which meant Wes had never seen this look on her face before. Something stung deep in Wes's heart, and it grew and pulsed.

Did he push this?

Help me, he prayed, and he immediately knew it was time to get some answers from Bree. He'd fallen in love with her. Was he going to live the rest of his life with lies about her family, never knowing the truth?

"Bree," he said as gently as he could. "I feel like you just lied to me."

"I—I can't."

"Sweetheart," he said, laying down his fork. "It's just me. Remember how I said I wanted to know all the good, the bad, and the ugly? I still do. I'm not going to judge you." He took a deep breath, ready to lay it all on the line. "I'm in love with you, Bree Richards. Whatever you say isn't going to change that."

Panic ran through her expression and she lifted her napkin from her lap and put it on her plate. He hadn't served the cake Annie had made for her yet. He hadn't held her close and danced with her in his kitchen. There was so much more he wanted this birthday to be for her, and he felt it and saw it all slipping away from him.

Bree was retreating from him, and Wes felt his whole chest start to cave in.

"Bree," he said again. "Please. You can trust me."

She stood up, her determination written on her face. "I do trust you, Wes. But this really will change everything between us. You'll...you'll think badly of me even if you don't want to. And I'll know that you know, and every time you look at me, I'll wonder what you're thinking, and if you really want to be with me."

She raised both of her arms to the side and let them fall again, a mirthless laugh coming from her mouth. "I fight against that inadequacy already. I just—I can't tell you. I'm sorry."

Wes stood as she spun. "Bree, wait."

But she was already moving toward the door, and there was no hesitancy in her step. She even ran the last few steps, and Wes just let her go.

He let her go, because the only thing his body could do was keep his heart beating as it broke in half, and then those pieces cracked again. Finally, when it shattered completely, Wes fell back into his chair, everything from his toes to his fingertips utterly numb.

Chapter Twenty-One

Bree could not stop crying. She sobbed the whole way back to the cabin from Wes's, but then she couldn't go inside. Not while Elise was still awake. She couldn't explain to anyone what she'd just done, because she didn't even understand it herself.

I'm in love with you, Bree Richards.

The words tortured her, and she pulled out of the parking lot at the lodge and went back down the canyon as if she'd go to town. She parked at the first pullout, left the air conditioner running, and cried.

She couldn't tell him about Bronson. She couldn't. He was so good, and so kind, and so perfect, and despite what he said, he *would* think differently of her once he knew. She couldn't stand the thought of Wesley Hammond knowing she'd been responsible for her brother's death, because that would ruin everything they'd been building.

She'd just calmed enough to think semi-clearly, and she had the distinct thought that she might have just ruined everything they'd been building by *not* telling him.

And that only made her trickle of tears turn into sobs again.

She stayed in the car for a long time, finally flipping around and going home. Only one light shone from within the cabin, which meant Elise was likely already in her room, fast asleep.

Bree looked at the place she'd called home for the past couple of years, admiring the long porch that spanned the whole front of the cabin. Laney had been so generous in letting Bree and Elise live here for free, though Bree knew it was part of her salary for working at the lodge.

She didn't want to go inside yet, so she got out, the chill in the mountain air sinking right into her lungs. She'd brought a light jacket with her, because she'd anticipated being with Wes until long after dark and needing it for the drive home.

She put the jacket on and zipped it up, a fresh wave of emotion threatening to overcome her. The urge to drive back down the canyon to Wes's house made her question every step she took toward the stables, the lights from the lodge shining the darkness too.

She went in the side door, the scent of horses, straw, and dust meeting her nose. She loved the outdoorsy smell, and she took a deep breath of it, the soft sound of a horse snuffling bringing new comfort to her.

"Hey, CC," she said to Cookie Crumble, and the black-and-white horse lifted her head over the door of the stall. Bree ran her hands up the sides of the horse's face and smiled at the beast.

"I really messed up," she whispered. "I just don't know how to tell him." She leaned her forehead against the horse's face, about halfway down from her eyes. CC had very long eyelashes, and Lionel must've given her a bath recently, because she smelled like the lavender animal soap they used in the wash shed.

"If he knows, he'll never look at me the same," Bree added. She couldn't stomach the thought of anyone knowing about Bronson and the true reason he'd died.

She often wondered what her life would be like if everyone knew. Would they hate her as much as she hated herself?

She believed they would, so she'd always put the brakes on any conversation, any question, from anyone, about her family.

Tears filled her eyes, and she let them fall. She didn't like imagining what people would think of her if they knew, because it felt like a hot knife slicing through the fleshy parts of her heart.

Several minutes later, her tears dried up again, and Bree pulled in breath after breath until it stopped hitching in the back of her throat. "Thanks, CC," she said to the horse. "You're such a great listener."

She backed away from the horse, and added, "I'll be back tomorrow afternoon, okay? Don't go telling anyone I was here, or about the crying." She smiled at her own joke, though it wasn't very funny, and left the stable.

* * *

The next day, Bree immersed herself in her work. Sometimes she and Willie didn't have long, in-depth conversations, so nothing seemed out of the ordinary. Willie didn't ask any questions, and Bree waved as she left the employment office.

Her stomach swooped to the right and then the left the whole drive back to the lodge. She didn't keep track of Wes's schedule, because he normally told her what he was doing when they made plans for the day.

She pulled into the carport and sat in the car, wondering if she'd ever just be able to get out and go inside somewhere without bracing herself for who she might see. She wondered how long it would take for the news of her and Wes to spread through the lodge, and down the canyon to Colton.

She gasped, her breath automatically hitching at the thought of Colton Hammond. She'd enjoyed his friendship, and now everything would be different.

Bree felt like she'd lost everything, all of it floating away like ashes on the wind though she tried to grab at whatever pieces she could find.

She eventually did go inside the cabin to eat a quick lunch and change her clothes. She had work to do in the stables, and that would keep her away from Wes. In fact, most of what Bree did around the lodge didn't involve her going anywhere near the podium at the front of the building. She'd only gone there to find him.

In the stables, she found that her crew had cleaned out the

required stalls that morning, and Lionel, her right-hand man, had everyone polishing the tack for that afternoon's ride.

"Hey," she said to him, and her voice sounded normal to her own ears.

Lionel didn't look at her like she'd spent more of the last twelve hours crying than she should've, nor like she'd only slept for a few hours. "Hey, Bree. Listen, we're almost out of self-adhesive bandages, and Double Mint will *not* stop chewing his off."

"I'll take care of it," Bree said. She looked around at the few guys getting the work done. In the summertime, she hired a lot of teenagers, and they'd all gone back to school. A couple still came up to the lodge in the afternoons to help with horseback riding, but their activities were less, so she didn't need as many people.

"What about the hay loft?" she asked. "Did you guys check that?"

"It's next on the list," Lionel said. "Patsy said someone complained about the condition of the saddles yesterday after the ride, so I thought we'd inspect it all today. Make sure there are no problems."

"They complained?"

"Yep." He shook his head. "We've found one pair of stirrups that should've been thrown away, but nothing else." He too surveyed the few men working through the equipment. "I'll let you know if we need to replace anything."

"Thanks," Bree said. She moved away from the tack room, noting that the fans above the stalls were slowly rotating. In the summer, they used the fans a lot, but now that the weather had started to cool, they wouldn't. It was quite warm today, and Bree started to sweat.

She didn't know how to act or be normal when she felt so out of sorts. Had Lionel noticed anything off about her? What would he do even if he did?

"I hear you've been being bad," she said to Double Mint. The big bay horse just looked at her with those almost black eyes. "You've got to leave the bandages alone."

Bree opened the door and looked down at his front legs. The hair there had been scraped away too, and the skin was bright pink. "Bud." She sighed and looped a rope around his neck. "You've got arthritis, okay? I know you used to be this amazing lead horse, who led all the winners out onto the track. But this is your life now."

She reached up and stroked her hand down the side of his face. "You can't get rid of the pain by scratching your teeth over your ankles. Come on." She led him out of his stall and down the aisle.

Outside, she tethered him to a post and went to get the first aid supplies. Sometimes, she'd talk to the horse and tell him what she was doing, but Double Mint had been through the bandaging process many times.

So had Bree, and she wished she could take the pain from his joints. He'd had a good career in Lexington, and he had worked at some of the premier training stables, where the thoroughbreds came through, race winners, Triple Crown horses that had been bought for half a million dollars.

"All right," she said to him once she finished. "Now, I put

that chili oil on there, so you're not going to want to taste that." The oil made it look like he was bleeding through his bandages, but he wasn't. Hopefully, it would stop him from taking them off and give his legs a chance to heal.

"Come on." She took him back into the stable, where she heard a man's voice she didn't recognize. She stilled instantly, panic welling in her stomach.

Wes had come looking for her.

What was she going to say? Would he press her to talk about her family again?

She looked around, trying to decide where to hide. She had the wild idea to simply leap onto Double Mint's back and set him into a gallop to get as far from here as possible.

Boots sounded against concrete, and Bree was still frozen.

"There you are," Beau said as he came around the corner. "Listen, the boys and I want to go horseback riding, but Lionel says we have to run everything through you to make sure we have enough horses for guests."

"Yes," Bree said, the word exploding from her mouth. "Let me put Mint away, and we can look at the calendar in the office." She gave him a smile, and when she took a step, she felt sure her leg would snap right in half.

He wasn't Wes, but her adrenaline was still sky-high, and Bree hated it.

She hated herself—and now she had two reasons and no way to ever stop.

She worked things out with Beau, and he said, "Thanks, Bree. You're amazing," before he turned to leave.

"Beau," she practically shouted after him.

He turned back to her, his eyebrows up. "Yeah?"

She knew this man; she'd known him for years. She'd worked at the lodge for eight long years, a couple of them while he'd lived there personally.

Her hands wrung around each other, and he noticed. "What's wrong?" He was the first one to notice Bree's complete unrest, and her eyes filled with tears.

"What if...I don't know," she said. "What if something goes wrong?"

"Wrong with what?" He took a step closer to her.

"Everything," she whispered.

Beau seemed to know what she was really asking, because he said, "Well, when I feel like everything is going wrong, I know I need to get down on my knees and figure it out."

Bree liked that answer, but she also hated it. She nodded anyway, the nervousness in her heart only serving to send zips through her bloodstream.

"Sometimes, if that doesn't work that well, I call my mother." He smiled and ducked his head. "She usually knows what to do. Never steers me wrong, at least."

Bree pulled in a breath and held it tightly in her lungs. Call her mother.

"Anyway," Beau said. "Let me know if I can help with anything, Bree." He held her gaze until she gave him a single nod, and then he left the office.

She couldn't call her mother. She released the breath, and that caused her to sag into the chair behind the desk.

She'd surrounded herself with friends to help in situations like these, and what she really wanted to do was call Elise and

Colton, buy a lot of ice cream, and have a night where the three of them got together to figure out what she should do.

But she knew she wouldn't do that either. All that was left was to put her head down on the desk, and cry. So Bree did that.

Chapter Twenty-Two

Cy Hammond inhaled the scent of concrete and grease as he finished replacing the carburetor on the motorcycle that had come in yesterday. It belonged to Curtis Hill, who'd served for sixteen years in the Air Force. He'd retired last year to California, and Cy had built him a motorcycle with the American flag painted on the gas tank and his plane's name stitched into the seat.

Cy loved everything about motorcycles. He didn't normally spend a ton of time in the shop these days, but he needed a distraction that cruising the coastal highway just couldn't provide anymore.

Mikaela had broken up with him a couple of months ago, and Cy was just now starting to wake up in the morning without her on his mind. He'd been planning to take her home to Ivory Peaks and introduce her to his parents, Grams, and all his brothers.

He'd loved her, plain and simple.

He'd been lost the day she'd sat on his front steps, holding his hand, and told him that she didn't think they would make it. He'd wanted to ask why. He'd wanted to argue with her. He'd wanted to lay out his case for why they would absolutely make it.

He'd said nothing, because Cy wasn't especially gifted with words and explanations. He was good with his hands, and he understood machines, which didn't speak English.

"Cy," Wade called from the doorway, and Cy lifted his head from under the motorcycle.

"Yeah?"

"Your brother's on the phone."

Cy felt his pockets for his cell, but he couldn't find it. Maybe he'd left it on the front counter, as he'd done many times. Or in the shop office, where Wade worked to keep the orders flowing, the accounts balanced, the details just right.

"All right," Cy said, reaching for a roll of paper towels. He tore off a couple and wiped his hands as he walked through the shop toward the door. His cowboy boots made odd slapping sounds against the concrete, but he absolutely loved them. They made him stand out, and Cy—as the youngest brother in a family of absolute winners—needed to stand out.

Not stick out. *Stand* out.

The longer hair helped him achieve that. The leather clothes he'd managed to find. The cowboy boots and hat he wore while riding his custom-built motorcycle. Cy turned heads, and he liked it. He'd never had a hard time catching the eye of a pretty woman, though he wasn't always interested in those looking.

In the past eight months, he hadn't noticed anyone but Mikaela.

"Thanks," he said to Wade, the burly, tattooed man who ran Cy's shop office.

"Yep." Wade handed him the phone Cy had been looking for a moment ago.

Cy looked at the screen to see which brother was calling. "Hey, Wes," he said. He loved all of his brothers, but Wes was the biggest enigma. The mighty older brother. The powerful CEO. The man who always knew exactly what to do.

"Hey," said Wes, and though not everything could be conveyed over the phone, Cy definitely heard some measure of unhappiness.

"What's up?" Cy asked when Wes didn't say anything else.

"Wondering what's going on with you," Wes said. "I'm thinking I'll be in California in, oh, I don't know." He sighed so heavily that alarms started sounding in Cy's head. "Three weeks or so. Maybe a month."

"You're coming to California?"

"Yeah, well, I've never been, so...." Wes let his words hang there, and Cy knew instantly that something was very wrong.

"I don't really know my schedule a month in advance," Cy said. "You tell me when you're coming, and I'll make sure I'm available." He did love spending time with his brothers. He was instantly transported back two or three decades to when they'd play basketball in the front driveway or all stomp out to the farm to do the chores when their father was in a bad mood.

He'd never longed for a friend, especially because Ames was only five minutes older than him.

"Maybe I'll be there for my birthday," Wes said. "Could we get a cake?"

"What's really going on?" Cy asked, walking away from the desk toward the front wall of windows. He had a whole showroom full of motorcycles, with two salesmen who both happened to be with customers.

He didn't want anyone to overhear this conversation, even if it was only his side.

"I'm just going to finish my state tour," Wes said airily. "And I thought we could spend some time together in California. Then it occurred to me that I'm not one-hundred percent sure where your shop is."

Cy pushed out the front door and into the sunshine. Even September in Southern California was beautiful, and Cy drew in a breath of the warm air, knowing it wouldn't be like this in the Mile High State. The air would be crisp and the leaves changing. Mom would be making peach jam and storing it for the winter, along with her famous Concord grape juice.

A fierce sense of homesickness filled Cy, and he forced himself to focus on what Wes had said. "I'm in Solana Beach."

"That's right," Wes said. "I'm sure I can find you now that I know the name of the town."

"Great beach," Cy said. "Great coffee shops. Great place for running."

"Oh, well, that's Gray's arena," Wes said. "I still haven't taken up the running."

"Gray will never leave Colorado," Cy said, taking a seat on the low wall around the fountain in front of the shop.

"He might," Wes said. "Things change, you know?"

"What do you know that I don't?"

"Nothing," Wes said, his voice a bit higher now. "I'm just saying sometimes what we think is going to happen, doesn't actually happen."

Cy's thoughts flowed to Mikaela. "Yeah, I understand that."

"Maybe I could meet your girlfriend," Wes said. "You never did set a date for us to get together in Ivory Peaks."

"Yeah." Cy sighed. "Listen, uh, we broke up."

Wes exhaled heavily, the end of it sounding like a hiss. "No."

"Yes."

"You liked her so much. You haven't brought anyone home since Abbie."

And she'd become Cy's wife. True, that marriage had only lasted ten months, but Cy had loved her. He didn't bring women home willy nilly, and he kept his relationships out of the family spotlight for a long time after they'd started.

"Did you end it?" Wes asked.

Cy didn't want to have this conversation, so he asked, "What do you think?"

"I'm sorry, Cy," Wes said. "I feel this on a deep, personal level."

"Did Bree break up with you?" Cy asked.

"Not yet," he said. "She...I can't even say it out loud. I'm thinking of leaving town for a bit. I just need some space."

"*You* need some space?"

"She doesn't trust me," Wes said. "I think she'd be happier if I left town, and I just want her to be happy."

Cy pulled in a breath and stood up, realizations streaming through him. "You fell in love with her."

"Yeah," Wes said miserably, not even bothering to deny it. "And it's been a few days since we had this horrible, horrible conversation, and I just think it's time for me to move on."

"I'm so sorry," Cy said, feeling more connected to Wes than he had in years.

"I am too," Wes said. "I'm going to be *forty-eight*, Cy. Don't be like me, okay? Find someone as soon as you can and make them yours."

Cy wished finding someone was only so easy. "I tried that once," Cy said. "I'm a little more cautious now. Maybe that's what's going on with Bree?"

"I don't know what's going on with Bree," Wes said. "I'll let you know when I'm getting close to Solana Beach."

"Okay," Cy said. "And Wes, call me, okay? I worry about you out there by yourself."

"Thanks, Cy," Wes said, and the call ended.

Cy stuck his phone in his back pocket and stared out across the parking lot. Beyond that, a row of shops blocked his view of the ocean. With just a hundred-yard walk, he could have his toes in the sand and an unobstructed view of the waves.

"What do we do?" he asked the empty sky in front of him. "Dear Lord, what do we do? Wes really loved Bree. Why couldn't that work out for him?" There was no one better than Wes, and Cy wanted nothing more than for him to be happy. "Please help him be happy," he added. "Bless him to be safe."

"Boss," someone said behind him, and Cy turned. He didn't care if someone overheard him praying. It wouldn't be the first time, that was for sure.

"Yep." He faced McCall, one of his best mechanics.

"Boston Bill is here, and you said you wanted to go over his bike with him."

A bit of joy blipped through Cy's bloodstream. "Yes," he said. "I do." He loved going through a custom bike with a veteran or someone who'd served his fellow beings in some way. Boston Bill had been in the police department for twenty-seven years before he'd been injured in the line of duty.

This bike was Cy's monthly donation to an individual or family who deserved recognition, and he definitely wanted to go over the bike with Boston Bill. As he did, he managed to get a few minutes of relief from his worries about Wes and his misery over Mikaela.

Chapter Twenty-Three

Wes moved his laundry from the washing machine to the dryer and returned to his bedroom to look at the bag he'd started to pack. He stared down into the bag, wondering if he could call Gray next.

Talking to Cy hadn't been terrible, but Cy didn't know Wes as well as Gray and Colton. If he spoke to either of them, they'd know something was off in the first five seconds. It had taken Cy at least five minutes to ask about Bree.

But Wes didn't want to deal with anything in Coral Canyon once he left. When he'd left Denver in February, he'd turned his bills and utilities over to Gray, who paid them every month from one of Wes's accounts that Gray managed.

He could do the same for the mortgage and bills in Coral Canyon—couldn't he?

"Only if you make the call," he muttered to himself, wondering if he really wanted to continue his quest to visit every state in the country. Living out of a bag wasn't exactly an amazing experience, especially now that he'd been stationary for a few months.

He sank onto the bed and ran his hands through his hair. He felt more stressed about this decision than any he'd ever made behind the desk at HMC.

"Why couldn't—?" He cut off the question, because he'd learned long ago not to delve into "Why me?" types of questions. But he really wanted to know how he'd fallen in love with a woman who didn't love him back. He wanted the Lord to tell him that everything would be okay. That the next person to ring his doorbell would be Bree, and she'd tell him how sorry she was, and that of course she loved him too.

No one rang the doorbell, just like the only people who'd been texting or calling him shared his last name.

Wes didn't even know how to classify his feelings, because he'd literally never been this upset before. Unhappy didn't seem strong enough, and misery didn't go deep enough. The closest thing he'd been able to come up with as he knelt beside his bed last night, begging God for a release, was heartbroken.

And he'd gotten no release.

He knew he wouldn't get one in Coral Canyon. Not while he worked at the same lodge as Bree and could run into her at any moment. He hadn't signed a contract with Graham, and he could leave any time. The right thing to do would be to give two weeks' notice and then leave town. But Wes wasn't sure he could even make it through another hour in the same town as Bree. Looking at the same mountains. Talking to all the same people she did.

"You have to go," he told himself, and he reached for his

phone again. He wasn't sure if he was going to call Colton or Gray until he started tapping and swiping. Gray's name came up, and the call started ringing.

"Uncle Wes," Hunter answered, and Wes felt a smile move across his face. He was glad he could still smile, and he started to relax.

"Hunter," he said. "What's goin' on?"

"My dad left his phone in the truck," he said. "He just ran in to get the Chinese food."

"I didn't think your dad was ever detached from his phone." Wes chuckled, and that felt good too.

"He's usually not," Hunter said. "He's just been on the phone all day, and it's almost dead."

So Gray wouldn't want to talk. "Rough day for him?" He rarely ordered food either, and both of those were giveaways for Wes.

"Yeah, I guess there's some problem at work. He didn't say much about it. He never does."

"That's true," Wes said, though Gray would unload on him. He just didn't want Hunter to ever know that sometimes Gray's life was hard. "Well, tell him I called, but it's nothing big. So if he doesn't want to call until later, that's fine."

"All right," Hunter said, his western drawl more pronounced than Wes had ever heard it. He'd spent the entire summer on the farm, and Wes could just see his nephew as the littlest Hammond cowboy. The thought brought a beam of joy to his life, and it was moments like these that allowed his shattered heart to keep beating for another day.

* * *

A week later, Wes had carried his last bag up the stairs to the second level at the lodge. He'd had the hard conversation with Graham, and the man had been nothing but kind and amazing. He'd asked if he could still call him and they could continue their business consulting, and Wes had agreed to that.

He'd made the embarrassing phone call to Gray, and then Colton. Only one of them had the power to show up on the front porch with four boxes of pizza and Wes's favorite soda—root beer—and Colton had done just that.

Surprisingly, Wes hadn't had to defend himself. Colton had told him once not to hurt Bree, and Wes had expected his brother to question him mercilessly about what had happened and why Wes was leaving town and the whole nine yards.

Instead, he'd plunked down on the couch, sans plate, and ate his way through a pizza while they watched *King Kong*.

Colt had hardly said a word, and when he'd finally gotten up to leave, he'd clasped Wes in a hug and said, "I wish you didn't have to go."

But he did have to go. Wes was dying here, a little more each day. He hadn't spoken to Bree in ten days, but he didn't want to leave town without at least talking to her. He wasn't sure why. Maybe he needed to be filleted alive again. Maybe he just wanted to make sure things between them were completely over.

No matter what, his conscious wouldn't allow him to just

load up and drive away, Coral Canyon and Bree Richards in his rear-view mirror.

He knew she didn't work at the employment office on Saturdays, so his only choice was to drive up the canyon one more time and face her at the lodge. Or rather, her cabin. To him, though, they were the same thing.

The drive passed quickly, and Wes found the turn-off easily. He kneaded the steering wheel as he inched along the road, and eventually a cabin appeared in front of him. Bree's sedan sat there, and Wes remembered the first time he'd seen that car in the parking lot outside the employment office.

He parked behind her, noting there wasn't another car in the driveway. Maybe he'd get to talk to Bree alone. And dang it, his stupid romantic heart actually thought he'd get to kiss her good-bye.

Gathering his every last nerve and every ounce of bravery he possessed, he got out of the truck and headed for the front porch. There was no doorbell, which Wes thought fit the mountain landscape perfectly.

There were so many trails he and Bree hadn't explored yet, and he doubted his decision to leave. Would she see him as a coward? Someone who ran away when things got hard? Wes didn't want to be that person. He wanted to fight for the relationship he'd wanted for nine months now.

He took a step back, but Bree opened the door in that moment, and Wes froze.

"Oh." Bree's hand fluttered up to her neck, and she rubbed along her jaw.

Wes's heart pounded in his chest. Violently. "Hey, Bree."

His voice creaked, almost a growl in his throat. He cleared it away, determined to be strong in a situation that made him feel weak. "I came to let you know that I'm leaving Wyoming. I have ten states still to see, and I think we'd both be happier if we didn't have to tiptoe around each other."

Bree started nodding about halfway through, her beautiful eyes filling with tears.

"I'm so sorry," Wes said, his own emotions conspiring against him. He employed his training as CEO and shoved them down, down, down, so they wouldn't show in his face or his voice. "I didn't mean to hurt you."

"Wes." She shook her head, her tears falling onto her cheeks, where she wiped them away.

"I'll miss you," he said. "I didn't want to be another man in your past that you reflect on and feel badly about yourself." He stuck his hands in his pockets and rocked back on his heels. "So please don't do that, okay?"

"Nothing about this is your fault," Bree said.

Didn't feel like it to Wes, so he shrugged. "I want to leave the door open. If you feel like we might be able to have a future together, all you have to do is text me. You don't even have to call. I know calling is hard sometimes." He took a deep breath. "I love you, Bree. Honestly, I do. If you feel any inkling at all that you'd like to see me again, please let me know."

She openly cried in front of him now, and Wes couldn't stand it. He couldn't look at her and know he was the cause of those tears. "I'm sorry," he said one final time before he turned and walked back to his truck, Bree as silent as ever.

Wes hated the silence in that moment, and as soon as he

reached the asphalt, he turned on the radio as loud as he could. Anything to get his thoughts to quiet, to dull them into something he couldn't think about for too long.

His phone rang, which was connected to the Bluetooth in the truck. The ringtone wailed in the truck, nearly deafening Wes. He jabbed at the radio screen to get the call connected, and he immediately turned down the volume before he said, "Hey," to Colt.

"You'll come back for Christmas, right?" his brother asked.

"Not to the lodge," Wes said. Unless Bree texted him. Then anything was possible. He loathed himself for the hope that still existed inside him, but his mother had taught him that if he had hope, he could do anything. He could endure anything. But sometimes hope hurt. It created unrealistic situations where his fantasies had room to grow. And fantasies were definitely dangerous.

"To our place," Colton said. "We'll have a big thing at my house. I've already invited Gray and Mom and Dad. He said he's going to talk to them and see if they'll make the drive."

"There's no way Grams will make that drive," Wes said.

"Maybe she'd fly."

"She can't even get out of bed by herself," Wes said. "If you want to do a Christmas thing, why don't we go back to Ivory Peaks? Last year was really fun. Christmas and New Year's at the farm."

Wes knew the hesitation on Colton's end of the line had everything to do with his wife, as it should. Annie was a Coral Canyon native; her parents lived nearby; her two daughters lived in town. Her friends gathered at the lodge for the holidays every year, and if Colton wanted to come to Ivory Peaks, that would mean they couldn't go to the lodge.

"Talk to Annie," Wes said. "I don't think you'll get Grams and Mom and Dad to Coral Canyon."

"I'll talk to them," Colton said. "You just focus on your bucket list."

Wes scoffed. "I don't really care about the bucket list. I should've put *get married and have kids* on my bucket list." He sighed miserably, hearing the ticking of a clock in the back of his mind.

His birthday was in three weeks, and the dreams he'd started to have where he and Bree had another romantic adventure together as he turned another year closer to fifty now tormented him.

"Wes, she's going to come around."

"Colt," Wes said, suddenly beyond annoyed. "I know you're really good friends with her. Really, I do. But you didn't see her. You haven't gotten to know her the same way I have. She's not going to tell me about her family. Period. And that's fine for you and her, because you don't have to have unconditional trust with Bree."

"Wes—"

"No," Wes said, almost shouting, though he was also already regretting his raised voice. He drew in a big breath. "Think for a minute if you found out Annie had been keeping a secret from you. A great, big secret that could and would change everything between you. And the reason she didn't tell you was because she doesn't trust you. So now you've got a wife who *doesn't trust you*. Now what, Colt?"

"I don't know, Wes," Colton said very quietly.

"Exactly," Wes said. "You don't know. So please don't tell me she's going to come around." Wes could see the last evening he'd been with Bree; he heard himself tell her he was in love with her; felt how great it had been to say it. To finally tell her.

He heard himself tell her she could trust him, and he'd watched her refuse to do that. Absolutely, positively refuse.

When he'd sat there, at that candlelit table for two—by himself—totally in love with Bree and honestly willing to do anything to be with her, Wes had found something he couldn't live with.

He would not pledge himself to a woman who couldn't be completely honest with him.

The hours passed as the miles rolled beneath his tires. He left Wyoming and entered Idaho, pulling over at a gas station to fill up on the other side of the Tetons. Coeur d'Alene looked beautiful, with rivers and lakes and plenty of places to stay. He found a five-star hotel where he could get room service, any channel on the television he wanted, a spa, and a door hanger that would keep everyone away.

He booked five nights, figuring he could find something fun and rejuvenating to do in the mountains and lakes in the area.

"Nine states to go," he said to himself, because there was no one else to talk to.

Chapter Twenty-Four

Bree paced in her cabin, feeling like a caged tiger. Wes had left hours ago, and Bree had called Lionel to get him to run the riding groups that day. She'd normally never do that, because she already felt guilty for being gone in the mornings during the week.

But Lionel had done a great job this summer, and he could handle the late September crowd at the lodge that weekend.

Bree was tired of dealing with people. No, that wasn't right. She was tired of dealing with herself.

The darkness inside her crept up and out of the box where she normally kept it. It had been doing that for days and days now, since her birthday. She didn't need to go down the hall to her bedroom and look in her top dresser drawer at the birthday card she'd put with the others.

She could still see her mother's handwriting, and Bree's chest collapsed as she thought about going another day without speaking to her mom.

"Do I have to do this?" she asked, her voice high-pitched and squeaky. And for maybe the first time since Bronson's death, Bree felt an overwhelming sense that yes, she needed to do this. In fact, she should've dealt with all of these issues and feelings a long time ago.

She craved peace, and she knew she'd only get it one way. Still, hours passed before Bree finally took her phone into her bedroom, closed and locked the door, and navigated to the contact that said Mom.

She stared at it for a long, long time, finally tapping to open a call. She held the phone to her ear, her hand shaking and her stomach rioting against her, though she hadn't eaten anything that day.

The line clicked, and then her mother asked, "Bree?"

Bree started crying—again—and she couldn't get any words out. Her throat felt so tight, and her regret so deep. She was drowning, and she sucked at the air, trying to find a way to breathe with the beautiful echo of her mom's voice in her head.

She hadn't heard that voice for so long, and it seemed to be able to heal so much.

"Bree, baby," her mom said, her voice pinched too. "Are you there?"

Bree nodded, though her mom couldn't see her. How could she speak without giving away how she felt? She couldn't, and she realized she didn't need to hide how she was feeling. "Mom."

Just saying that word broke something inside her, and she

started a mental prayer. *I'm sorry, Lord. I'm so sorry. How do I fix this? What do I do?*

It seemed like the years of silence from the Lord had come to an end, and her mind raced now with things she should say. Things she needed to do.

"I'm sorry, Mom," Bree said. "I'm so sorry for everything. I need to come home." She didn't even know where the words had come from. She hadn't ever seriously considered returning to Vermont. Ever. She'd left and never looked back, and now that she'd witnessed someone doing that to her, she knew how deeply that action cut. How badly it stung.

"You can come anytime," her mom said, obviously weeping. "Anytime, Bree."

"I have two jobs," Bree said. "Because I make so many mistakes, and I'm so tired, Mom, and I can't pay for a ticket to get there." Her emotions surged, and she let the hot tears burn in her eyes until they fell. She sniffled and sobbed, everything in her life crashing down around her.

"We'll pay for it," her mom said. "Tell us when, Bree."

She pulled back on her fear, her sorrow, her guilt. "I need to talk to my bosses. Can I call you after I do that?"

"Of course, yes."

Bree knew she didn't deserve her parents' forgiveness, and she'd never truly felt like she deserved to be forgiven by God either. She'd accepted that. It would be hard—beyond hard—to walk into the house where she and Bronson had grown up, face her parents, and admit her failures.

But Bree also knew she couldn't take another step forward

in her life until she did all of those things. She'd reached a point where she could go no further until she dealt with her past. And she desperately wanted to take the next step with Wes, and she couldn't.

"Okay, I'll call you as soon as I know. It might be Monday, because I work in an office, and I don't want to bother my boss on the weekend."

"Bree, are you okay?"

"Physically," Bree said. "But Mom, I met a man, and he's just—wonderful." She blew out her breath. "And perfect, and I haven't been able to tell him about anything that happened in Vermont, and I lost him." Her tears started trickling down her face again. She wiped them again and pressed on her sinuses, everything in her head feeling so dang hot.

"And I miss you and Dad so much," Bree said. "I hate being alone, and only having myself to rely on. I need you. I love you."

"We love you too, Bree. Please come home as soon as you can."

"Is Dad there?"

"He's out with a new horse," her mom said, her voice growing in strength. "He'll be thrilled you called. You want me to go get him?"

"No, Mom, it's okay." Bree knew how her father acted when he got a new horse.

"He'll come in, Bree. He misses you so much." Her voice broke again, and Bree could not shoulder the fact that she'd hurt her parents for so long.

"Okay," Bree said. "Maybe you could go get him and call me back. Or I'll call back in fifteen minutes or something."

"I'll go get him and call you back."

After ending the call, Bree sat on the edge of her bed and cried. She'd done so much of that in the past ten days, she hardly had anything left to give. At the same time, she hadn't truly been this humbled in all the time since she'd left Vermont, and she'd needed to hit the very bottom of her life before she'd feel like she'd have to make that phone call.

"Did You put Wes in my life to send me as far down as I could go?" she asked, lifting her eyes to the ceiling. She imagined she could see through the plaster and roofing tiles to the sky above, then all the way to the heavens. "Well, it worked if You did."

She shook her head, feeling God's powerful presence in her life so strongly. She wasn't living with numbness anymore. She could feel everything, and it was raw, and painful, and never-ending.

Her phone rang, and Bree flinched at the shrill sound. Then she picked it up and said, "Mom. Dad?"

"I'm right here, honey," her father said, his voice so deep and so warm, and exactly the thing that could heal everything that had broken inside Bree all those years ago.

"Get me a ticket for Monday morning," she said, deciding on the spot. "If you can."

"Did you talk to your bosses already?" Mom asked.

"No," Bree said. "But this is a family emergency, and they'll have to understand."

"I love you, honey," her dad said. "I'll forward everything to your email. It's the same one you've had for a while now, right?"

"Yes," Bree said. "Thank you, Dad. I'm so sorry. But thank you."

"You don't need to apologize," her father said.

But she did, because he'd sent her emails over the years that Bree had never responded to. She'd done so much wrong, and it felt impossible to set it all right. But she sure was going to try, because she needed her soul to be cleansed. She wanted to feel closer to God. She needed her parents in her life.

And then, maybe if she could fix all that was wrong within her, she could fix her relationship with Wes.

* * *

"Thanks, Elise." Bree sat in Elise's compact SUV for a moment before reaching for the door handle. It had been a whirlwind past couple of days, while she washed everything she owned, called Marc and Graham multiple times, got email confirmations of her plane tickets, and talked to her parents a few more times too.

"Sure thing," Elise said. Only she wouldn't be annoyed by having to drive Bree an hour to the airport in Jackson first thing in the morning on a Monday. She wore a smile on her perfectly pink lips, a feat Bree knew she achieved from a particular lip gloss that never ran out.

"Good luck, Bree." She got out of the vehicle too and

came around the back to help Bree with her bag. She took Bree into a hug and held her tight. "This is a good thing, Bree."

"I'm so scared."

"I know you are." Elise clung to her. "I am too, because I don't like sleeping in the cabin by myself."

Bree half-laughed and half-sobbed. She stepped back from her best friend and wiped her eyes. She didn't want to go into the airport a weeping mess. "Colton already said you could go stay with him and Annie. She drives up to the lodge every day too."

"I know," Elise said, glancing toward a truck that pulled up to the curb behind her. "I'm just trying to decide if I should go or not."

"Why wouldn't you?"

"Oh, he asks me about Gray all the time." Elise sighed and put a smile on her face that almost looked real. Bree knew exactly how that felt, because she'd been doing it for far too long.

"Well, one piece of advice: don't let him set you up with his brother," Bree said. "You'll fall for him, and then who knows what will happen." She smiled at Elise, who just shook her head as she chuckled.

Bree hugged her again and then drew in a breath. She faced the airport and walked inside, her mind racing as fast as her nerves. But she could do this. She *had* to do this.

It was time to do this.

Hours later, she walked off the plane, her carryon rolling along behind her. She'd checked a bag too, and the airport in Montpelier wasn't that big. It seemed like she'd walked down one hall and then a short flight of steps, and she was past security and into the baggage claim area already.

"Bree," her father said, and Bree hadn't even seen him. She turned to the left, her heart bobbing against the back of her tongue.

"Dad?"

He stepped out from behind another couple waiting for their loved one, and Bree dropped everything in her hands. She didn't care who saw her crying now, and she barely had time to open her arms to embrace her father before he swept her into his strong arms and crushed her to his chest.

"Oh, my Bree," he said, and Bree had never felt so loved. The hug didn't last nearly long enough, and then her father said, "Mom's here. She's right here, Julie."

Her mother stepped between them and hugged Bree with everything she had too, and Bree wondered why in the world she'd stayed away for so long. Her parents clearly didn't hate her. They didn't blame her. They'd told her all of that for so long, and she hadn't believed them.

Because she hated herself. She blamed herself.

"I'm sorry," she whispered over and over, hoping they could feel how much she loved them too. But Wes had taught her something—she needed to tell the people she loved that she did indeed love them.

"I love you, Mom," she said, the words barely making it out of her mouth.

Her mom stepped back and cradled Bree's face in both hands. She cried openly too and said, "I love you, too, dear."

"I love you, Dad," Bree said, and the three of them formed

a huddle-hug, with Bree's head between both of theirs. They breathed together, right there in the airport, as if no one else was around.

Bree couldn't adequately describe how she felt, only that she knew without any doubt that she'd done the right thing by calling her mom and coming home. Not only could she feel their love, which she desperately needed, she basked in the glow and warmth of the love of the Lord too.

"Ma'am?" someone asked, and Bree turned toward the airport worker. "Is this your bag?"

"Yes." Bree wiped her eyes and stepped away from her parents. "Sorry." She picked up her purse and took the water bottle from the woman in uniform. She reached for the handle of her carryon and gave her a smile. "Sorry."

"It's fine." She glanced at Bree's parents. "Welcome to Vermont."

A new kind of excitement entered Bree's awareness, and she allowed a smile to cross her face. She turned back to her parents, a fierce love for them and how they'd stood by one another all these years moving through her.

"What did you make for dessert?" Bree asked her mother. She may not have spoken to her much in the past, but she knew some things about her mother would never die. And that included her dedication to having a delectable dessert at the conclusion of every evening meal.

"Apple pie," she said without missing a beat. "Our trees produced beautifully this year."

"With maple cream?" Bree asked, her mouth already watering.

Bree's mother put her arm around Bree's waist as they fell into step. "You may have been gone awhile, Bree, but you still know how to eat apple pie."

Bree grinned and looked toward the bright sunshine streaming through the glass doors in front of her. She finally felt like the future held something amazing and wonderful and shiny in it...for her.

Chapter Twenty-Five

"And now I'm here." Wes pressed the power button on the side of his phone, and the television in front of him, Hunter, and Gray went black. He'd just finished an hour-long travelogue of where he'd been for the past six weeks, and he could admit he had some impressive pictures.

He even looked happy in some of them, especially the ones with him and the massive fish he'd caught during his deep-sea fishing expedition off the Alaskan coast. He'd loved Alaska with every fiber of his being.

It wasn't hugely populated, for one. He enjoyed the small-town feel of the communities there, though he could do with more than a few hours of light—and he hadn't even been there during the height of winter.

"What was your favorite thing?" Gray asked.

"Oh, it's impossible to pick," Wes said. "Mount Saint Helens was really fun. The lakes in Idaho were beautiful. I even liked the cruise ship up to Alaska."

"And that's saying something for a man who washes his hands if he's anywhere near other people." Gray grinned at him, and Wes had healed enough to smile back, though his brother was poking fun at him.

"I even ate at the buffets."

"Hoh-boy," Gray said, chortling. "I barely know who you are anymore."

Wes didn't know who he was anymore either. Somewhere between Wyoming, Idaho, Oregon, Washington, Alaska, California, Nevada, Utah, Arizona, and New Mexico, he'd lost himself.

He knew exactly where he'd left the best version of himself. The man he wanted to be, with the life that man wanted to live.

The shadow or ghost or spirit of that man stood on Bree's porch, desperate for her to apologize and then tell him everything she'd refused to tell him before.

But she hadn't done that, and while Wes's world had shattered that day, he'd been picking up one piece every day and fitting it back inside himself. Some of the edges were really sharp though, and sometimes he had to take pieces out. Examine them. And find a new spot for them.

The whole ordeal had left him weak in a lot of ways, and Wes hated feeling weak.

"Uncle Wes?" Hunter asked, and Wes blinked back to the living room in Gray's comfortable house. He didn't live downtown in an apartment or penthouse the way Wes and Colton had, but out in a suburb, with other families and a good elementary school for his son.

He did live back in the corner of a subdivision, with a broad, long driveway back to his house that looked a lot smaller than it actually was. His backyard encompassed the whole corner, and he had a dozen fruit trees he cultivated in his spare time.

As if Gray had any of that.

But he did love the trees, and Wes had gone with him through the yard as he explained how he'd gotten them ready for winter.

"Yeah, bud," Wes asked his nephew.

"Are you gonna come to Coral Canyon for Christmas with us?"

Wes's eyebrows shot up, and he looked from Hunter to Gray. "You're going to Coral Canyon?"

"Colton can be very convincing," Gray said. "And I'm determined to be finished at HMC before the holidays."

Wes was dying to know how Gray felt about having only a few weeks left at the job he'd held for twenty years, but he wouldn't ask in front of Hunter. Gray wouldn't answer if he did.

"Grams is going?"

"Grams is going to stay with Uncle Roger."

"Holy cow," Wes said, deeply surprised. "And Laura and Jill and Kent?"

"I don't know all the details," Gray said coolly. "What I know is Mom called me last week and asked if I could stand driving with her and Dad to Wyoming, because they didn't want to drive themselves. I said yes. Then I called Colton to find out what the devil was going on."

"Oh, this has Colton written all over it," Wes said darkly.

"He didn't even tell you yet."

"That's because he thinks I'm still on the road." Wes looked away, up to the mantel where Gray had a picture of him and Hunter. They looked infused with joy, their smiles wide and their eyes crinkled with laugh lines as water sprayed between them.

Wes wondered what it would feel like to be a father. Or even to feel like he wasn't one breath away from the end of his life. He hadn't tried to text or call Bree, not even once. Problem was, he hadn't heard from her either. Not even once.

Honestly, he'd expected to hear from her. The silence sliced into him every day, every hour, every minute.

"We're going on the twentieth," Gray said. "Tentatively. Barring anything happening at HMC, and of course, the weather."

Thirty days. Wes had no idea what condition his heart would be in by the time another month passed, and he supposed he could put on a brave face and cross the city limits of Coral Canyon. He could hunker down inside Colton's house and refuse to go to town, to any restaurants, or anywhere near Whiskey Mountain Lodge. He could.

Everyone would understand, without any explanations needed.

"So will you come with us?" Hunter asked.

"Did Grandma put you up to asking me?" Wes asked. "Or Uncle Colton?"

Hunter exchanged a glance with his dad, and Wes got his answer. "Gray?"

"I knew you wouldn't want to come, that's all." Gray got up and padded into the kitchen, where low lights shone down from beneath the cabinets. He put his coffee cup in the sink and busied himself with cleaning up the takeout containers and plates on the island where they'd eaten dinner.

"You should come," Hunter said. "Everyone is going to be there, and Uncle Colt has a new dog."

"Yeah," Wes said, trying to keep the darkness out of his voice. "I've heard all about this new dog." And he wasn't really upset about the dog, or the fact that Colton wanted to have a holiday celebration at his house. In fact, he wanted to meet Colton's dog, as Wes had a soft spot in his heart for canines too. And Colton had a cute one—some sort of designer breed with good fetching instincts. He'd trained the dog to jump off the dock as he threw a ball out into the water, and Sparky loved getting the ball and swimming back to shore to please Colton.

"I guess I'll go," Wes finally said, causing Hunter to look up from his tablet. "But you have to help me go shopping for everyone between now and then."

"Shopping?" Hunter asked as Gray came back into the living room.

"Yeah, at like stores and stuff," Wes said, grinning at the two of them. "Where do you think your dad got that amazing tablet?"

Gray didn't normally let Hunter have devices, but he was getting close to twelve, and a lot of kids had phones and e-readers and more starting about now. Gray monitored what Hunter did on his tablet, and in the day Wes had been there, he'd seen it plugged in more than not. Hunter maybe spent thirty minutes on it each day, and he usually read a book and played a quick game until Gray told him to put it away.

"I ordered it online," Gray said. "But you can help Uncle Wes, Hunt. He's been gone practically all year, and he won't even know what to get everyone."

"I've already got a few things," Wes said. "From my travels."

"Tea towels for Mom?" Gray asked, smiling.

"If you must know, yes," Wes said, suddenly feeling like he'd gotten their mother the worst gift possible.

"Anything for me?" Gray asked.

"I'm not telling," Wes said. "Because you'll just guess what it is, and what good is a gift if it's not a surprise?"

"Dad hates surprises," Hunter said soberly, looking back at his tablet like they were talking about the weather.

Wes grinned then, because Hunter had Gray pegged, all right. "That he does," Wes said.

"Oh, I do not," Gray said. "Just surprises in the courtroom, Hunter."

Hunter shrugged one shoulder and kept reading. "That's what you said last week."

Wes stood up and looked back into the dark, clean kitchen. "Do you have any ice cream?"

"Nope," Gray said. "I'm in training mode again."

"All right." Wes reached for his keys, though he wasn't too keen on going outside in the cold. Darkness had fallen a couple of hours ago, but Wes knew the ice cream shops would be open still. "Hunter, you want to come with me?"

Hunter stood up without missing a beat. He left his tablet on the couch and asked, "Can I have that banana caramel crunch cone?"

"You have to go all the way to Dairyland for that," Gray said. "It's too far."

"Sure," Wes said, putting his arm around Hunter's shoulders. "It's not that far."

"There's school tomorrow," Gray said, practically growling at Wes.

"Dad, you said I didn't have to go," Hunter said, turning back to his father. "It's the last day before Thanksgiving break, and all they do is show movies. It's stupid."

Gray looked like he was trying to stare into the winds of a hurricane and could somehow will it back into a breeze. He finally broke and said, "Fine. But don't stay out too late."

"You sure you don't want anything?" Wes asked.

Gray shook his head and bent over to stretch. "No, I'm going to actually go get on the treadmill again."

"Your funeral," Wes said, though he could probably stand to get on the treadmill even once a day. Gray had already been on that morning, and he seriously looked like he could run a marathon every day for the next month and not even be winded.

As soon as Wes and Hunter were in the truck alone, Wes said, "So tell me, Hunter. How is your dad really?"

"He's good," Hunter said. "Though...I don't know if I should tell you this."

"Which means you really should," Wes said, backing out of the driveway.

"I heard him talking to Uncle Colton a few weeks ago, and he said something about a woman named Elise. When I asked about her, Dad turned all dark and stormy, you know how he does sometimes."

"Oh, I know," Wes said. And he knew exactly who Elise was too.

"Anyway," Hunter said with a sigh. "I told him that he could date, but he said he doesn't want to." Hunter looked at Wes with wide, innocent eyes. "Do you think that's true, Uncle Wes? That he really doesn't want to date anyone?"

"I don't know, Hunter," Wes said thoughtfully. "Why do you think it might not be true?"

Hunter shrugged and looked away. "There's this girl in my class, and I don't know. I think if I could hang out more with her, I'd like to." The way he just stated it so matter-of-factly made Wes's heart happy.

He smiled as he navigated the suburban streets back to the more main thoroughfares and got them headed toward Dairyland.

"What's her name?" Wes asked.

"You can't tell my dad."

"Please, Hunter," Wes said. "I don't tell your dad everything."

"Promise?"

"Pinky swear," Wes said, holding his pinky up and extending his hand toward his nephew. Hunter hooked his around it, smiling.

"Her name is Molly."

"And she's nice?"

"Yeah, she's nice."

"She's pretty?"

"Yeah." Hunter sighed, and Wes grinned at the pure innocence of his nephew's first crush. He wished his relationship with Bree could be so easy. Checkmarks next to *nice* and *pretty*, which she was both.

But there was so much more to an adult relationship, and Wes found himself glancing at his phone just to make sure he hadn't missed any texts or calls.

He hadn't.

So a lot of ice cream, he told himself as he drove. *And Lord? Could you give me a bit more patience? Maybe she just needs more time.*

But Wes didn't know how much more time a person could possibly need, and he felt like he was operating on the last reserves of his hope.

Chapter Twenty-Six

Gray hadn't told Wes not to stay out too late because of Hunter. But for himself. He did have to go to work in the morning, and he wanted to talk to his brother about a few things before he did.

Dairyland was definitely too far away, but Gray put in four miles on the treadmill, estimating that Wes and Hunter had to be at the ice cream parlor by then. He showered, and he figured they'd be on their way back.

He dressed and made coffee, thinking they'd walk in within ten minutes.

When they did, a sense of pride moved through Gray. He got down mugs, though he knew Wes wouldn't have coffee. Only Gray seemed to be hooked to the stuff intravenously, and only Gray seemed to be able to tolerate it after six p.m.

Wes and Hunter laughed about something, and Gray did like the look and sound of that. He was grateful for his brothers' influence on his son, though he did wish sometimes that there were other Hammond cousins to play with. It was just Hunter, and sometimes Gray wondered if the boy knew how much of an island he was.

He didn't seem to, as everyone loved him—including Gray.

"Dad, you should've seen Uncle Wes tonight."

"Hunter, we don't need to tell your dad anything about what happened tonight." Wes wore a disgruntled look on his face, and when he turned his attention to Gray, he wiped it all away.

"What happened?"

Hunter looked at Wes and then back to Gray. "Uh...Uncle Wes got pulled over."

A great hiss came from Wes's mouth, but Gray could only laugh. "I told you Uncle Wes wasn't a great driver."

"Hey," Wes said. "I managed to make it to forty-nine out of fifty states, almost all of them behind the wheel of a truck."

"And we've all been prayin' mightily for you," Gray said. "A whole army of Hammonds, down on their knees so Wes won't die on some highway across Kansas."

"Oh, stop it," Wes said with a scoff. "I'm a great driver."

"So why'd you get pulled over?" Gray poured his coffee, his smirk stuck to his face.

"Ames," Wes said, stepping into the kitchen and opening Gray's freezer. He put a carton of ice cream there. "And you shoulda seen him. He was like, 'Wes, I can't believe you weren't driving the speed limit.' At first, I thought he was kidding."

"He wasn't," Hunter said.

"He lectured me about having Hunter in the truck, and I kid you not, he gave me a ticket."

Gray laughed, because that totally sounded like something Ames would do. "How fast were you going?"

"Six over," Hunter said.

"Six?" Gray let another wave of laughter come out of his mouth. "Wow, Ames must really be hurting for his quota of tickets. We've still got another week left in the month."

"He's just sticking it to me," Wes said.

"It's not like you can't afford it," Gray said.

"Oh, I'm not paying," Wes said. "No way. I'm going to traffic school and getting those points taken off my license." He wore a look of one ready to go into battle, but Gray found the whole thing hilarious.

"Then he started asking me how we could get Uncle Ames back," Hunter said.

"Oh?" Gray poured cream into his coffee, but no sugar. Sugar—even a little bit—would undo what he'd done on the treadmill that day.

"And I told him Uncle Ames was mighty afraid of snakes." Hunter laughed too, and Wes leaned against the counter, a wicked smile on his face.

"Okay," Gray said, still chuckling. "Time for bed, Hunt. Go get changed. Brush your teeth."

"Can I get on the computer for a few minutes?" he asked.

"Twenty minutes," Gray said, and Hunter nodded.

"Yes, sir." He went down the hall toward his bedroom, and both Gray and Wes watched him until he disappeared.

"He's a great kid," Wes said.

"Yes, he is," Gray said, reminding himself to thank the Lord for Hunter that night during his prayers.

"Talk to me about HMC," Wes said. He'd gotten in late last night, and Gray had run that morning and bustled off to work, so they hadn't had much time to talk business.

"It's good," Gray said. "Laura is bringing in a lawyer named Maisey Knight, and she's worked for Amazon and IBM."

"Oh, wow."

"She'll be fine," he said. "She starts after Thanksgiving, and I'm hoping I can show her around the filing cabinets, give her some permissions on our websites and software, and be done."

"Tired of it?"

"Beyond," Gray said. At the same time, he knew he'd miss his job at HMC. A lot. It had been different this year, of course, without Wes and Colton there. But Laura and Jill had stepped into the empty shoes beautifully, and their stock prices were up two percentage points over last year.

"And then what?" Wes asked, and that was the question that struck fear way down deep in Gray's heart every time he even thought it.

"And then...I don't know," Gray said. "I'm going to try to qualify for the Boston Marathon next year, I know that."

"Wow, Gray." Wes's eyes lit up with respect. "That's great. What do you have to do for that?"

"You have to get a qualifying time," he said. "At a major marathon. And apply."

"Does Colorado have a qualifying race?"

"Yeah, Colfax," Gray said. "It's in May, and that's the one I'm training for."

"When do you find out if you made it into Boston?"

"September is the application date."

"So you've got time."

"It's all about time in a marathon," Gray agreed. His phone chimed, and his heart pinged along with it. He'd texted Elise earlier, and she hadn't responded.

"Oh, boy," Wes said, beating Gray in reaction time. He swiped Gray's phone from the countertop and danced away. "You're still talking to her?" He looked up from the phone while Gray's heartbeat hammered out of control.

"I just asked her about Bree," Gray said. "I wanted to find out what we were dealing with this holiday season."

"Yeah, you just want to talk to Elise." Wes didn't even react to Bree's name, but Gray thought he was probably putting a brave front. Wes had been the CEO of their massive conglomerate, based in dozens of countries around the world, and he knew how to hide how he was feeling. Gray did too, and the skill allowed him to lean into the counter and fold his arms, one eyebrow cocked as Wes read the text.

His own curiosity about what Elise had said headed toward the stars, and Gray only allowed himself to admit his attraction to the petite, white-blonde waif of a woman in the single minute before he fell asleep at night. Otherwise, he lost too much time during his day thinking about her.

His mind wanted to build a bridge from where he was with Hunter, to where Elise lived in Coral Canyon. They'd never talked about a long distance relationship, nor about either of them relocating to be near the other.

Gray was satisfied with keeping their brief and infrequent texts to be about Colton or Bree, because that was all he could afford to do at the moment.

Wes frowned as he put the phone back on the counter. The pain and tension in his mouth and radiating from his shoulders was the answer to Gray's question for Elise.

"So she'll be in town," Gray said, and he wasn't asking a question.

"She's apparently only going to Vermont for Thanksgiving. But she loves the traditions at the lodge too much to be gone for Christmas. She's bringing her parents there for the holidays." Wes turned away from Gray and walked toward the back door, which had a big window that looked out over the yard.

Gray heard the disappointment in his oldest brother's voice, and he didn't know how to erase it. Wes had never tried to cheer up Gray when he was going through something tough, but Gray wanted to help him.

In the immediate months after his divorce, it had been Wes who'd shown up to take Hunter to soccer practice so Gray could work on the case against Sheila. Wes who'd ordered groceries and had them delivered to Gray's house. Wes who'd bought Hunter his first backpack for kindergarten, and Wes who came over after a long day of work and let Hunter read to him in his stilted, little-boy-learning-to-read voice while Gray stared at the TV for hours and hours.

So he walked over to the door too, looking out the flanking windows. "What are you going to do?"

"I don't know," Wes said.

"You own a house there."

"I need to sell that," he said.

"Maybe that's where you start," Gray said. "Maybe you just need to take the first step, and then the path will appear."

The two of them stood there for a couple of minutes, each brother lost inside his own head, and finally Wes turned around. "You'll want to look at the texts, Gray. That woman likes you."

Gray spun around too, his heart suddenly bobbing in his chest like it wasn't attached with veins and arteries. "She does?"

"For sure," Wes said, his back still to Gray. "And how do you feel about her?"

"That's irrelevant," Gray said, striding over to the counter where Wes had left his phone.

"I won't tell her you said that," Wes said. "And don't say that to Colt. They're best friends, you know." He poured a cup of coffee and started stirring it, his eyes finally coming back to Gray.

He held Wes's gaze for a moment and then looked down at the phone. *Yes, Bree will be here for the holidays. She's inviting her parents while she's in Vermont this weekend for Thanksgiving. I'm sure they'll come.*

Gray's muscles tightened and then relaxed as he read her words, imagining her delicate fingers tapping out the message. He could picture her perfectly in his mind, and he couldn't help thinking that he'd really like to get to know more about her.

Are you coming for the holidays? her next message said. *If so, I'd love to get coffee with you, if you have time. Or lunch. Or whatever you have time for. There will be a lot of activities at the lodge, and we're doing Cupcake Wars this year. We could be partners.*

Gray took a breath, and the air felt like dry ice, spreading an absolute chill through his whole body. "She wants to get together with me."

"Yep." Wes just kept stirring and stirring. "You seem surprised."

"I am, I mean, yeah. A little."

"Why? Seems like she's not even embarrassed to ask." Wes gave him an expectant look, and Gray didn't like it. He didn't want to talk about Elise, because then he'd have to admit he liked the woman.

"We've talked over the months since Colt's wedding," Gray said. "Little things here and there. Mostly about Colton and Annie, or Bree, or something going on at the lodge. She asked me a legal question, and I sent her that favorite movie quiz I sent to everyone."

"Mm hm." The clinking of Wes's spoon against the side of the mug was slowly driving Gray mad. "You like her, though, right?"

"Sure," Gray said, and Wes grinned. "What?"

"Nothing."

"Oh, come on. You lit up like a Christmas tree when I said that."

"That's because you gave away everything in that one word," Wes said, taking his cup of coffee and pouring it down the sink.

"How?"

"I asked you how you felt about her, and you said 'that's irrelevant,' and this time when I asked, you said you did."

Gray rolled his eyes. "You're reading way too much into that."

"What I know, lawyer brother of mine, is that your feelings for the woman are *very* relevant, and your dismissal of them speaks very loudly. So I knew you liked her when you said that your feelings for her were irrelevant."

"You're annoying me."

"I bet I am." Wes grinned at him.

"They *are* irrelevant," Gray said, shooting a glance toward the mouth of the hall, though Hunter wouldn't likely come out of his bedroom again that night. In fact, Gray should go check on him and make sure he wasn't still staring at a screen. "Because she lives there, and I live here, and Hunter needs the stability in his life, and he's got friends here, and Mom and Dad are here, and—"

"Okay," Wes said. "Enough."

Gray wanted to keep going, because his argument for why his feelings—whatever they were—for Elise were irrelevant was strong and multi-faceted. He glared at Wes, almost daring him to say something more.

"There are a thousand reasons not to be with someone," Wes said, his voice barely loud enough to be heard in the cavernous kitchen. "But sometimes you have to put all of that aside and take a leap of faith."

Gray had plenty of faith. He'd been living with its guidance every day for the past six years. He couldn't be a father without constant prayer, and he took Hunter to church every week. They read their scriptures, and he'd taught his son to listen in case God wanted to lead him somewhere.

He looked down at his phone again. He'd never truly taken a leap of faith. Gray studied things out before he took a single step, and he always knew where that step was going to land. He definitely wasn't the leaping type.

"I'm going to bed," Wes said. "Thanks for letting me crash here, Gray."

"Anytime," Gray said automatically, and then he was alone in the kitchen. He looked down at his phone again, trying to decide what to say to Elise.

Surely he'd be able to slip away for a couple of hours. He'd have plenty of help with Hunter, and he was left trying to decide if he wanted to commit to a cup of coffee or a meal. Or a whole afternoon at the lodge, doing whatever Cupcake Wars was.

He snapped his fingers, something he did when trying to make a hard decision. The steady rhythm of it kept his thoughts from wandering.

He finally picked up his phone, and used both hands to tap out a message. *Sure, Elise. I'm sure I can find some time to get coffee or go to lunch.*

He stared at the words, his heart now thumping to the rhythm his fingers had made.

He literally felt himself leaping as he added, *Not sure what Cupcake Wars is, but if it involves chocolate, I'm sure I'd be interested.*

He sent the text without giving it too much time or thought. If he did, he'd erase it all, delete the text string, and lay awake for the next couple of hours. He read over the sent words again, realizing he'd just told Elise he was interested in her.

I'm sure I'd be interested.

"You *are* interested." He took his phone and headed toward the master bedroom. He had to get up and run before work, and he was already up too late.

Chapter Twenty-Seven

Elise couldn't knock as she carried a bottle of apple-grape cider under one arm, a pan of potatoes in that hand, and a bowl of salad in the other. Thankfully, Colton had somehow been alerted to her presence, and he opened the door a moment after she arrived.

Sparky barked at her, growling low in the back of his throat. "Shush," Colton told the dog, reaching for the bottle of cider Elise was about to lose. He took the salad too, and that freed up Elise to hold the heavy pan of potatoes with both hands.

"Morning," she said to him as she eased past him. "Where's Annie?" She wasn't worried about being alone with Colton. Since Bree had been traveling more the past several weeks, she'd been staying with Colton and Annie, as she really didn't like being in the cabin alone.

"She's over at her daughter's," Colton said, closing the door behind her. "I guess Em is supposed to take a dessert to her in-laws for dinner, and she burnt the first one. Annie went to help her."

"Smells like she got the turkey in here first," Elise said, setting the pan of potatoes on the counter. "These need a couple of hours, so if we're eating at one, I can put them in about ten-thirty."

"We're definitely eating at one," Colton said. "That way, Eden can go to Mitchell's at four."

"I can't even imagine eating two Thanksgiving dinners," Elise said.

"That's because you barely eat," Colton said.

"How many cupcakes have you eaten this morning?" she asked.

"Who says I've had cupcakes?"

Elise laughed, because Colton ate cupcakes every day, it seemed. "I'm sure it's at least three," she said. "Now, Annie said she'd get the cream cheese I needed for the cheesecake. The store I went to was out, if you can believe it."

"People seem to go crazy around the holidays," Colton said. "Annie managed to get the last of the Chex she needed for that mix we like."

"Tell me she made a huge batch." Elise looked around for it, her mouth already watering.

"She sure did." Colton grinned as he opened a cupboard and pulled out a big bowl of the chocolatey and nutty mix made with cereal, peanut butter, chocolate, and powdered sugar.

"I'm so grateful for Annie," Elise said, grinning as Colton

put the bowl near her. She took a handful of it and started eating, everything in her life aligning.

Especially since Gray had agreed to see her while he was here for Christmas. She hadn't told anyone about that, and she strengthened her resolve not to say anything to Colton about his brother. More than likely, though, Colton would bring up Gray, and Elise would have to decide how to play it.

She and Colton were close enough that if he was looking at her at all, he'd see the nervousness in her expression or hear the hesitation in her voice before she answered. And Colton saw and heard everything.

Elise started making the cheesecake they'd eat for dessert after their traditional Thanksgiving meal and getting out the ingredients and tools she needed gave her a distraction from consuming the entire bowl of sweets—and from thinking too long about Gray Hammond.

She'd told herself a dozen times she wasn't going to date her best friend's brother, because so many things could turn awkward so fast. She would not put her friendship with Colton at risk, and she'd already seen the impact Bree's relationship with Wes had had on her and Colton's friendship.

They hardly talked anymore, and even Colton had noticed and asked Elise what was going on with Bree.

She hadn't known what to say. Maybe because Colton looked a lot like his brother, or maybe because he definitely possessed a similar spirit as Wes. No matter what it was, Bree didn't seem to want to spend much time with Colton anymore.

She didn't spend much time with anyone, and Elise didn't

like that. She'd done everything in her power to stay as close to Bree as possible. She made sure to eat breakfast with her in the morning. Send her funny memes throughout the day. Make sure Bree knew about all the meals at the lodge, though they didn't ever eat a whole lot with the guests.

Bree had changed a lot in the past couple of months, and she now wore freedom on her face that she hadn't before. She laughed easier. She told Elise she was making good progress on forgiving herself, as she went to therapy every week and spoke to her parents daily.

Elise was happy for her. So happy. She still didn't quite know what Bree needed to forgive herself for, or why she went to therapy, but that didn't matter. Elise had always loved Bree, and she missed her when she left town. She missed the threesome she and Bree and Colton had once been.

If Colton did too, he'd never said.

"My brother says I need to watch Hunter for a bit while he's here," Colton said, and Elise dropped the rubber spatula she'd been using to scrape the filling down closer to the beaters. She looked up, her eyes wide, to find Colton smirking at her from across the counter.

"He said that?"

"Want to see the text?"

"No," Elise said quickly. She picked up the spatula and finished the job before turning on the mixer again. "And? Can you do it?"

"Of course I can do it," Colton said. "What I want to know is why. I asked him, and he said he'd rather not say."

"Well, then I'm not going to say either," Elise said. "Not

that I know." She was practically yelling above the noise of the beaters. "I mean, it's not like Gray tells me everything he's doing." In fact, Elise wished Gray would communicate with her more. They'd been texting a little bit since she'd asked him if he'd like to get together with her over Christmas.

She'd honestly been shocked—a pleasant shocked—when he'd said yes. And to find out that he'd already texted Colton to make arrangements for Hunter made Elise's face start to warm. She attempted to pull back on that, because heat in her face meant she'd soon turn red, and then Colton would know she definitely had feelings for his brother.

Elise couldn't even believe she had feelings for Gray, but literally no one had intrigued her as much as he had, and she'd only met him the one time, when he'd come for Colton's wedding.

She'd gotten his number through a sheer miracle, and she thanked the Lord every day for that amazing coincidence that Colton had said, "I can't deal with that. Gray, will you work with Elise on the sound?"

So she'd gotten his number, and they'd been talking since. *Just a little bit*, she told herself as the cheesecake batter reached peak creaminess. She switched off the mixer, very aware of Colton's eyes still on her.

She glanced up as she removed the beaters. "What?"

"What? Nothing."

"You're staring at me."

"I'm just sitting here."

"Could you go sit over there?" she asked. "Or set the table. Or something."

"Lunch isn't for four hours," he said. "I don't need to set the table right now."

"You don't even know *how* to set the table," she said.

"No, I don't," he said, grinning.

Elise couldn't help smiling as she lifted the bowl to pour the filling into the crust. "You're pathetic."

"I know," Colton said, still smiling. He didn't move hardly at all. "I know how to peel potatoes, but you made those already."

Elise tapped the springform pan to get all the air bubbles out of the cheesecake, and then she set it in a deep sheet pan. She slid that into the preheated oven and picked up the tea kettle. She poured hot water into the shallow pan surrounding the cheesecake and closed the oven. "There."

"I can't wait to eat that."

"You eat more sugar than any human should," she said.

"I like it." He tapped the counter at the spot next to him. "Come sit by me."

"Why?" Elise reached for a towel and wiped her hands on it. "So you can tease me about Gray?"

"Yes." Colton rested his chin on both of his hands. "Tell me about you and Gray."

"I'm not having this conversation," she said. "And just because we're friends doesn't mean you get to make this awkward for me." She gave him the hardest look she could, and Colton's smile slipped off his face.

"Okay," he said, holding up his hands now. "It's just...I feel like I should sign something or get you to sign something that says I'm not responsible for how Gray treats you. If you end up hurt, Elise, and we can't be friends...." He shook his head. "I've already lost Bree."

So he did know. Sometimes Colton painted over hard things with a quick laugh, that infectious smile, and a lot of cupcakes. Elise tended to do the same, but she didn't have as much room on her frame for extra sweets as he did.

"You haven't lost Bree," Elise said. "She's still with us."

"It's not the same," Colton said. "Maybe for you, because it wasn't your brother who hurt her."

"Wes didn't hurt her," Elise said, rounding the counter and sitting next to Colton. "*She* hurt *him*. He left because she couldn't tell him about her family."

"But she's talking to them now."

"Yeah," Elise said. "I think she'll be ready to get him back soon, but I don't know. We don't talk about specifics with that."

"Has she told you about her family?"

"No."

"Me either." Colton sighed. "And I don't really care. But I know Wes does."

"As he should," Elise said. "He was right, Colton. She wasn't. So I know it's been weird with you and her, but that's on her. Not you. Not Wes."

"Feels like it's on me." He reached over and covered her hand with his. "Gray is an amazing guy, Elise. You're an amazing woman. I think you two would be great together, but you should know, he—"

"Please stop talking," Elise said, shouting over him. "I'll find out about Gray when I talk to Gray." She turned her hand

and squeezed Colton's. "It's not your job to fix up all your friends with your brothers. I met Gray on my own, thank you very much, and I can't help it if he was so taken with my beauty that he gave me his number." She grinned at him, because that wasn't what had happened at all.

Colton chuckled and shook his head. "All right. So I stay out of it."

"That's right, Colt. You stay out of it." At the same time, Elise thought she could probably use the inside scoop on Gray Hammond. He exuded confidence and power, and Elise withered in his presence. She'd been working on that, but it was hard, because she felt confident around the lodge, with her job and her friends.

"What's your biggest hang-up with him?" Colton asked.

"I have two, actually," Elise said.

"Oh, you've thought about this."

"Absolutely," she said.

"And they are?"

"He lives in Colorado," Elise said.

"That's a big one."

"And he's a cowboy."

Colton whipped his attention back to her. He reached up and adjusted the big, white cowboy hat he wore day and night. "I forgot you don't like cowboys."

"It's not that I don't like them."

"Yeah, yeah," Colton said. "I remember about that guy who cheated on you."

"Yeah." Elise remembered that too.

"Gray doesn't cheat," Colton said. "On anything. Ever.

The guy graduated top of his class in law school because he's a freak of nature when it comes to remembering things."

Elise giggled and slid off the stool. If he wasn't going to set the table, she could. "Now I'm going to have three things. He'll be too smart for me."

"Nonsense," Colton said, joining her in the kitchen as she got down plates and opened the drawer to get out silverware. "You're a catch, Elise."

"I'll keep that in mind." Thankfully, the conversation moved away from Gray, and the activity around the house picked up when Annie returned with her two daughters. Both of them brought their significant others, which only made Elise feel smaller than her five-foot-one-frame. They were ten years younger than her and had managed to find someone to spend their lives with.

Eden wasn't engaged—yet, but Emily and Kelly had gotten married a month or so ago, after several setbacks when the venue they'd booked had gone out of business suddenly in the spring.

Elise pushed aside the feelings of inadequacy. It wasn't like she'd never had a boyfriend before. She had. Of course she had.

But she'd never had a *man* like Gray.

Elise's excitement for the Christmas holiday doubled as she thought about the sexy cowboy-lawyer and hopefully spending a couple of hours alone with him.

Chapter Twenty-Eight

Bree put the plate with a stick of butter on it on the table and turned back to her parents. Her mother had invited her parents to their Thanksgiving feast too, and her father had invited his dad. His mother had died a decade ago, and Bree hadn't come to Vermont for the funeral.

A wave of uneasiness rolled over her, but she kept her shoulders square and strong. Her parents had been gracious and kind and forgiving, and with weekly therapy sessions, Bree was starting to believe that the Lord could forgive her too.

The really tricky part was forgiving herself.

Every once in a while, she believed she'd accomplished that, and she had a very good day. She toyed with the idea of texting Wes and asking him what his Christmas plans were. Then, the next morning, she'd be back at square one, almost crying because of the things she'd done, the pain she'd inflicted, the turmoil she'd caused.

And not just because Bronson had died the day he'd fallen

through the ice. But because of how Bree had chosen to handle every moment since.

Help me today, she prayed silently as her mother lifted her eyes from the salad she was constructing. "That's everything," Mom said. "My parents should be here in about five minutes. Did you want to take Collie out for a minute?'

"Sure," Bree said. She moved over to the cupboard where her father kept the leashes, dog treats, and clothes their little corgi wore. Today, Dad had dressed the eight-year-old dog in a bandana with turkey feathers on it, and Bree liked the way the animal seemed to know his special cupboard had been opened.

Collie perked up and managed to get himself off the couch where he'd been snoozing. He stretched and yawned and trotted toward her, by which time Bree had selected one of his many leashes and picked up a bag of cheesy sausage treats.

"Come on, boy," she said. "Let's go down to the river for a second." She couldn't believe she could even get close to the Marble Falls River. But she could. She had. She'd been to the place Bronson had fallen through the ice, and she'd stood there for a long, long time, crying and begging God to forgive her.

Her mom and dad had initially gone with her, and they'd stood at her side and said, "We don't blame you, Bree. Accidents happen."

Dad had said, "God must've needed him in heaven."

Bree wasn't sure what God needed. If He was such an all-powerful being, why hadn't He saved Bronson? Why hadn't He communicated with Bree more clearly over the past twenty-three years since her brother's death?

Slowly, as she came back to her roots and made amends,

Bree realized the blocks she'd put in her own ears. Perhaps the Lord had been calling to her all this time, and she simply hadn't heard Him.

She carried no blame anymore. Her guilt rode the same roller coaster her self-forgiveness did. Her therapist told her to be patient with herself, and kind, and to expect this process to take a very long time.

Bree clipped the leash to Collie's collar and she led the dog out the back door. She paused and took in a deep lungful of the clear, fresh air in Marble Falls, Vermont. There wasn't air as crisp anywhere else.

"Except maybe Coral Canyon," she murmured. She and Collie crossed the deck and went down the steps to the backyard. From there, it was a straight shot back to the stand of trees. Vermont seemed to have trees everywhere, and Bree walked under their skeletal branches, her fingers turning cold.

She'd forgotten to grab her gloves, but she didn't mind. She actually liked the bite against her skin, as it reminded her that she was human. Humans made mistakes. Humans could try again. Humans could be forgiven.

"Can I call Wes?" she asked the empty horizon in front of her. She'd taken to praying out loud as she walked with Collie, as he never asked her who she was talking to and never gave her any answers. Her mind was free to wander, and her heart was open to hear.

"Will he really come if I ask him to?"

Just like all the other times Bree had asked that question, verbally or not, she felt the same answer: Wes wasn't a liar.

He'd said she could call or text when she was ready, and he'd be waiting.

But what if that's not true? What if something has changed?

Bree hated what-ifs. She'd lived for so long with so many, and she frowned as she tried to change the two she'd allowed into her mind.

"What if it is true? What if nothing has changed, and he's just waiting for you to call him?"

She let Collie off the leash and he scampered around, frolicking in the nearly frozen grasses and shrubs along the water's edge. He seemed to know exactly how far he could go without falling into the water, though there wasn't much flowing in the river right now.

He took care of his business, and Bree turned around to go back through the orchard and the yard to the house. She'd definitely been gone for more than five minutes, and she suspected her mother wanted her grandparents to come while Bree wasn't in the house to greet them.

She knew Mom had been talking to everyone in the family. She'd been to Vermont a few times in the past seven weeks, and she'd rekindled relationships with aunts, uncles, and cousins. She'd seen her father's father a couple of times, but her mom's parents actually lived in Maine, and this would be the first time Bree would have to face them.

"Come on, Collie." She continued walking, grateful for the warm boots she wore that protected her feet. The back door had been cracked, and she heard voices the moment she stepped out from under the apple trees. Everything carried so well in the silence when there were no neighbors close by to absorb the sound.

Bree's heart pounded harder and harder with every step she took, and not only because the way back to the house was slightly uphill. She mounted the steps as Collie ran ahead of her, and the corgi nosed open the door to enter the house first.

The talking stopped, and Bree had a few seconds of complete doubt while she crossed the deck. Her fight or flight instincts kicked in, but she wouldn't run away. Not again.

She knew better than that now.

She inched open the door too and stepped inside, Collie's leash hanging from her fingers.

"There she is," Mom said, wearing a bright smile with her festive apron and dark brown sweater. Her mother had a sweater for every occasion, and Bree loved the stripes, the jewels, the patterns, the intricate snowmen and trees knitted into them. She wore a pair of turkeys as earrings, and she looked like a professional had done her makeup so she could do a TV interview.

Bree felt put together a bit wrong as she scanned the people in the kitchen. Her parents. Grandpa George, her father's dad. And then her mother's parents.

They seemed to have shrunk quite a bit from the two people Bree held in her memory, but instant tears came to her eyes.

"Hey, Gramma," she said, dropping the leash on the table though it was already set and the leash was dirty. She hurried around the table and counter to her grandmother and leaned down to hug her.

A sob burst from Gramma's mouth, and Bree didn't hold back her tears. That was another thing she'd learned. She didn't have to hold everything so tight. She didn't have to hold anything at all.

The Lord could—and would—carry anything she couldn't. Anything she could too.

"Oh, sweet pea," Gramma whispered. "We've missed you so."

A warm hand landed on Bree's back, and she knew that belonged to Pops. She didn't want to let go of Gramma quite yet, because while she'd aged, and her hair had changed colors, and wrinkles appeared around her eyes, and she carried more weight, she smelled exactly the same.

Like, sugar and coffee, with a hint of freshly baked bread in there too.

"I missed you too, Gramma," Bree said, feeling movement around her.

She opened her eyes and turned into Pops, who was still taller than her though not quite as big as she remembered. "Pops."

He said nothing, but Bree's body vibrated slightly as his did, and she didn't mind all the crying. For a while there, she'd thought she'd spontaneously combust if she didn't figure out how to stem the tears. But now, they cleansed her. They made her whole for a few minutes, and then they washed away the bad and left room for the good.

"Welcome home, buggy," Pops whispered, and then he stepped back.

Bree busied herself with wiping her eyes and cheeks while

her mom welcomed everyone for their Thanksgiving feast. As she explained that the sweet potato casserole had walnuts in it, Bree looked around at everyone. There were six of them there. Only six.

She couldn't even imagine a holiday with so few people, as she'd spent almost the last decade with the Whittakers at the lodge.

But this small family gathering possessed a healthy spirit too. God was here too. She enjoyed this too.

"All right, Jerry," Mom said. "Say a prayer, and let's eat."

Bree bowed her head, glad when Pops slipped his hand into hers and squeezed. The acceptance they freely gave her made her marvel, and then fresh tears to fill her eyes with gratitude. She wanted to accept and forgive others too.

"Amen," she said when her father finished the prayer.

"We'll do what we're grateful for at the table," Mom said. "And Bree has asked that it not be her." She cut her a look, not truly making eye contact.

"So," Gramma said, latching onto Bree the moment Pops let go of her hand. "I hear you're seeing a man in Wyoming."

"Kind of," Bree said. "We're on hold at the moment." She picked up a plate, noting that it was Gramma's fine china. "You brought your plates."

"Yes." Gramma gazed fondly down at them, and Bree did too.

"I always loved eating on these as a kid," Bree said, not holding back the thoughts of her past when they came into her mind. "They're beautiful."

"They don't make them like this anymore," Gramma said. "That's for sure."

"That's because they can't make yellow paint that hideous color anymore," Dad said, picking up his own plate. He grinned at Gramma, who scoffed at him as she smiled.

Bree liked the "hideous" yellow rim on the plates. They also had depictions of a bounteous harvest—grapes, pumpkins, corn, and pheasants—painted on them, and she did love them. They spoke of easier times, when she'd have to call the armchair before dinner so she could sit in it afterward. Otherwise, Bronson would do it, and then she'd be on the floor while they watched their traditional after-feast movie.

"I hope you can push play again with your cowboy," Gramma said, going with Dad over to the table to take a spot. Bree watched her, and she found herself hoping for that exact same thing.

And she knew it was up to her to push the right button to make it so.

Or in this case, start tapping and swiping on her phone.

* * *

After dinner, after the movie ended, after pie and ice cream, everyone went home. Bree helped her mother clean up, and the sun had started to set by the time she had a moment to stand and think about what she might do next.

"Mom?" she asked.

"Hm?" Her mother looked up from the book she'd picked up.

"Do you think...I mean, I've told you about Wes."

Mom put down the book and scooted to the edge of the couch. "Are you going to call him?"

"I'm thinking about it."

"And? What are you going to say?"

"That's the part I can't quite figure out."

"I wish I could help you." She indicated the couch beside her, and Bree went to sit by her.

"Maybe I should just, I don't know. Find him a gift and show up at the lodge at Christmas."

"Will he be there?"

"I don't know why he would be." If she were him, she wouldn't go to the site where her heart had been shattered. "But I can ask Elise. She'll know if he'll be there."

You should ask Colton. The thought ran through her mind, unbidden. Yes, she'd put Colton in a box of his own for the past couple of months. She'd needed the space from him to figure out what to do about his brother. To figure out who she was without the touch of a Hammond in her life.

See, they were made of pure gold, and sometimes that glint could be blinding.

She needed to apologize to him too.

"I'm going to go make a call," she said.

"I'll be right here," Mom said, reaching for her book again, as if this would be a simple call. As if Bree would come back from the bedroom where she stayed when she came and be smiling and happy.

She wouldn't, and they both knew it.

But she went down the hall and into the bedroom. She

closed the door and locked it. She plugged in her phone and started doing that tapping and swiping she'd been thinking about earlier.

Wes's and Colton's names both came up on the screen, as they shared a last name.

She reached down and tapped on the top one. The line held its breath, and Bree did too.

Then it rang.

Then Colton said, "Holy stars in heaven, it's Bree Richards," in that playful, cowboy voice she'd missed so much. "What are you doin' callin' me?"

"I wanted to talk to you," she said, her voice somewhat hoarse. "I wanted to apologize, Colt."

"Oh, come on," he said, the teasing quality of his voice nearly gone now. "You don't have anything to apologize to me for."

"Yes, I do," she said. "I pushed you away, and we both know it. So don't act like you weren't upset or that you didn't miss me."

Colton chuckled, and Bree felt the first rays of laughter in her soul too. "Fine," he said. "I missed you."

"I miss you too," she said. "So when I get back, will you take me to lunch? We can talk more then."

"Of course I will," he said. "I can't wait."

Bree took another deep breath as a little bit more of the negativity in her soul filtered out. "And Colt, I wanted to ask you something."

"Ask me anything, Bree."

"It's about Wes."

"I was hoping it would be."

Bree's chest tightened, because she missed Wes so much. She couldn't even adequately describe how much she longed to see him, and talk to him, and kiss him.

"I might have more than one question," she said, her voice pitching up.

"Ask them all," he said. "He's here for the weekend, but he went with Hunter and Gray to the lodge to get ice cream sandwiches. Did you know they're doing crazy contests during Thanksgiving too?"

Bree burst out laughing, more sunshine pouring into her soul. "And you didn't go? You love ice cream sandwiches."

"I needed a break from the twins. I stayed here with my parents and Annie. We like the quiet."

"I think you've aged a decade since you retired."

"Ha ha," he said, but he didn't deny it. "No," he said to someone on his end of the line. "It's Bree."

"Anyway," Bree said. "First question: do you think Wes will forgive me?"

"Yep," Colton said.

"Second question, and it's really two parts. First, will he be there for Christmas?"

"I'm working on that," Colton said. "Keep going."

"If he is," Bree said. "Will you get him up to the lodge?"

"By any means necessary."

Bree smiled. "And then, will you help me find the perfect gift for him, so I can show up at the lodge on Christmas Eve, when we do the gifts and the stockings and the tree lighting? Then I can give it to him in front of everyone, and tell him how much I love him, and beg him to forgive me. I figure he might not walk out if there's an audience."

Colton let a couple of seconds go by, and then he burst out laughing. "Bree, he's not going to walk out anyway, but I actually think that's a great idea."

Bree thought so too. Wes didn't mind being in the spotlight, she knew that. And he loved the people at the lodge—and more importantly, they loved him.

"So you won't be in Vermont for Christmas?" Colton asked.

"Nope," Bree said, deciding on the spot. "In fact, I'm going to invite my parents to the lodge, and get them there by any means necessary. Then they can meet Wes."

"I think you meant then they can meet me," Colton teased.

Bree giggled, and it had been a while since that had happened. "Ohh, is that what I meant?"

"I'm liking this plan," Colton mused.

"Put your thinking cap on," Bree said. "The gift has to be *really* good."

"Oh, whatever," Colton said. "You're the only gift he needs." Something loud sounded on his end of the line, and he said, "Oh my heck. They're back already. Gotta go."

"Okay," Bree said, but Colton didn't hang up. Something scuffled and scraped against the microphone on his phone, and she suspected he'd shoved the device in his pocket.

So the call was still open when she heard Wes ask, "Who were you talking to?"

"No one," Colton said, and even from thousands of miles across the country, Bree heard the false note in his voice.

But she fixated on the other male voice, the one that made her heartstrings hum and her pulse pounce.

"We brought you four ice cream sandwiches," Wes said. "My favorite is the mint one."

"You're not supposed to say your favorite," Colton said.

"Yeah, okay," Wes said, his voice dripping with sarcasm. "I didn't get that memo."

"He's not, right, Annie?"

"You're really not," she said.

Bree suddenly felt like a stalker—not to mention an outsider—as she listened to their conversation happening so close to her, and yet so far away.

"Didn't someone tell you that?" Annie asked.

"No, I bet they didn't," Colton said. "Remember how it was always Bree to lay out the rules for things like ice cream sandwich competitions?"

"Yeah, well, Bree wasn't there," Wes said darkly. "And don't think I haven't noticed how you try to work her into every conversation we have."

"I do not," Colton said.

Bree's heartbeat picked up steam.

"Uh huh," Wes said. "I can't wait to go home."

"And where is that, exactly?" Colton asked, his voice a bit acidic. "You don't have a place in Denver. Your house is a half-mile from here. Are you moving back here?"

"I don't know," Wes said. "But then at least I won't have to try to dodge you when you're all Bree-this and Bree-that."

"I do *not*—"

Bree cut off the call by touching the red phone icon on the screen. The resulting silence held equal parts excitement, hope, and fear.

"You have a plan," she coached herself. "This is going to happen." She got up and headed for the door. She had a lot to do to put the plan together, and the first step would be convincing her parents to come to Whiskey Mountain Lodge for the holidays.

Chapter Twenty-Nine

"I can*not* believe I'm doing this." Wes rode in the back seat of Colton's SUV, the scenery outside his window as familiar as his own face.

Because he was going up the canyon to Whiskey Mountain Lodge for Christmas. He had a packed bag in the back and everything. He, Hunter, and Gray were staying in a room in the basement that had two queen beds, and Annie had said it was quite nice. Apparently, she'd stayed in that room with her two daughters last year.

No one in the SUV said anything. Colton and Annie rode up front, and they'd all but shoehorned him into the vehicle while Gray had tossed their luggage in the cargo space behind the seat. Hunter rode next to him, smart to stay out of adult conversations and situations, and Gray sat on the other side of the SUV, also looking out his window.

He hadn't said a word about Elise in weeks, and Wes

didn't want to ask. He was sick and tired of Colton asking him about Bree, and he didn't want to make Gray feel the way he did. A certain level of tension also rode in the SUV, even when Colton flipped on the radio and *Jolly Old Saint Nicholas* came belting out of the speakers.

Hunter started to hum along, and then sing, and before he knew it, Wes's spirits had started to lift. Colton had told him a dozen times that Bree wouldn't be at the lodge. She was once again off to Vermont to see her family, and Wes should've been happy for her.

He *was* happy for her.

He was also extremely disappointed she hadn't called or texted him yet. Not even once.

His heart broke again, right there in the SUV as Colton rounded a corner and the towering Tetons came into view. Wes had given up on picking up the pieces and trying to stitch them back together. His heart would only break again the next day. Sometimes in the next hour.

The littlest things reminded him of Bree's silence, and the woman seemed to be *every*where in Coral Canyon. Literally, everywhere. He'd run into her friend from the employment office last night while buying sodas, and he'd seen a black sedan exactly like hers in the grocery store parking lot not ten minutes later.

Each time, his heart had started to beat again, throbbing painfully against all the shards that were stuck in there wrong. In the end, it hadn't mattered, because when he realized it didn't matter if he saw Willie or Bree's car—she hadn't called him. She hadn't texted him.

They weren't getting back together this Christmas.

He wondered how small pieces could get, because with each re-breaking of his heart, they seemed to get finer and finer, the edges sharper and sharper.

So he wasn't picking them up anymore. If his heart wanted to keep beating, it would have to figure out how to heal itself.

Colton pulled into the parking lot, where many other cars and trucks already were. He didn't bother with a spot but pulled right through the driveway where Wes used to check people in, take their bags upstairs, and then come back to move their cars to a space as part of the valet service at the lodge.

He'd learned all about the holiday traditions here at the lodge, but they hadn't come up on the twenty-first with the rest of the Whittakers.

No, today was Christmas Eve, and apparently, there were gifts to exchange and a tree to light. Then dinner. Wes didn't care about any of it. He actually thought Christmas was a great big waste of time if he didn't have anyone to spend it with.

You're spending it with your family, he thought as one Christmas song ended and another began. Colton cut the engine though, before the song could really get going.

But Hunter kept right on singing. "...and Prancer and Vixen. Comet, and Cupid, and Donner, and Blitzen."

"But do you recall?" Gray sang, joining in with his son.

"The most famous reindeer of all?" everyone chorused. Everyone except Wes, that was.

He did smile as they started in on, "Rudolph the red-nosed reindeer."

"Reindeer," Colton shouted, sending a wave of annoyance through Wes.

He opened his door and got out of the vehicle, ready to be back in his own house already, and they'd committed to staying at the lodge for a week.

A whole blasted week.

He had gone back to Denver after Thanksgiving, and he'd been staying at the farm with his parents. He still had his house here in Coral Canyon, and he was trying to decide how often he'd see Bree now that she wasn't working in town anymore.

At least he'd benefited a bit from running into Willie last night. She'd told him that Bree had quit last week, and that she'd just be back to her one job at the lodge. She lived up here, and she worked up here, and maybe they'd never see each other again, even if he did move back into the house he'd bought over the summer.

Gray opened the back of the SUV, and Wes took his bag. He did not want to be the first to enter the lodge, so he let Colton and Annie go first, and when they opened the front door, a literal wall of noise hit them.

A cheer went up, and calls of "Hello," and "Welcome" came from inside. Wes entered last, immediately swallowed up by the enthusiasm and energy pulsing through the huge living room. Most people seemed to have gathered there, and a couple of them were still hanging ornaments at the top of the tallest, broadest pine tree Wes had ever seen.

"Ho-ly cow," he said, tipping his head back to look up at it. "That thing is incredible."

Graham laughed and drew Wes into a hug. He clapped him on the back and said, "It's so good to see you. How have you been?"

"Good," Wes said, but he couldn't help feeling like it was a lie.

"How were the other ten states?"

"I only went to nine," Wes said. "Still have Hawaii on my list."

"Oh, maybe Laney and I will go with you." Graham beamed at him. "We've been wanting to get out of the snow for a while."

"Deal," Wes said. He liked Graham a whole lot, and he wouldn't mind lying on the beach next to the man. His kids were calm, and his wife was kind, and Wes maybe needed to trade in his annoying, loud brother for someone like Graham.

"Come in, come in," Graham said. "The stockings are all around the hearth and the walls. We're going to start in about a half an hour."

Wes glanced around, finding several people carrying boxes that they removed small gifts from and dipped them into the stockings. Annie and Colton had warned him, Hunter, and Gray of this, so they had little trinkets for everyone too. Wes fully expected to find a stocking with his name on it, but a slip of surprise still stole through him when he did.

"This is amazing," Hunter said from behind him. "Dad, was it like this when you came a few years ago?"

"No, son," Gray said. "Not quite." He seemed filled with

wonder too, and Wes knew the feeling. "Grab Uncle Wes's bag and take them downstairs for us, okay, son?"

"Yes, sir."

Wes handed his bag to Hunter, who did as his father asked. Wes didn't know where to stand or where he belonged. So he stuck close to Gray as his brother went around and passed out the Hammond candy they'd brought from Denver. Hunter returned, but he got swept up by Annie, who was standing with Graham's oldest daughter and Eli's oldest son. They were a few years older than Hunter, but they were the closest to his age.

Everything blurred, and finally, Gray said, "Okay, let's sit by Colton."

Their brother had saved a few spots in the back, and Wes was glad for a chair as more people started piling into the room.

The speaker system dinged and donged, and Pasty said, "It's time for the tree-lighting. Please gather in the great room for our annual Christmas Eve celebration."

Wes's heart started to tingle with the magic of Christmas, and he could grudgingly admit he was glad he'd come to the lodge for this.

Graham stood and raised both hands, which started to calm the loud crowd. "Welcome to Whiskey Mountain Lodge," he said, his voice booming over everyone. A toddler fussed somewhere, but Wes didn't try to find where.

"We're thrilled to have even more Hammonds with us this year, and we welcome them." He grinned at the corner where

Wes, Colton, and Gray sat with Hunter, and Wes did his best to put a smile on his face. Everyone here seemed so happy, and he wondered how they did it.

"Oh, there's Elise," Colton whispered, and Wes watched Gray jerk to attention, his eyes immediately tracking the blonde woman as she scurried toward the front of the crowd and sat on the floor in front of a couch. She took a little girl from someone, and Wes lost sight of her.

Graham continued with, "And we have more visitors I'll introduce in a second. Most of you know we do a tree-lighting every Christmas Eve. A lot of us have had a turn to flip that switch and make this behemoth shine for all the world to see. Every year, it's a chore to try to decide who should light the tree."

He surveyed the crowd. "Someone even suggested we should have a contest to see who should do it." Laughter and chuckles raced through the crowd. "But then I was informed that we do far too many contests, and we're doing Cupcake Wars this year, so Laney and I simply wrote down all the names and put them in our Bingo basket."

Wes knew it wasn't going to be him, so he didn't much care who flipped the switch. His stomach growled, and he knew that after this, he'd get his gifts and get to eat. Honestly, sometimes he forgot to eat, and the only way he remembered was with an alarm on his phone or his mother telling him it was time for dinner.

"And our winner this year was Bree," Graham said, and that got Wes to come back to life. His heart jumped and jolted as if someone had attached him to a live battery. He expected Graham to say, *But she's not here. So someone else will have to flip the switch.*

But he didn't.

He waited a second, then two, then three. The time dragged on and on, and Wes grew more and more nervous.

"So let's get her out here to do the honors."

He pulled in a breath, very aware of both of his brother's eyes on him. In fact, as Wes searched the only two entrances in this room—the front door to his right, which also allowed him to see the staircase coming down from the second floor—and the wide doorway that led back into the kitchen—more and more people looked at him.

Until everyone was looking at him.

And he still didn't see Bree.

She couldn't be here.

He couldn't be in the same room with her and not be with her. It was too hard, too painful, simply too much.

He stood up to leave at the same time Bree walked through the doorway from the kitchen.

Time froze, stilling Wes with it.

She looked amazing in a tight pair of dark jeans and a bright red sweater with snowflakes on it. Her hair was dark, and long, and held the wave he loved to run his fingers through when he kissed her.

She seemed to shine with an inner light he hadn't seen before, making her more beautiful than even he remembered. In her hands, she carried a box about the size of a loaf of bread, and she didn't have to look very hard to find him.

He had to leave.

Now.

"Excuse me," he said, practically shouting the words as he tried to step over one of the Everett sisters. Then their parents. Only a few more people to go, and he'd have a free path to the front door.

His lungs hurt, and he started to see spots in his vision.

Free of the row of people, he took one step before he met a wall of cowboys. Graham, Eli, Andrew, and Beau all blocked his exit now. Todd stood up too, a little boy in his arms, and behind him came Colton and Gray.

"Wes," Bree said. "Could you stay for a second?"

He spun toward her, the feelings of being trapped escalating, growing, choking him. Their eyes met, and something inside Wes calmed. A voice shouted at him that he'd said his name. That same voice reminded him that he'd told her all she had to do was call or text.

This was in-person, and so much better.

Or is it? he wondered. Maybe it would be so much worse.

She raised the gift in her hands slightly. "I got this for you, and I was hoping you'd open it in front of everyone."

Wes felt the weight of dozens of eyes, but he couldn't look away from Bree. She was the same woman he'd fallen in love with, but...better. Happier. So much more beautiful, and not only physically.

He found himself picking his way through the people in the room until he stood four feet from Bree, both of them standing in front of the magnificent Christmas tree. He looked at her, his cells vibrating at her nearness.

The hope inside him that had gone dormant screamed now, lifting and shooting toward the sky.

"I know gifts don't make up for mistakes," she said. "Heaven knows I know that better than most people." She spoke in an even tone, not a hitch of emotion in her voice at all. She moved the gift closer to him. "I know it won't make up for everything, but I'm hoping it's a start. And I'm hoping that you and I can start over. A fresh start. A second start."

She swallowed as Wes took the package. It was much heavier than he expected it to be, and he looked down at the bright green bow and back to her. "I don't—"

"I know you don't need it," she said. "After all, what does one buy a cowboy billionaire?" She grinned and looked out at the crowd. "Thankfully, there's a few women here who understand my dilemma, and we've been brainstorming for a few weeks."

"Just women?" a man asked, and somewhere in the back of his mind, Wes knew it was Colton.

"Not just women," Bree said. "Colton has helped a lot, actually."

"No wonder he wouldn't let me stay home," Wes muttered, and Bree giggled.

Wes was completely entranced by her, and he wondered if he could skip the presents and the apologies and go right to kissing her.

"I hope you can forgive me," Bree said. "For my silence. For any hurt I've caused. For being so dang slow to figure things out." Her voice broke then, and Wes balanced the gift in one hand and swept the other around her.

The crowd sighed then, and Wes did too. In fact, everything inside him sighed in absolute relief that she was here.

"Come here," he whispered, and he drew her to his chest while she cried.

"I'm fine," she said, but she clung to him like she wasn't fine.

Someone cleared their throat, but Wes had pressed his eyes closed so he could memorize the way this woman felt next to him.

"Okay, that's a lie," Bree said, stepping back slightly. She kept her arms wrapped right around him though. Looking up at him, she said, "I'm not fine, nor will I ever be fine, without you. I love you." She smiled a wobbly grin at him. "I love you so much, and I really just need a yes or no answer."

"What's the question?" Colton called.

"Can you forgive me?" Bree asked.

"And a follow-up question," Elise said.

Wes knew then that she'd planned this with them. Joy burst through him, and he let it spill onto his face in the form of a smile.

"Can we please start again?" Bree asked.

Wes couldn't imagine ever telling her no. Not to these two questions, and not ever.

"Yes or no answer?" he asked.

"That's right."

"And I can keep the gift no matter what?"

Bree giggled again and swatted his chest. "Yes."

"Oh, all right," Wes said. "Then I guess my answer is yes."

Cheers like he'd never heard filled the air, with loud men

whooping, and applause that could deafen anyone. Wes grinned at her, handed the gift to someone else—he didn't know who—and lowered his mouth to Bree's.

Heaven, he thought as he kissed her, this woman he loved so much and hadn't stopped loving despite their three months apart. *This is what heaven feels like.*

Chapter Thirty

CORAL CANYON

Bree had forgotten how beautiful and wonderful it felt to be kissed by Wes. She didn't mind that literally everyone she knew—including her parents—was watching, and she kissed him back with as much passion as she dared.

"All right," Graham finally said. "All right. Let's settle down again."

Bree broke the kiss with Wes, who leaned his forehead against hers, the very real presence of his body next to hers almost too much to fathom. She'd dreamt of it for so long, and while she'd been over every scenario of what might happen when Graham said she got to light the tree, she had not imagined Wes wouldn't even open the gift before he accepted her and forgave her.

And she knew it was because he'd already accepted her, forgiven her, and loved her.

No gift needed.

She was still going to make him open it though.

"I love you," he whispered while Graham said Bree really did get to light the tree.

"Come flip the switch with me," she said, slipping her fingers into his and tugging him toward the bank of light switches near the doorway she'd come through. Standing on the other side of that wall had been one of the hardest things she'd ever done, and she knew she still had a couple of hard conversations to have with Wes.

"Okay," she called to the room, her voice nowhere near as loud as Graham's. "One...two...three!" She pushed the switch, and the Christmas tree lights burst to life, filling the branches and boughs with heavenly, white light.

A chorus of *oooh*'s filled the air, and Bree took a few moments to admire the tree before she turned her attention back to the man she admired.

"This is great," he said.

"Is it?" she asked. "Because I think Colton told me, and I quote, that you were 'being a wolf' about coming."

Wes rolled his eyes, a stitch of tension coming from him. "He's been annoying me lately."

"That's because you need your own place," Bree said.

"So you know everything, then. Is that it?" A flicker of hurt entered his expression. "Everyone knew you were going to be here but me."

"Yes," she said. "But that was because we all thought you wouldn't come if you knew."

"I told you all you had to do was call or text."

"I know," she said, her own hurt feelings and fluttering

anxiety pulsing through her. "But I didn't know how. This—I knew how to do this."

Wes just looked at her, those dark eyes devouring her over and over and over.

"Are you going to open your present?" she asked as Laney, Vi, and Amanda started handing out the stockings.

"If you want me to," he said. "I have something I want to ask you first."

"All right."

"Are you going to tell me about your family?"

"Yes," she said with certainty. "And if you don't mind waiting to open the present, you can meet my parents right now."

Hope lit Wes's face. "Is that right?"

Bree looked over her shoulder, where her mom and dad had their eyes glued to her and Wes. "That's right. They're right there."

He followed her gaze, and she felt him shake off his nerves and tighten his hand in hers. "What are their names?"

"Come find out." Bree led him over to her parents, and she grinned at them and then him. "Mom, Dad, this is Wesley Hammond. Wes, this is my mom and dad, Julie and Jerry Richards."

"It's so great to meet you," he said, his voice rich and rolling with pure sophistication. "I'd say Bree has told me a lot about you, but she hasn't."

"Oh, we know," Dad said, grinning. "She's going to fix that, though." Dad shook Wes's hand, and looked at Bree with little bolts of electricity in his eyes. "He's amazing, Bree."

"He's standing right here, Dad."

"Yeah, and he should know he's amazing." Her father smiled at Wes again, but he was shaking her mom's hand.

"Ma'am," he said.

"So nice to meet the love of Bree's life," Mom said, and Bree thought she might be laying it on a bit thick. "We have heard a whole lot about you, Wes, and it's all been wonderful."

Wes glanced at her. "Is that right?"

"One-hundred percent right," Bree said. "I told them you're the reason all of this started. The reason I'm able to talk to them. The reason I went home to Vermont for the first time in twenty years. The reason we have our family back."

Wes did not smile. In fact, his eyes grew more serious. "What? Why?"

"Without you," Mom said. "Bree would still be limping through each day. But you showed up, and fell in love with her —a woman who has never felt loved—and she wanted to be the woman you thought she was."

Wes shifted his feet, glancing at her and back to her parents, still searching for an answer Bree knew made no sense.

"Wes," she said gently. "When you refused to just let me keep my secrets, you forced me to examine what I really wanted. Who I really was. What I'd really done." Bree's first instinct kicked in again, and that was to shut down this conversation and hurry back to her cabin. She fought against the feeling, and she'd won several times before, so she knew she would again.

"And I did that. I learned that I really *didn't* want to be alone. I wanted to talk to my mother and father. I wanted to heal. I wanted *you*."

"It's true," Dad said. "I did hear that a lot. 'I want Wes'."

"And I really am a child of God, and He loves me, and he wanted me to be the kind of woman you already loved. So I've been working on that. It's slow, I'll admit."

"It's fine," Wes murmured, his eyes down and his head down, his cowboy hat concealing his face.

"And I just have to tell you what I've done, and I pray you'll understand." Jitters romped through her, because this still wasn't over.

"He will," Mom said. "I get a good feeling from this one."

Wes lifted his eyes to her mother's, and before she knew it, her mom stepped forward and hugged Wes. He embraced her back, and she whispered something in his ear. He nodded, and when he looked at Bree again, he nodded toward the doorway that led away from the chaos still happening with the stockings.

"Don't forget your gift," Dad said, handing it to her. Bree took it and went with Wes down the hall toward the master suite. Amanda and Finn stayed in there during the holidays, but she'd already spoken with them about using the room if she needed to speak to Wes privately.

With the door closed and locked behind them, she handed him the gift again. "Please open it."

He did, taking his time with the ribbons and wrappings, finally getting to the cylindrical container. "You didn't." He lifted his eyes to hers, and they glowed with an inner fire. "I love this ice cream cake."

"I know you do. Colton's told me about fifty times."

"Ah, so he annoys you too."

Bree burst out laughing, and she didn't deny it. "He just wants us to be happy." She nodded to the squat, wide tube. "There's more in there."

"There is?" He opened the top and pulled out the envelope she'd had to fold in half to get it inside. He unfolded it and smoothed it out before opening the flap. He took out the paper she'd placed inside, his eyes scanning, reading, absorbing.

"You're going to take me to Hawaii." He looked at her, and Bree found all the desire, all the love, the entire world, in Wes's expression.

"Yep," she said, grinning. "State number fifty. Your quest won't be complete if we don't go."

"I can't wait." He set the ice cream cake down and drew her into another hug. "I really do love you, Bree. So much."

"I love you too." She kissed him, and this time, because there was no audience, she didn't have to stop any time soon.

* * *

A couple of hours later, they sat on her front porch, in the swing that used to rest on the back patio at the lodge. He kept them gently rocking back and forth by touching his toe to the ground every so often. They'd talked through almost everything that had happened over the last three months. He'd told her about his adventures in the nine states he'd visited.

She only had one more thing to tell him.

"Okay," she said. "Are you ready?"

"If you are." He pressed his lips to her forehead.

"I'm ready." Bree leaned into his body and told herself this was what she'd been working for. This moment, right here. To put her complete faith and trust in Wes, the man she loved.

"When I was fifteen years old, I disobeyed my mother," she started. "It was wintertime—February—and very cold outside. Or so I thought, because it was always cold in Vermont in February. But my mom watched the news, and she knew we'd had a week or so of warmer-than-usual temperatures. And in Vermont, where there are a lot of lakes and rivers, warm temperatures means the ice starts to melt."

She worked not to let her voice slip into a monotone. Her therapist had asked her to be present when she told the story, especially for Wes. Let herself feel. Relive what had happened.

"I didn't know any of this, of course. My mom told me and my brother—I have a brother—not to go on the ice. But I wanted to cross the river and get over to the beaver dam, because the baby beavers had just been born. So Bronson, who was thirteen years old, and I left the house and ran through the yard and the orchards to the river, which goes right behind our house."

She looked at Wes, but he had his gaze out in front of him, focused in the darkness.

Bree blinked, and she could see Bronson standing on the riverbank, his eyes wide and hopeful. "Bronson didn't want to cross the river. I'd already started across, and I told him it was fine. The ice was strong. Mom didn't know what she was talking about."

She saw him hesitate.

"I saw him struggling to make a decision, and I called back to him, 'don't be a baby. Come on. The beavers had their pups,' and I kept going. When I was only a few feet away from the opposite bank, I heard the first, terrible cracking sound. It's awful. It's unlike anything you've ever heard before. Almost like a whip, and it echoes in the surrounding silence."

Bree shuddered, and Wes kneaded her closer to his chest. "I can still hear it to this day. I spun around, and the ice was breaking. I had a few feet to go, and I jumped with everything I had. Behind me, I heard Bronson yelp. I heard the tell-tale splash of water. I knew he'd gone into the river of ice."

"Bree," Wes said softly.

"I have to finish," she said, her tears burning the backs of her eyes. She'd made it farther in the story than ever before without crying. So that was something. "I was on my hands and knees, and I turned around, screaming his name. I saw him go under once, then twice. He came back up one more time, his hair plastered to his forehead. He sucked at the air and sputtered, trying to find something to grab onto." She stared out into the darkness now too, so glad it wasn't inside her anymore. She had no idea how she'd carried it for so long.

"And then he went under for the last time. I screamed and screamed, sobbed and sobbed. I got a branch and tried to go out to help him." She shrugged like she'd lost something that didn't matter. "He was gone. No one could help him. My parents came, and so did two neighbors, because they heard me screaming. We found his body four days later, down the river about half a mile."

She let her tears fall then, because while she had never been allowed to see Bronson's body, she almost thought it would've been better if she had. Then she wouldn't have to try to imagine what he'd looked like.

"I killed him. At least that's what I thought. I've carried this huge weight my whole life, hating myself for what I did. For taking him from my parents. For not listening to my mom. His death was my fault, and I'm learning to deal with that now."

"Bree, sweetheart," Wes said, folding her into his arms. "It's not your fault."

"I thought everyone would hate me as much as I hated myself," she whispered into his coat. "So I left Marble Falls the moment I could, and I didn't go back. I barely spoke to my parents, and I thought I could make a life for myself with the door closed solidly on my past."

"I'm so sorry," Wes whispered. "I didn't mean to make you open that door."

"I'm *glad* you made me open that door," she said, inching back and settling back into his side. "Please don't hate me."

"Of course I don't hate you."

"I did not think anyone could love me until you said you did," she whispered. "That moment changed everything for me. It devastated me and gave me hope at the same time."

"I do love you."

"Even now?" Bree's tears tracked down her face as she tipped her head back to look into Wes's eyes.

"*Especially* now," he said, dipping his head to kiss her. "I will always love you, Bree. Always."

"Thank you, Wes," she whispered, and then she kissed him again, her gratitude and faith in the Lord strengthened by his good soul, his kind spirit.

And thank you, she said to the Lord. She knew without Him, she wouldn't be where she was today. She wouldn't have Wes. And she wouldn't be the woman He needed her to be.

Thank you.

Chapter Thirty-One

Wes rolled over, the light coming through his blinds bright enough to tell him morning had arrived. He took his time opening his eyes, and he'd just sat up when he heard a door in his house slam.

"It's me," Colton yelled, and Wes whistled between his teeth to call his brother's dog. Sparky came trotting into the bedroom, as it wasn't his first time in the house. He jumped up on the bed and Wes lifted his arm as he chuckled. Sparky had soft, semi-curly fur, and Wes had learned he was a labradoodle, and a smart one at that.

"You're still in bed?"

"Yes," Wes said. "Technically." He stood up and faced the dog. "Now I'm not." He scrubbed Sparky, and the dog flopped on his back and stretched out his front legs so Wes could scratch his belly and chest. He grinned at the dog, because Sparky was just so lovable.

"Your plane leaves in five hours."

"Yeah," Wes said, looking up. "I own a clock."

"You have to leave in an hour." Colton glanced around, his eyes landing on the suitcase Wes had started packing last night. "Oh, good. You're packed."

"Almost, *Mom*," Wes said, chuckling. "I'm getting in the shower. Why are you here?" He rounded the bed and started for the bathroom, knowing his brother would just follow him.

"We need to talk about Gray."

"No, we don't," Wes said, pulling his shirt over his head. But Colton would talk anyway. Wes grabbed his toothbrush from the shelf in the shower and slid some paste on it before stepping back inside the stall. He let the hot water pour over his head as he scrubbed his teeth clean, as Colton talked.

"He's miserable in Denver. He doesn't have anything to do but run, and honestly, who can do that twenty-four-seven? He should move up here. I keep telling him we have schools with the seventh grade in them."

"Mm," Wes said, his mouth full of foam.

Colton took that as agreement and kept going. "I'm going to talk to Mom and Dad too. They're too old to keep that farm, and it's time to sell."

That was never going to happen, and Colton knew it. They both did. Wes spat and rinsed, finally saying, "They're not going to sell it."

"I know." Colton sighed so loud, Wes could hear him above the spray of the shower. "Maybe Ames will buy it. Keep it in the family."

"Maybe," Wes said. "Any of us could buy it if it's a matter of keeping the house and land in the family. Heck, Mom and

Dad could keep it if that's the case. They don't owe any money on it."

"True." Colton fell silent for a minute. "Would you talk to them about it?"

"Maybe when I get back from Maui," Wes said, moving onto his hair. "Why do you want them up here?"

"Because I think we're all going to live here anyway," Colt said. "They can't take care of those animals. They need to sell them and come up here. Get a nice house they can take care of. Be by me and Annie and you and Bree."

"Sounds nice, actually," Wes said. He soaped up, waiting for Colt to keep going.

"So you'll talk to them, and I'll try to get Gray to tell me what really happened with Elise."

"She won't tell you?" Wes finished bathing and turned off the shower. He opened the door and reached for a towel, running it through his hair and across his shoulders before cinching it around his waist.

"No," Colton said quite crossly. "Neither one of them will say."

"Well, they're still talking," Wes said. "Not everyone falls in love in eight days, Colt."

His brother shot him a death glare, but Wes just shrugged one shoulder and stepped over to the mirror. "I don't want to shave."

"Then don't. You're just going to be lying on the beach."

"I'm not going to." Wes stepped into his closet and picked up the clothes he'd reserved to wear today. He dressed while

Colton continued to muse about Gray and Elise and if they were talking or not.

"And I just don't know. I have this feeling like he's sabotaging again, and you know how I am when I get a feeling."

"Yes, I do," Wes said, finally looking fully at his brother. "Listen, Colt. You're an amazing brother, and it is pretty special how you have these gut feelings about us. But Gray is a grown man, with a son, and he knows what he's doing."

"Does he, though?"

"Better than you," Wes said. "Please don't say anything to him while I'm gone."

"But—"

"Colton."

"Okay," Colton said, but he didn't look happy about it.

"We'll talk when I get back, and we can decide if an intervention is needed then."

Colton folded his arms. "Fine."

Wes didn't doubt Colton. If he said he wouldn't say anything, he wouldn't. Wes put the toiletries he'd just used to get ready for the day in his suitcase, rolled up his phone charger and added that to the bag, and stood there, trying to remember what else he needed.

Nothing.

He was ready to visit the fiftieth state in the United States of America, and the trip was extra-special because he was going with Bree.

"Do you have the ring?" Colton asked, as if Wes had lost his mind and couldn't do anything without Colton's constant reminders.

"Yes," Wes said. The diamond engagement ring he'd bought for Bree was one of the first things Wes had packed. He'd had it for two weeks now, and Colton had done some very clever sleuthing to get her ring size so Wes could get the engagement band perfect before he asked her to be his forever.

He'd had the ring back for a couple of days now, and he reached into his bag and past his T-shirts just to quadruple-check that he had the ring. He did.

He zipped his bag closed, added his tablet to his backpack, and took everything out to the truck. Colton followed him and loaded Sparky in the back of his truck.

The two brothers faced one another, and Wes found he had nothing to say. He embraced Colton and just hugged him tight.

"Have fun," Colton said. "Ask her tonight when you get there. Then it's over with."

"We'll see," Wes said as he stepped back. He loved Bree, and he wanted to get married with his whole heart and soul. But it was almost February, which he now knew was a very hard month for Bree. They'd be in Hawaii for seventeen days, through the start of the month, and he'd been hoping and praying he could give her new memories for the month of February.

They'd talked about marriage and family, and Bree would be thirty-seven in a couple of months. Plenty of time to have kids, she'd told him, but Wes wanted to get started right away. He didn't want to be seventy years old before his kids started graduating from high school.

You already will be, he told himself, not for the first time.

He sat on the front steps while Colton drove away, and he only waited a couple of minutes before Bree's black sedan pulled into his driveway.

He got up to help her with her baggage and kiss her hello, and he wondered if he could ask her to be his wife right there in the garage. No, he wasn't going to do that.

"Ready?" she asked.

"Sure am. You?"

"I've been looking forward to this for weeks." She gave him a bright smile, the happiness pouring off her.

Wes basked in it, because he loved how strongly she felt things now. "It's a long flight," he said. "I hope they let me stand up on the plane."

"We're flying first class," she said. "They let you do what you want up there."

He chuckled and shook his head. "All right, let's go do what we want, then."

Hours and hours later, they'd flown from Wyoming to Hawaii, across the wide, beautiful Pacific Ocean, landed, and gotten their rental car. Wes turned where his phone told him to, and a charming cottage came into view.

"Oh, this is nice," Bree said.

"The reviews were good." Wes peered out the windshield at the cottage. "It's not huge, but we'll have our own room and own bathroom."

Bree just pushed her fingers through her hair and smiled, and Wes pulled up to the house. He got out, the air filled with humidity he wasn't used to. "Wow, it's hot, yeah?"

"It's not cold," she said. "It's so weird it's not cold." She giggled and took her smaller bag toward the house. "How do we get in?"

"There's a code," he said, pulling the rest of the luggage from the back of the SUV. "Just a sec." He swiped and tapped on his phone to find the email, and then he read the code to her. She got the lock open and entered the cottage first.

"Hot in here too," she said.

"No air conditioning," he said, following her. "Just fans." He went inside too, and while the space was small, it was clean. A living room expanded in front of him, with just enough room for one couch and one chair. To his right sat the kitchen, complete with a quaint round table with two chairs. Perfect for him and Bree.

A hall ran down the middle of the house, with two bedrooms at the end of it, one on each side. One had a bathroom attached; the other bathroom sat in the hall. Wes put Bree's bag in the bedroom with the attached bathroom, despite her protests.

He couldn't help thinking that if they were married, he could be in that bedroom with her. He kept his back to the door as he unzipped his bag and dug for the diamond. Colton had been right; Wes needed to do this immediately.

Not only that, but a crazy idea had occurred to him just now, and he couldn't shake it.

"Getting your swim trunks on already?" Bree asked, her hands snaking around him as she pressed into his back.

"Not quite yet," he said, his fingers meeting the velvety box that held the ring. He pulled it out and took a steeling breath. "I wanted to ask you something first."

"All right."

He shifted, and she moved with him, allowing him room to turn around. He didn't waste any time opening the box. "Bree, I'm in love with you, and I want you to be my wife as soon as possible."

He gazed down at the gorgeous diamond. It was set deep in a thick, gold band, and sparkled like the sapphire cut it was.

Raising his eyes to her face, he asked, "Will you marry me?"

"Wes." She pressed both hands to her chest, staring at the ring. Her eyes were wide, excited, and afraid when they met his. "Yes."

He grinned at her. "Just like that?"

"Just like that, cowboy." She leaned into him, threading her arms around him again.

"I had a crazy idea," he whispered, leaning closer to her. "You put this on right now, and we go find someone to marry us tonight."

She stiffened in his arms, but she didn't step away. "That is a crazy thought."

"Completely wild," he said, touching his lips to her neck, then up by her ear. "I love you, and I can't stand the thought of you sleeping across the hall without me."

Bree swayed with him, letting him lightly kiss along her earlobe, then her temple, and down to her collarbone again. "All right."

Wes pulled away, sure his hearing had malfunctioned. "What?"

"You call your mother and make sure it's okay with her,"

she said. "I'll livestream the ceremony with my parents so they can see it."

"Are you serious?"

"Are you?" Bree lifted her eyebrows, almost a challenge.

Wes thought fast, trying to decide if his family would be upset if they didn't get to attend the wedding. "Let me call my mother." He reached for his phone, his heart pounding. When he'd woken up that morning, he hadn't anticipated today being his wedding day.

What would he wear? He hadn't brought anything nice—only shorts and T-shirts, swim trunks and flip flops.

"Wes," his mother said, and Wes pulled his thoughts together. "Did you make it to Hawaii, baby?"

"Sure did, Mom," he said. "It's beautiful." He gazed at Bree, who'd sat on his bed and was texting on her phone, her fingers flying over the screen.

"All fifty states."

"In less than a year," he added with a chuckle. "Hey, I wanted to ask you something, and you just be real honest with me, okay?"

"Okay."

"We got here, and I'd already bought Bree an engagement ring, and I just asked her to marry me. She said yes, and well, I had this wild idea that we should get married tonight." He didn't want to get into too many details. "But I don't want you to be upset you aren't here."

"Oh." His mother said nothing more, and Wes knew he'd hit her with something big. Mom always had something to say, and when she didn't, that was newsworthy.

"Bree is going to livestream it to her parents."

"Maybe we could watch with them," Mom said. "I'm going to talk to your dad. Chris, Wes is on the phone, and he and Bree want to get married tonight."

"Tonight?" his father said, and the next thing Wes knew, his dad was on the phone. "Wes, what's going on?"

"Exactly what Mom said," Wes said.

Bree rose from the bed, giving him a thumbs-up. He pulled the phone away from his mouth. "Can my mom and dad watch too?"

"Sure," she said. "We just have to send them the link."

"So everyone can watch," he said.

"Yes."

"Let's send it to everyone," Wes said. "If they can watch, great. If not, well, that's life."

"Wes," his dad said.

"We're going to send you and Mom a link so you can watch the wedding," Wes said, giddiness starting to fill his chest.

"When?"

"Not sure," Wes said. "Soonish."

"All right," his father said, his voice somewhat resigned.

"Love you guys," Wes said. "Did Mom hear?"

"I heard," his mother said. "We love you too." The call ended, and he looked at Bree. A strange, almost hysterical laugh came out of his mouth.

"Now we just need to find somewhere to get married," he said.

"You do that," Bree said. "I'm going to make our link and send it to everyone in Wyoming, Colorado, and Vermont."

Wes felt like he'd gotten the harder job, but he dutifully got out his computer, connected to the Wi-Fi at the cottage, and searched. Surprisingly, at least a dozen places came up within a single second. He had no idea it was that easy to get married on such short notice. They'd gone to Maui, not Las Vegas.

He called the place at the top of the search results, and said, "Hey, I'm wondering if my fiancée and I can get married tonight."

"Do you have a reservation?" the man asked.

"Nope," Wes said. "We just landed less than an hour ago."

"Let me check something," he said, and the line went silent. Only a few seconds later, he came back and said, "We have an officiant that just finished a wedding, and he's willing to wait for you guys if you can get here within an hour."

"Tell me where," Wes said, his heart thumping now.

"White Rock Beach," the man said. "He just got back to our office, but he's ten minutes away."

"We'll be there. What's his name?"

"Adam Garland."

"Thank you," Wes said. "How do I pay for this?"

"Come to the office. I'll hold Adam here, and then you guys can go to the beach together." He rattled off the address, and Wes quickly put him on speaker and typed it into his phone when he said it the second time.

"Okay," he said, and he hung up a moment later. He turned to Bree, feeling somewhat numb. "We've got a beach and an officiant. We need to be there in an hour, and it's...." He looked down at his phone. "Fifteen minutes from here."

"Let me change and put some makeup on," she said, ducking into her bedroom.

Wes stood there, stunned. All at once, he turned back to his suitcase and started pulling clothes out. Surely he'd brought one pair of pants. "Ah-ha," he said, pulling out a pair of jeans. He changed into those and his nicest polo, which happened to be a smooth gray that matched his cowboy hat, which he'd also brought.

Ready, he picked up the ring he hadn't put on Bree's finger and went into the living room. Ten minutes later, she came out of the bedroom wearing a white maxi dress that had wide straps running over her shoulders.

"You actually have a white dress," he said, drinking her in.

"It's got peach flowers on it," she said, holding the gauzy material out. Wes caught the edge of the flowers, but they didn't erase his grin.

"It's beautiful," he said. "You're beautiful."

She stepped easily into his arms. "You really want to do this?"

"More than anything."

"You look nice."

"I'm wearing jeans and a polo."

"And the hat." She reached up and touched it, gently taking it off so she could kiss him. And Wes had absolutely spoken true. He wanted to marry her more than anything. "I don't have a ring for you," she whispered.

"We'll go get one tomorrow," he whispered back. "You really want to do this?"

"Yes," she said. "More than anything."

"Then let's go get married, gorgeous." Excitement skipped through Wes like a flickering flame, and when Bree started laughing, he joined in.

She sighed once they were in the rental car. She reached across the console between them and took his hand in hers. "I love you, Wes."

"I love you too, Bree."

* * *

Read on for a sneak peek of **GRAY,** featuring single dad Gray Hammond and Colton's best friend, Elise Murphy. **You can read it in paperback right now!**

Sneak Peek! Gray - Chapter One

Gray Hammond checked his teeth one more time in the rear-view mirror, though he hadn't had anything in them when he'd left Wes's house. Gray never went anywhere without all the proper pieces in exactly the right place—at least he hadn't for the past twenty years.

Now that he was done at HMC, he had no idea what his days would hold. Probably a lot of time spent in pants with an elastic waistband and hours on the farm his parents refused to sell. A frown marched through his eyebrows at the thought of them on that piece of land, with all those animals, none of which they could take care of. His father tried, but he was almost eighty years old, and Gray had started talking to Ames about staging an intervention.

If there was a brother who would take such a thing seriously, it was Ames. The man took *everything* seriously, and most of the time, that grated on Gray's nerves. And *he* was the lawyer in the family. He, by profession, took things seriously.

But an intervention with Ames involved would have steps and rules, and Gray had told him his concerns for a reason. Their parents simply couldn't stay on the farm much longer.

Ames and Cy had gathered to the farm in Ivory Peaks for the holidays, just to give Gray and Hunter a break. Gray felt like he needed a vacation from his life, and he was having a hard time not to take one. The only thing anchoring him in one place at the moment was Hunter. Hunter's school.

He couldn't just pack a bag and board a plane and come back to his life when he felt like it, the way Wes had after he'd retired from the family company. He couldn't move to Coral Canyon at the drop of a hat for a woman, the way Colton had done.

Gray loved his son very much, but he alone knew that his life wasn't entirely his own. "It's fine, Lord," he said to himself. "I don't mean to complain. I love Hunter, and I'd rather he be with me than his mother." He let out his breath, hoping some of the negativity he harbored inside would go with it. A bit of tension released from his shoulders, and he added, "Guide me to what I should do next."

Gray's future was wide open, he knew that. Hunter would keep getting up in the morning and going to school. There would be science fair projects, and math homework he didn't know how to do, and a brand new challenge for both of them —junior high. Multiple classes, dances...girls.

That last one Gray barely knew what to do with himself. His first marriage had been one long fight, and when it had finally ended, he hadn't even recognized himself anymore. He'd tried a couple of relationships since, and both of them had been nothing but disaster after disaster. He should've known he couldn't date in the greater Denver area—at least not anyone who used the Internet or drove down the freeways. His surname was everywhere there, and the two women he'd been out with since Sheila's departure from his life had been after only one thing: Money.

That had hurt Gray, sure. But the worst part was knowing that Hunter had started to bond with Maddie. She'd known it, too, and she'd exploited the boy to get money from Gray for her. He'd never been so angry in his life. And having to explain his failures and shortcomings to a seven-year-old?

Gray hadn't dated in years. Four years, to be precise. Which was why he still hadn't gotten out of his truck either.

Elise would likely be here already. He'd pulled in right at the time they were set to meet, and he'd been sitting in the vehicle for at least ten minutes. She hadn't called or texted yet, but he knew he was probably causing some anxiety in her soul too. And he didn't want to do that.

"Help me," he begged as he got out of the truck. The chill in Wyoming in December was not to be trifled with, and Gray flipped up the collar on his coat to keep the wind off his neck. Someone had cleared the sidewalks, but he had to traverse snow and sleet to get there. His leather cowboy boots kept the dampness off his feet, and he hurried the rest of the way to the entrance of the restaurant.

He'd let Elise pick where she wanted to eat, because he didn't live here and didn't know what was good. By the level of noise and the amount of people waiting inside the reception area, he knew this place must be popular.

Glancing around, he searched for the beautiful blonde who'd first caught his eye at Colton's house. Elise was light everywhere Gray was dark, and he wondered if their opposites extended to other things. He hadn't spoken to her a whole lot over the months, little things here and there. The woman loved memes, and whenever Gray saw one he thought she'd like, he sent it to her.

They talked about Colton and Annie, her work at the lodge, and Bree. He did know she loved to bake and was good at it, and that she could literally cultivate any plant back to life. But most of what he knew about Elise hadn't come from her, but Colton.

Her best friend.

Gray wasn't sure what he was doing, getting involved with her. If things went badly—and Gray had no reason to think they wouldn't—he'd have to deal with Colton.

He couldn't find Elise among the crowd, as she had a way of slipping through the cracks. Still, he'd never had a problem locating her at the lodge or among all the guests at his brother's wedding.

"Hey," a woman said, and he turned toward the voice. Elise stood there, her cheeks pink and those light green eyes making something unhitch in his chest that he hadn't even known was so dang tight.

"There you are."

"Sorry I'm late." She glanced around, nerves pouring off of her. Gray was exceptionally good at reading a person, and he could tell she didn't like this.

"Want to go somewhere else?" he asked.

Hope filled those beautiful eyes. "Did you put our name on the list?"

"I only just got here myself," he said. "I was looking for you. So no."

"Sure, we can go somewhere else." She turned and left the restaurant, and Gray followed.

"There's a great steakhouse over on March," she said.

"Okay."

"Meet you there?"

"Yep." Gray separated from her and got behind the wheel of his truck again. His heart beat a little faster than it normally did, because now he'd have to coax himself out of the vehicle one more time.

"Make a right turn on Seagull," his GPS said, and he obeyed. But when he arrived on March Street, it didn't go all the way through. "Your destination is on the right."

"But it's not," he said, pulling to the curb and picking up his phone. He was on a residential street, with homes on both sides. No steakhouse. He looked left and right out the windows. Definitely no steakhouse.

But this was definitely March Street. He typed in the search term "steakhouse" and got several results. Of course he would. This was Wyoming, after all, and they raised a lot of beef cattle here.

Frustration started to lick through him as he tapped and studied the addresses. In the end, he had to dial Elise, who picked up with, "I think I lost you."

"I'm on March Street," he said. "There's no steakhouse

here." He swung his truck around to get out of the cul-de-sac. "What's the name of the place?"

"The Branding Iron," she said. "And it's not on March Street. It's on *Marks* Street."

"Shoot," Gray said, embarrassment moving through him powerfully. "I'll be right there."

"Take your time," she said. "They're busy here too. I put our name on the list, and they said forty minutes."

"Oh, wow." Gray's stomach growled as if telling him he better feed it sooner than forty minutes from now. "See you in a sec."

Turned out that, no, he wouldn't see her in a second. He'd somehow navigated clear out north of town, and it took a good half an hour to even get to the steakhouse.

Something here was definitely wrong, but Gray pulled into the parking lot anyway. Easing around the restaurant, his phone started pinging, shooting out at least a dozen notifications for text messages in the space of two seconds.

"I hate the reception here," he grumbled. He was used to lightning-fast Internet and text messages that went through the moment he sent them. His provider didn't operate well in Coral Canyon, and half of Gray's messages spun and spun, never going through at all. "Oh, wow."

He stopped when he saw the crowds of people standing outside the steakhouse.

And the big plume of smoke rising from the roof. When he heard the sirens for the fire engine, he got out of the way and picked up his phone.

He'd been gone from Colton's for over an hour now, and

he barely had time to eat with Elise at this point. She'd texted several times about a kitchen fire at The Branding Iron, and that she'd gone somewhere else.

"Be...right...." Gray dictated as his thumbs typed out the letters. Before he could finish the text and send it, he got thrown forward, the horribly loud sound of metal on metal crunching through his whole body, crackling in his ears, and imprinting on his soul.

He gripped the wheel, his phone gone and forgotten, the text not sent. He sucked at the air, trying to figure out what had happened.

An angry man appeared through the driver's side window. "You've got to move this." He gestured, his face angry and his clothing indicating he was an emergency worker. "Now."

Gray punched the button to roll down his window. "You hit my truck."

"You're parked in a red zone, Mister," the man said. "Now move immediately. We've got two more ambulances coming and another fire truck."

"I am *not* in a red zone." Gray knew better than that, and he got out of his truck, his own anger spiking. "I moved out of the way when I saw the smoke."

"Just move," the man barked, walking away.

"Who's gonna pay for my truck?" Gray called after him, but he didn't break stride or wave or anything.

Gray circled the back of the truck to access the damage, and sure enough, he was not in a red zone. Not even close. Fine, close, but at least ten feet away.

He'd been hit by an ambulance, which had since been

backed up. The tailgate had bent inward in the middle, and that whole assembly would have to be repaired. The fender hung off the truck completely on one side, and the whole thing leaned precariously to the right.

He looked up to see if the ambulance drivers were still there, but they weren't. Gray returned to the cab, frantically searching for his phone. He was a lawyer; he knew what to do to protect himself. And billionaire or not, he shouldn't have to pay for damage to his vehicle that wasn't his fault.

He first made sure the date and time feature of his camera was activated, and then he took at least forty pictures ranging from where he was parked to where the ambulance was—and the license plate of it—to the extent of the damage to his truck.

His fingers ached from the cold, and he'd forgotten about everything and anything else but the pictures and the icy chill threatening to overpower him.

He finally climbed into the cab again, but it was as cold in there as outside, because he'd left the door open. His phone rang, and it didn't connect to the Bluetooth and play through the speakers, which only made him more furious.

"What?" he barked at Colton.

Ohhh, Colton. Maybe something had gone wrong with Hunter. The fight left him, and Gray's pulse pounded.

"Where are you?" he asked. "Elise just called me crying."

Sneak Peek! Gray - Chapter Two

Elise Murphy had never been so mortified in her life. Not even when Brandt had broken up with her via a text while she sat in the stands before one of his rodeos. She'd driven for two hours to be there, and she hadn't told him she was coming.

The text had jolted her back to reality, not this make-believe place where women as plain and quiet as Elise married bull riding champions. Just one look at Violet Everett confirmed that. She was a country music star with platinum albums. That was the kind of woman a billionaire bull rider wanted on his arm.

Elise sniffled, because she needed to calm down before she got back to the lodge. She drew in deep breath after deep breath, horrified that she'd called Colton to ask him if Gray didn't like her.

"What a mess," she said, her voice cracking and tears

slowly leaking down her face again. She wasn't fourteen. She didn't need to ask her best friend if his brother liked her.

A sting moved through her lungs, making breathing difficult, but she clenched her fingers on the steering wheel and kept the car on the mountain road. This Christmas wasn't nearly as snowy as last, for which Elise was grateful. She didn't like the snow that much, and driving in it especially terrified her.

She'd seen Gray walk into Devil's Tower ten minutes late. She'd followed him after counting to twenty-five, a random number she landed on because if she let herself go higher, she might not have gone inside at all.

He'd barely looked at her, barely said two words to her, and then he'd gotten right back in his truck like he had a checklist to get done that day, and lunch with her was an inconvenience.

She'd listened to her affirmations all the way to the steakhouse, and when he didn't come, and didn't come...Elise knew now that she'd started to spiral then.

"But he called," she said to the towering Tetons in the distance. The pine trees stood guard on the sides of the road too, never losing their needles and creating the perfect Christmas backdrop.

The big event had been yesterday, and Elise had skipped the rowdy present-unwrapping in the main living area of the lodge. She did love watching the little children open their gifts, but for some reason, she hadn't been able to face going this year.

She pulled off the road, her car fishtailing a bit when she

hit the snow on the shoulder going a little too fast. Her pulse picked up, but the vehicle came to a stop a moment later. With a sense of hysteria moving through her, she dug into her purse to find her phone. Her fingers shook while she swiped and jabbed, finally getting a call to go through to her mother.

"Elise, dear," her mom answered, her voice rich as clover honey. Elise started to relax just with the sound of it in her ears. "How are you?"

"Okay," she said, but her word wobbled. "Actually, not great."

"Not great? I thought you were going out with Gray today?"

"Yeah, me too," she said, her cheeks getting wet again with a fresh set of tears. "It didn't work out."

"Oh, no," her mother said. "You were so excited about it." She sounded genuinely upset on Elise's behalf. "Tell me what happened."

"Maybe I should leave Wyoming," Elise said instead of getting into the story. "Go somewhere warm, where rich people will pay me to design their yards. Put my degree to some actual good use."

"You think that's what you want?" Mom asked. "Eh?" The Canadian came out in her whenever she asked questions, and that "eh" caused a smile to bloom on Elise's face.

She shook her head. "No, though I would like somewhere warm about now."

"Still snowing up there?"

"Not for a couple of days," she said. "It's just really cold now. Clear sky. Subarctic temperatures."

"You could come to Vegas," she said. "I know you're not working around the lodge right now, while the Whittakers are there."

Elise let the thought roll through her mind, really examining all sides of it. "I could," she said, because she didn't hate the idea. "Let me think about it a little more."

"I'll be here until the third," her mom said. "Plenty of time to shop, get a pedicure, lounge by the pool...Henry has a pool in his backyard, dear. You wouldn't even have to go out in public."

Elise didn't even own a swimming suit, so the shopping trip would have to come before the lounging. She leaned her head back against the rest. "Sounds nice," she said, letting her eyes drift closed.

"What happened with Gray?" Mom spoke with a quieter voice now, and Elise had calmed enough to start the story. She detailed how things had gone at Devil's Tower, and how Gray had gotten lost.

"And then he didn't show up," Elise said. "I texted him and called him, and nothing. It was like he just disappeared. And then smoke started pouring out of the kitchen, and people started yelling and running out of the restaurant. I left, and I texted and called Gray again to let him know to meet me somewhere else."

Elise paused, reliving the frustration at so much silence. She'd thought she craved silence, especially after dealing with the huge crowd at the lodge, then more people in town. Apparently, no one made lunch for themselves on the day after Christmas, as every restaurant Elise had been to that day had been jam-packed.

Even the third one, which wasn't even that good.

She'd stood by the door, literally getting smashed behind it when people went in and out, as if she were invisible. In so many ways, Elise *was* invisible. She'd perfected how to be invisible, and most of the time she liked it.

But not behind a door, and not with Gray Hammond.

"And he never showed up," she said. "Never called. Never texted. I think he saw me at Devil's Tower, and was like, 'Wait a second...I'm not attracted to her.'" She sighed, because sometimes living inside her own head was very hard.

"I'm sure that's not true," her mom said. "Elise, you're a beautiful woman."

"I'm thin," Elise said. "Mom, there's a difference between being thin and being beautiful."

"Sweetie," she said. "I'm sure he didn't run away from you on purpose. Something must've happened."

Elise opened her eyes and looked at the bright blue sky, without a cloud in sight. "I called Colton."

Her mother didn't say anything, which was an indication that Elise shouldn't have called Colton. "He said he hadn't heard from Gray. So whatever happened, he didn't know about it." Elise didn't either. "It's fine. I have spaghetti and meatballs at my cabin, and plenty of ice cream, and I'll be fine."

"You said fine twice."

"Well, it's a two-fine kind of day," Elise said, a smile

perking up her lips. "Thanks for letting me vent, Mom. I love you."

"Anytime," she said. "Maybe try calling him from the cabin? Maybe he was in a place of poor reception. That place is like a pocket for my network. Only works half the time."

"Okay, Mom," Elise said. "I've got to drive now. Love you." She hung up, because she didn't want to get in to the fact that her mother had only been to Coral Canyon once in the last four years that Elise had lived and worked in Wyoming. Once—and that was to help Elise move from Jackson Hole to the lodge, just about three years ago now.

She continued up the mountain, the road in front of her like a shiny, black snake through the snow. She went past the lodge to an access road only she and Bree used, as it led to their cabin. She parked under the semi-permanent canopy Graham and Eli had erected for her and Bree, as there was no garage at the cabin.

Bree's car wasn't there, which indicated she'd likely gone down the canyon to her boyfriend's house. Another Hammond, this one the oldest and the former CEO of the company that had made all the brothers billionaires.

Elise didn't care about Gray's money. She blinked and she saw him standing in Colton's kitchen, shirtless, pouring coffee. Another blink, and their eyes met through the crowd. Another, and she witnessed him laugh with his son.

He made her feel something she hadn't in a long time, and she'd liked him. He'd been smart and kind, soft but clearly an alpha male. He wore the cowboy hat and the boots, and while

Elise had told herself she didn't like cowboys, she now knew she'd been lying to herself for years.

"It's fine," she told herself as she went inside. "Fine, fine, fine." Four fines didn't make anything better, but they did help get her inside and get the plastic container of spaghetti into the microwave.

She put her phone on silent, left it in her room, and changed out of the cute checkered slacks she'd specifically bought for this date. She hadn't worn them except to try them on, and Gray probably hadn't even noticed them.

"It's fine," Elise told herself again. And then again. And then again.

* * *

The days passed, and Elise helped Celia in the kitchen and stayed out of the way. The Hammonds came up to the lodge on New Year's Eve—the day of the Cupcake Wars—and Elise made a silent escape only a few minutes before they arrived.

She'd texted Gray between Thanksgiving and Christmas about what the Cupcake Wars entailed, and he'd said he'd compete with her. But she found she couldn't handle the noise and crowds in the lodge, and she texted him to say so.

Her phone rang with his name on the screen, and she only hesitated for a moment before she answered it.

"Elise," he said, his voice as smooth as a still lake. "You don't feel well?"

"It's just so noisy at the lodge."

That noise came through the receiver on his phone. "It sure is."

She didn't know what else to say. He'd called the other night too to explain about the fire engines, and getting hit by the ambulance, and all of that. He claimed not to have gotten her texts until hours later, and Elise had just nodded during the conversation.

He hadn't asked her out, and she certainly wasn't going to ask. Not again.

"I'm going home tomorrow."

"Yes," she said, wondering what she'd thought they could become. He wasn't like Colton; he couldn't just leave Ivory Peaks whenever he wanted. She didn't know Gray well, but she knew he felt a great responsibility for his parents, and she knew his son was nearly twelve and in school.

"Colton says you make a mean chocolate cake," Gray said. "Maybe I could come to your cabin and taste it."

His suggestion gave her pause for a moment, but then his voice reverberated in her ears. *I'm going home tomorrow.*

"I don't think so, Gray," she said. "I'm not up to it."

"Okay," he said, his voice giving nothing away. "I'm real sorry it didn't work out for lunch."

"Me too," she said. "'Bye, Gray." She ended the call and let her hand fall to her side. There was nothing more to say.

* * *

A couple of weeks passed, and Elise found herself at the courthouse one afternoon, a jury summons in her hand. She really couldn't sit on a jury, as the very thought of having to decide someone else's fate made her sick to her stomach.

But getting arrested for not showing up did too, so she'd put on her checkered pants—might as well wear them for something—and driven down the canyon. The wind whipped at her scarf, and Elise tried to tuck it under her hood and walk at the same time. She stumbled, but righted herself and kept going.

She glanced up to see how far she had to go before she'd find relief from this wind, but her eyes stung.

Ducking her head, she focused on the ground at her feet. As long as there was flat cement, she'd be okay. She'd make it.

A cry filled the air, and Elise looked left to see a blue and yellow awning bumbling down the street toward her. It sent glass shattering when it hit windows on cars, and Elise froze.

Don't stand here, she thought. Or maybe it was the voice of the Lord telling her to move so she didn't get hurt.

No matter what it was, she obeyed, and she darted forward at the same time a huge gust of wind blew into the square, bringing the awning closer and practically lifting Elise off her feet.

She cried out as she fought the wind. She wasn't going to win this battle against Mother Nature, and she hunched her back and faced away from the wind so it would simply push her ahead of the awning.

Push her it did, right into the very solid form of someone else. "Sorry," she said automatically, but her voice got lost in the rush of air.

"Come on," the man said, grabbing onto her with very

strong hands. "Let's hunker down here." He pulled her several steps back the way she'd come, and then down to the ground. The wind and chill lessened, and Elise pulled in a breath, feeling like she'd just run a marathon. She had no idea where she was or what they hid behind, other than it was made of bricks.

"Elise?"

She looked up from beneath her hood, that voice making her eyes widen. And when she looked into the dark, gray, stormy depths of Gray Hammond's eyes, time froze.

* * *

Christmas at Whiskey Mountain Lodge in Coral Canyon™

Colton (Book 1): All the maid at Whiskey Mountain Lodge wants for her birthday is a handsome cowboy billionaire. And Colton can make that wish come true—if only he hadn't escaped to Coral Canyon after being left at the altar...

Wes (Book 2): She broke up with him to date another man...who broke her heart. He's a former CEO with nothing to do who can't get her out of his head. Can Wes and Bree find a way toward happily-ever-after at Whiskey Mountain Lodge?

Gray (Book 3): She's best friends with the single dad cowboy's brother and has watched two friends find love with the sexy new cowboys in town. When Gray Hammond comes to Whiskey Mountain Lodge with his son, will Elise finally get her own happily-ever after with one of the Hammond brothers?

Cy (Book 4): A cowboy billionaire beast, the woman he asks out in front of everyone, and the family traditions that softens his heart and bring Cy and Patsy together.

Ames (Book 5): A cowboy billionaire who's rough around the edges, the woman he ghosted last Christmas, and their second chance at happily-ever-after.

Coral Canyon Cowboys Romance Series

Visit stunning Wyoming for another family of cowboys... The Youngs! The series includes second chance romance, friends to lovers, family saga, Christian values, clean and sweet romance, single dads, equine therapy themes, police dog training, brotherly relationships, return to hometown, fish out of water, and country music stars!

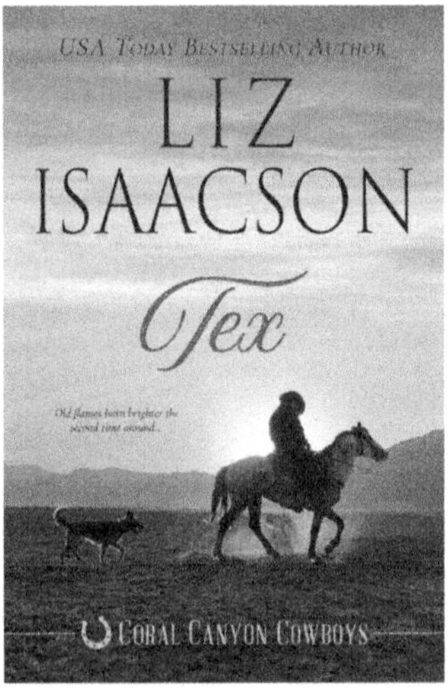

Tex (Book 1): He's back in town after a successful country music career. She owns a bordering farm to the family land he wants to buy...and she outbids him at the auction. **Can Tex and Abigail rekindle their old flame, or will the issue of land ownership come between them?**

Ivory Peaks Romance Series

Experience true Rocky Mountain life in the Ivory Peaks Romance series! You'll get more Hammond family romance, second chance romance, and all the heartwarming and uplifting family fiction you're craving. Ivory Peaks is the perfect escape for anyone looking to feel loved, cherished, and like they belong. You belong right here in Ivory Peaks!

His First Love (Book 1): She broke up with him a decade ago. He's back in town after finishing a degree at MIT, ready to start his job at the family company. **Can Hunter and Molly find their way through their pasts to build a future together?**

Seven Sons Ranch in Three Rivers Romance Series

Meet the cowboy billionaire brothers at Seven Sons Ranch. The Walkers are new in Three Rivers, and they've got the women circling. Every contemporary romance in this series features a fake marriage that turns to more, family holiday traditions, and the family saga that will create a space for you in the Walker family too!

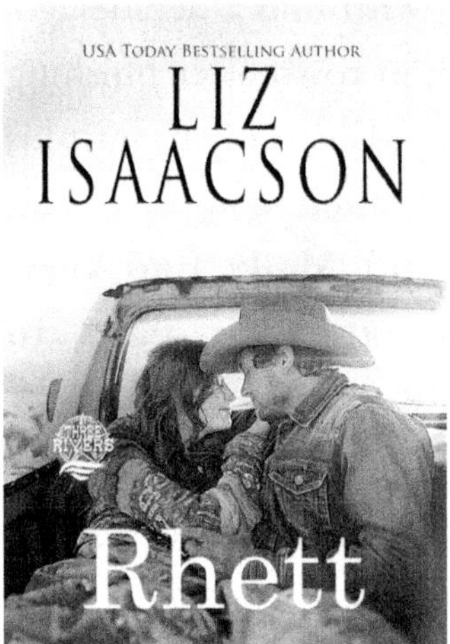

Rhett (Book 1): To save her business, she'll have to risk her heart. She needs a husband to be credible as a matchmaker. He wants to help a neighbor. **Will their fake marriage take them out of the friend zone?**

About Liz

Liz Isaacson writes inspirational romance, usually set in Texas, or Wyoming, or anywhere else horses and cowboys exist. She lives in Utah, where she writes full-time, takes her two dogs to the park everyday, and eats a lot of veggies while writing. Find her on her website, along with all of her pen names, at feelgo-odfictionbooks.com

Printed in Dunstable, United Kingdom

63419949R00214